THE RAIDER

THE RAIDER

CHARLES ALDEN SELTZER

WILDSIDE PRESS

CHAPTER ONE

It was not until Ellen came in sight of the cabin that the awesome and austere history of the Ballinger family assailed her memory. The background of her ancestry was peopled with solemn-visaged men and women who watched her with formidable disapprobation. They were dignified ancestors whose mode of living was as sacred as a religious ritual. They never did anything wrong. They were moral, staid, and undemonstrative. The men were stiff necked; the women never permitted an adventurous gaze to stir the jealousy of their wedded mates. No scandal marred the fair record of the Ballinger family.

No scandal until now. At least Ellen's father, Matthew M. Ballinger, had insisted that she was disgracing the family, and of course he ought to know for he was more familiar with the family history than Ellen.

Ellen was not interested in the family history as much as she was interested in knowing what was going on in the courageous heart which had sent her to search for Jim Kellis's cabin. She had ridden twenty miles into the wilderness seeking it. And here it was, standing in a grove of pine and air balsam not more than a hundred yards from where she sat on her pony. The wilderness through which she had been riding encompassed the grove. It spread an endless number of miles to the purple mountains southward, eastward, and westward. This wilderness was featured by rugged cliffs and crags that appeared suddenly; it was dotted here and there by bastioned towers of polychromatic granite, slender spires and huge battlements. The dun earth was gashed by wild gorges, sandy arroyos, barrancas.

It had seemed to her that something had followed her from the instant she had left her father's ranch house. The something was invisible. An atmosphere. A threat or a menace. An imponderable something like a whisper which is stilled at its inception. Ellen grimly wondered if it were the Family breathing its disapproval.

Well, of the family there still remained her father and a brother. Her mother she had never known. Her mother had not been a Ballinger and in dying while giving birth to Ellen she had escaped the rigorous, silent scrutiny of the family, and perhaps the blame for Ellen's unconventional escapades.

Ellen had refused to inherit the dignity and the austerity of her ancestors, and back East in a long gallery where the walls were adorned with the portraits of beautiful ladies, she had often mocked at their solemn faces.

Something of theirs she had inherited at least—their beauty. And yet she was not entirely conscious that she possessed it. For now, sitting on her pony, while her cheeks crimsoned with embarrassment, she was not vainly thinking of how delighted Jim Kellis would be to see her again, but of how eager she was to look upon him.

She hadn't seen Jim Kellis in five years. She had been twenty and Kellis twenty-three when he had come West. He had belonged to her "set," and he had been improvident and weak. Yet she had loved him then and during the separation she had invested him with the character of a hero. He had been the only man of her acquaintance who had had the courage to journey to a new country. He had been weak and careless, yet he had grit enough to endure hardship and loneliness in an attempt to fight back to his former position. She loved Jim for that. The others, being merely men, were nothing to her. She wanted Jim Kellis and she meant to have him in spite of the solemn-visaged ancestors who at this moment seemed to be standing in the background wagging their heads at her.

She was not usually conscious of her ancestors. There had been many times when she had calmly ignored her father's advice. As in the present.

"No woman of the Ballinger family ever chased after a man!" Matthew M. Ballinger had told her.

"Would that explain why the men they did get were so spiritless?" she naïvely asked. "I shouldn't care to have a man unless I wanted him badly enough to make an effort to catch him."

"Are you sure Jim Kellis wants you?" questioned Ballinger.

"I am not sure. He told me he wanted me. But I want him. That is why I am going to him," she told her father on the day following their arrival at the Hour Glass ranch.

"Has Kellis kept you informed of what he has been doing?" asked Ballinger.

"He has written me letters."

"You know where he may be found?"

"Yes."

"This is the first time you have been out here with me," said her father. "You know nothing whatever about the country. I'll send Jim Peters with you." Jim Peters was the Hour Glass foreman.

"I'm going alone. Thank you for offering Peters, Dad."

Ballinger's lips tightened. In his business organization there were five thousand men with business brains who accepted his suggestions and commands with deferential bows. But his daughter stood straight and looked him squarely in the eye and declined to be guided by him.

He flushed, turned away.

"All right then," he said. He faced her again.

"What are you going to do when you find Kellis?" he asked.

"Marry him."

"To-night?"

"Of course."

Ballinger frowned.

"There is a justice over at Randall. It's thirty miles from here. A new town. I've never been over there, but I hear it's tough. You could have Kellis take you there. If you don't find Kellis you'd better ride right back here. Don't you want me to have Jim Peters come after you to-night? If you have gone on to Randall to marry Kellis of course Peters could come right back."

There should have been a certain wistfulness in Ballinger's eyes just now. What Ellen imagined she saw was a gleam of mockery.

"I'll manage without Peters," she said. "Thank you again, Dad."

Ballinger ejaculated something that sounded like "Bah!", and left her.

Now she sat gazing at the cabin which she felt belonged to Kellis. She sat in the saddle, half expecting that presently Kellis would hail her and come running toward her. His eyes, naturally, would be alight with amazement and delight.

However, Kellis did not appear, and no sound came from the cabin.

There was no sound anywhere. A flat, dead silence surrounded Ellen, seemed to press in upon her, to enfold her. The sky was white and cloudless. There was no breeze and the leaves of the trees dropped inertly. The denizens of the thickets were quiet. When Ellen's pony had sagged to a halt all motion had ceased.

Yet the invisible menace which had followed her all day seemed to surround her. It seemed to be in the atmosphere; a brooding calm, as if nature was waiting patiently and grimly for something to happen.

A great deal of dust had accumulated upon Ellen's riding habit, which she had brought with her from the East. The cloth was brown, matching her hair and her eyes and blending harmoniously with the peach bloom of perfect health that shone in her cheeks. There was the great calm of self-confidence in her mannerisms; intelligence and not too much worldliness was in her gaze as she waited in the silence.

She was positive she hadn't made a mistake in direction, for while Jim Kellis's letters had been more or less sketchy they had explained fully enough about the trail that led from the Hour Glass to the cabin where he professed to lead a "lonely existence." She had made no mistake, for there was the flat he had written about; there was the river wandering through the centre of it, and there was the cabin with its log walls and its roof of adobe.

She rode forward through the trees to a small door-yard in front of the cabin, where she pulled her pony down and sat motionless in the saddle, staring.

There was a small porch built of poles. It had an adobe roof and its floor was of earth packed to a rock-like consistency and cracked with the dryness. A bench with a pail and a tin basin stood against the wall under the porch. From one of the slender porch columns to a tree about fifty feet distant was stretched a line from which were suspended several nondescript pieces of cloth which had evidently been washed and thrown over the line to dry. The water in which the pieces of cloth had been washed had been thrown upon the ground near the edge of the porch. It was steaming in the sun and its odour was unpleasant. Sitting on a grass matting which was spread over a section of the earth floor of the porch was a dark-skinned young woman holding a child of three or four.

The young woman was handsome. Her face was oval, her eyes were black and lustrous. Her coarse black hair was combed smoothly back from her forehead and coiled in glistening curves at the nape of her neck. A bright coloured mantilla was lying loosely upon her shoulders, disclosing a necklace of turquoise stones. She wore a loose dress of violent green and red cloth which was caught together at the waist with a coloured embroidered girdle. Grass cloth slippers were on her feet. The child was arrayed like the mother.

Neither moved. The mother watched Ellen with uncompromising steadiness in which there was no suggestion of warmth; the child stared with frank curiosity.

"I beg your pardon," said Ellen. "It seems I have made a mistake, after all. Perhaps you will be able to direct me? I am looking for a man named Jim Kellis."

The woman's eyes gleamed, chilled.

"What you want weeth Jim Kellis?"

"Why I merely wish to see him."

"What for?"

"My reasons for wishing to see him cannot concern you," said Ellen.

"Jim Kellis my man," stated the woman, jealously, defensively.

Ellen gasped. The peach-bloom colour fled from her cheeks.

"Your man!" she said in a weak voice. "Do you mean to say that Jim Kellis is your husband?"

The woman nodded vigorously.

"He marry me before the Padre four year ago," she answered. "Now you tell me what you want weeth him?" she added.

"Nothing," returned Ellen.

CHAPTER TWO

For a reason which Ellen could not at once explain the atmosphere had chilled and an unsmiling sky stretched over a section of country that had suddenly become grim and bleak. She had definitely declined her father's advice and assistance, and now she was deep in the wilderness, alone, and facing the prospect of a ride of more than twenty miles through the night.

She observed that the sky was already darkening, that the sun had gone down and that purple shadows were stealing around her. Moreover, mingling with her inexpressible disappointment over the dereliction of Jim Kellis was a conviction that the Ballinger ancestors were watching her and derisively laughing at her.

Her pride had been hurt, also. She had carried the Ballinger family honour into the wilderness to see it contemptibly ignored. Worse, there was nothing she could do about it.

Obviously, she could not seek Jim Kellis and demand an explanation. There could be no explanation. And she didn't want to see Kellis again.

She couldn't cry. She wouldn't. But her cheeks had whitened from the conflict that her emotions were waging, and there must have been something in her appearance to arouse the pity and sympathy of the Mexican woman, for the latter invited gently:

"You tired. You rest."

"Tired? Oh no!" Ellen's laugh was far from being the spontaneous lilt it had always been. There was now a grim note in it.

She had been shocked, of course, and the sympathy of the Mexican woman was a humiliation. But the Ballinger brain was still functioning with its customary energy, the Ballinger dignity had not deserted her; and the cool calm of the sophistication she had spent years in acquiring was concealing her mental distress.

"Thank you," she added. "But I can't stop. I am on my way to Randall. You see, I knew Mr. Kellis slightly some years ago. I heard he was out here and I merely wished to inquire about him."

"Jim away."

"Yes; I understand." She smiled sweetly. "When he returns you may tell him that Ellen Ballinger passed. He will be surprised."

"You Ballinger girl, eh?" There was new interest in the woman's voice. "You father own the Hour Glass?"

Ellen nodded.

The woman seemed to brighten; her voice became eager.

"Then mebbe you father send for me for work, eh?"

"Have you worked at the Hour Glass?"

"Many time. Jim know you father—well. Me too."

Ellen's pulses leaped but she smiled disarmingly.

"But father does not know that you and Jim are married, does he?"

"Oh yes; he know. Him give me present, many time. *Ya se ve!* He know!"

So that was why her father had suggested sending Jim Peters as an escort! He knew Jim Kellis was married and that she had been starting upon a fool's errand. He had permitted her to go, not volunteering to tell her. Perhaps he had wanted her to find out for herself, thinking such a shock would be good for her. He had often spoken of what he had been pleased to call "the cockiness of the girls of the present generation," intimating that a great deal of it should be knocked out of them.

She had heard much of that gospel. All of it resulted from clouded vision and forgetfulness of the shortcomings of the youth of the preceding generation. Twaddle! If she had been as impudent as her father she could have reminded him that he had never been exactly perfect. She could see him from a different angle than that from which he viewed himself, just as he could see her. The difference was that she knew it and he didn't.

But this trick had been a mean one. He knew that she had always liked Jim Kellis, and telling her of Kellis's marriage should have been his duty. He had deliberately humiliated her!

Her lips settled into straight lines and the peach-bloom colour again flooded her cheeks.

She smiled at Jim Kellis's wife.

"I wish you every happiness," she said.

"*Gracias*, señorita."

Ellen rode southward, past the cabin, continuing in the direction she had travelled all day. She certainly would not return to the Hour Glass that night. Perhaps she would not return at all. What a senseless attempt at discipline. How crude, how brutal!

The peach-bloom cheeks were a flaming red as Ellen rode southward into the darkening world. The more she reflected upon her father's action the more bitter became her resentment. Considering the hatred she now bore her parent she wondered if she had ever loved him.

Ballinger had never been like other fathers. He had done things toward her that shouldn't have been done. Petty things, mean things—like sending her on this wild goose chase. He'd never given her the love and the consideration he should have given her—that he owed her. Fancy his playing with her affections like that.

But that was a Ballinger family trait—derision. She had observed how it had appeared upon the faces of the ancestors in the photographs. Cold pride, arrogance. She wondered if her mother had known; if that had been the reason her mother had set aside a separate fortune for her, making her independent of the Ballinger money? She silently blessed her mother, as she now vividly remembered the wise, tender, knowing eyes that always gazed out at her from various pictures she treasured.

She rode into a forest which was so dark and forbidding that she would have been frightened had she not been so furiously angry. She had been betrayed by Kellis and mocked at by her father.

She got out of the forest, crossed the river at a shallow and sent her pony through a swale whose southern side was topped by a bare ridge. By the time she gained the crest of the ridge her mood had changed and she was indulging in silent laughter which was inspired by a strange and reckless impulse which had seized her.

She had always been reckless. Some wild and perverse strain in her had made her contemptuous of the code of laws which people referred to as the conventions. Laws were made for people who were not original enough to think for themselves. "No woman of the Ballinger family has ever chased after a man, eh?" she said, aloud, nodding her head at the deep shadows that were slowly closing around her. "Well, Matthew M. Ballinger, this member of the Ballinger family is going to get herself a man before she goes back to the family circle! I will get the first man that looks good to me! And after I get him I'll make him ride with me to the Hour Glass. And then——"

How it happened she never discovered. She only felt the pony stumble, try to recover his equilibrium, slip and fall. She went out of the saddle, struck on her head and a shoulder and sank into an abyss whose atmosphere was vivid with dazzling flashes of light. She did not see the pony roll to the bottom of the ridge, nor was she aware that she was stretched out, flat on her back, a few feet from the animal.

CHAPTER THREE

For a long time Ellen had been conscious of motion, although the darkness was so dense that she could not determine whether her eyes were open or closed. There was an excruciating pain in the top of her head, her right shoulder was throbbing, and her arms were so heavy that she could not lift them. Also, she seemed to be suffocating. Something was covering her mouth. From its width she judged the something was a handkerchief. It was drawn tightly and when she attempted to lift her hands to remove it she was amazed to discover that her arms seemed to be bound to her sides.

Her legs were not bound. She was astride a horse, for she could feel the animal's muscles writhing under her. The horse was not her own because she could not bind herself in this manner and mount him. Besides, she could hear somebody breathing over her shoulder. A man.

She speculated upon the man's identity and tried to remember what had happened to her. She finally recalled that her pony had stumbled and that she had fallen out of the saddle. That would account for the pains in her head and shoulder, but there was still the presence of the man to be explained.

The man was probably Jim Peters. He had been following her and when she had not returned toward the Hour Glass after leaving the Kellis cabin he had trailed her. He must have been close when her pony stumbled and had taken advantage of her helplessness to bind her so that she could not resist. Possibly Jim Peters was a man who did not care to argue with a woman.

She was furiously indignant. Because she could not speak and tell Peters what she thought of him for binding her she kicked savagely at his shins with the heels of her riding boots. Moreover, she kicked a shin, for he growled:

"Awake an' kickin', eh? Well, you kick me in the shins again an' I'll fetch you a wallop alongside the jaw that'll knock some of the nonsense out of you!"

The man was not Jim Peters!

She was startled, chilled with apprehension, but not intimidated. She tried to express her opinion of the man but her words were muffled into unintelligible mutterings.

"That's all right," said the man. "Talk as much as you can. It won't bother me any because I can't understand you. All women ought to be gagged, anyway. Just keep your shirt on. I'll take that gag off after we get where we're goin'. Then you can shoot off your gab as much as you please."

She wanted to tell him that she was Ellen Ballinger and that all the power of the Ballinger fortune would be exerted to make him suffer for what he was doing. But the sounds she made could not be interpreted. And he went on, calmly:

"This is one time I even things with Matthew M. Ballinger! If he likes you as well as he ought to he'll be throwin' a fit when you don't go back to the Hour Glass!"

So the man was not afraid of the Ballinger power. In fact, he was deliberately challenging it. And she was not to return to the Hour Glass! This man was an enemy and was striking at her father through her. Obviously, he intended holding her for ransom.

She wasn't frightened now. She wasn't even angry any more. If it hadn't been for the handkerchief that covered her mouth she would have been amused. For she knew something of her father's methods, of his temper when aroused to wrath, and she anticipated that her abductor would get neither enjoyment nor money out of his adventure with her.

As for herself—she didn't care. She was rather glad something had happened to her, for if they found her and took her back to the Hour Glass she would not have to make any embarrassing explanations about Jim Kellis. Only she would rather escape than be rescued or ransomed.

She was not romantic. She was getting no thrill whatever out of her present predicament. Nothing but discomfort. She didn't even speculate about the personal appearance of her captor. He might be handsome, but she had met any number of handsome men and had never liked any of them. What she had always looked for in men she had never found—sincerity and naturalness. Even her father posed for her benefit. She had heard him lie and equivocate and boast. She had heard other men say things they had not meant; had seen them pose when they thought they were watched. She had seen them affect politeness and sympathy when they thought such acting would impress others. She was tired of them all and she had liked Jim Kellis because he was weak and didn't pretend. And even Kellis had failed her.

She would have liked to ask this man what he had against her father. But she couldn't talk. He was a coward, anyway, or he wouldn't have tied her. She couldn't see his face, of course, no more than she could see other objects, but of course when daylight came she would see him, and he couldn't keep the handkerchief around her mouth forever. And when she finally did get the handkerchief off she would tell him just what she thought of him.

Meanwhile, they were going somewhere, though she didn't know where. Of course he was taking her to some secret retreat where he could hold her in safety while he collected the money he was after. He probably belonged to a band of outlaws.

He didn't talk any more, but she assured herself that she would never forget his voice; that she would know it wherever she heard it. She had never heard another voice like it. It had a burr in it. The key to his enunciation was in the word "shirt." He had said "shurrut."

She hadn't any idea how long she had been riding with him and there was no way of her determining in which direction they were going. He was riding behind her, and now and then he placed a hand on her shoulder to steady her, indicating that the trail was rough and that he was no stranger to it.

Once they crossed a river at a shallow, for though she could hear the water splashing it did not touch her. Again they were going through some long grass; she felt it and heard it as it rasped against her boots. Then through some timber, for he told her to "stoop low" and pressed a hand heavily upon her shoulder.

She felt they must have been riding more than an hour when he pulled the horse to a halt.

"We'll get off here," he said. "Don't try any monkey-shines or I'll slap your mouth."

He pulled her out of the saddle and deposited her on the ground. She felt he had held her unnecessarily tight in getting her down and she showed her resentment by trying to wriggle out of his grasp and by attempting to kick his legs. He merely held her tighter and laughed at her.

And now for the first time she feared him, and she did not resist as he led her into the darkness. It was not until she felt a shoulder come in contact with a wall that she decided he was taking her to some sort of a house.

She heard a door creak on its hinges and she was pushed through it and across a floor to a bed or a trunk. He forced her to its edge and left her, saying shortly:

"You'll stay here for a while!"

He went out and she heard him close the door. She sat quietly in the silence and the darkness, listening, trying to penetrate the blackness around her.

She heard no sound and finally became convinced that she was alone. She now realized that she had been afraid he had been bringing her among men of his kind. She trembled a little, but her chief emotion was that of resentment for her father's action in permitting her to get into this sort of a predicament. For if he had been frank with her she would not have undertaken the journey.

She had been sitting on the edge of the bunk for about an hour when she observed that the moon was rising. At first the darkness was tinged with a luminous glow which grew and expanded until, looking out of a window—which she perceived was barred—she could see some trees just outside, and a small clearing.

She was in a room in which there were a number of bunks similar to the one upon whose edge she was sitting. There was only one door, that through which she had entered, and it was tightly closed and evidently barred from the outside. There was only one window, and that also was barred.

There was bedding in the bunks, which was eloquent evidence that men were in the habit of sleeping here. No woman could sleep in any of the bunks. At least no woman would.

She could not see the entire length of the room, for only a square of moonlight entered, and that merely struck the wall near her, disclosing the bunks and a section of the floor.

The floor was dirty. Mud which had been turned to dust had left the prints of men's boots here and there. She was certain no woman had walked in the room.

But she grew weary of the silence, so she got up and walked about the room and peered out of the window.

She could see very little of the outside, and what there was of it seemed to have no living thing in it. But as she stood at one side of the window, leaning against one side of the frame, her head came into contact with something hard and unyielding. Turning, she saw that a small shelf had been built against the wall near the window frame. Looking at the shelf she was seized with an inspiration. She backed against the wall and found that the edge of the shelf reached the back of her head just above the point where her captor had knotted the handkerchief which covered her mouth. By standing on tiptoe she got the edge of the shelf under the knot, and by rubbing it and working her head up and down she succeeded in slipping the handkerchief over the top of her head.

She could breathe freely now, and she stood for some time at the window filling her lungs with the keen, bracing air that floated in.

Leaving the window she searched the room in the hope of finding some article which would aid her in freeing her arms. But she was unsuccessful and again went back to the window.

She stood there for a long time, watching, listening. No sound reached her and she grew tired of standing. Her head still ached and her arms were numbed from the ropes which were wound tightly about them, but she fought against the inclination to lie in one of the bunks, knowing that once she stretched out she would go to sleep. And she didn't want to sleep until she discovered what her captor's intentions were.

She went to sleep standing beside the window, though, for she caught herself nodding and became aware of distant sounds at the instant her mind resumed its activity. The sounds were the crashing of brush, the rushing clatter of hoofs, and two pistol shots, the first closely followed by the second.

She stiffened, listened intently.

The sounds of crashing brush continued and the clattering of hoofs seemed to come nearer, but there were no more shots.

The sounds appeared to come from the timber which she could see from the window, and she got the impression that a number of horsemen were rushing through the trees and the thick, wild brush.

Then she saw a horseman burst out of the edge of the timber on the far side of the clearing, observed him, crouching over the animal's head, coming straight toward the window. He was furiously spurring the horse he was riding, and his cursing could be heard above the thunderous rataplan of hoofs. He swerved when within fifty or sixty feet of the window, passed the door through which Ellen had entered the room and went on, somewhere, into the country beyond.

Silence swept in behind him. Five minutes of silence which was heavy with portent. Then again came the thunder of hoofs beating upon the hard earth of a distant open stretch of country, followed by a heavy crashing as of a band of horsemen concertedly breasting the natural forest barriers. Then the timber at the edge of the clearing became animate with leaping, plunging horses and their riders.

There were six riders, Ellen observed. They crossed the clearing and were racing past the door when one of them shouted. There was a prodigious scuffling and grunting and snorting from impatient horses pulled to a sudden halt. Then a silence. After that a voice:

"Well, he's got away."

A laugh.

"One didn't," said another voice.

"He sure was fannin' it," said still another voice. "The devil couldn't ketch him, the way he was ridin'. I was sure I'd burned him, the second shot. But I reckon not, or he wouldn't be so active."

"We throwed a scare into that guy, anyway," said a fourth voice. "An' we can be mighty certain Hank Kroll won't steal any more hosses."

The horsemen seemed to be grouped near the door. Ellen heard a match strike, detected the odour of a cigarette.

"It's off for to-night, I reckon," said the first voice. "That second guy will keep goin', if his horse don't break a leg."

"What did you holler for, Jeff?" asked one man. "We might have ketched him."

"Horse," replied the one addressed as "Jeff," "in that clump of juniper. Hobbled, ain't he? Look at his brand."

There followed a silence and then a voice, fainter than the others, called out:

"A bay. Blaze face. Hour Glass."

Ellen's horse. The one she had ridden all day. She had wondered what had become of it; now she realized that her captor had led it to this place. She had not been able to see in the darkness, nor had she heard the horse following.

"Hour Glass, eh," said Jeff. "Ballinger hardly gets here when they begin to steal his horses. You didn't get a look at the fellow that came through here?"

"Not a look," came the answer. "An' I ain't sure he was with the guy we swung. He swore he was alone, you recollect."

"Lying to save his hide, I reckon," came Jeff's voice.

Standing beside the window, Ellen gasped.

These men had hanged a man! They were murderers!

"Whew!" exclaimed a voice. "Kroll sure showed yellow, didn't he? It made my hair raise to watch him! Far as I'm concerned I'll be seein' Kroll to the day I cash in!"

"Kroll can't blame nobody but himself, Bill," said one of the men. "He had it comin' to him an' he knowed it was comin'. An' if a man keeps stealin' horses an' the law don't take a hand—an' won't take a hand—why folks has got to do their own hangin'!"

"Sure, that's right," agreed the other. "But I keep seein' him. Seein' the way he——"

"Bill," said the other speaker, "Kroll didn't feel as soft as you when he shot Ed and Tim the night he was 'most caught runnin' off them Bar K hosses!"

"That's right," agreed Bill.

There was a creaking of saddle leather, and Ellen knew from the sound that someone was dismounting. She had feared the riders would enter the house and find her, and for the first time since the beginning of her adventure she trembled with apprehension.

However, there was no place to conceal herself. She would *not* get into one of the bunks! And she certainly would not cower into a corner! She wasn't afraid, even if she was trembling. So she held her position at the window, although she was hoping that none of the men would enter.

And then she heard a sound at the door. The door opened inward, slowly, and a man stood on the threshold, peering into the room. He was a tall man, lithe and well built. The moonlight that flooded the doorway revealed his broad shoulders, his gauntleted wrists, the leather chaps on his long legs, the heavy Colt low on his right hip. His hat was pulled over his forehead.

He did not enter the room, but stood in the doorway. He was motionless, rigid, and Ellen knew her presence in the room had amazed him. He almost bowed to her, she was certain.

She expected him to enter, but instead he turned in the doorway, laughed, and stepped out, closing the door behind him and barring it.

Ellen breathlessly waited. She expected now to hear him tell his companions what he had found in the room. They would swarm inside. And then, considering that they were murderers, they would——

"Nobody in there, boys," he said.

The voice was Jeff's. He was undoubtedly the leader. He had halted them; he had ordered one of the men to examine her pony. And there was authority in his voice when he again spoke.

"You boys scatter!" he said. "Some of you can trail the fellow that passed here—if you feel like riding some more. I'll see you to-morrow. I'm staying here to see if number two comes back after that Hour Glass horse."

One of the men laughed.

"No use chasin' number two," he said. "That guy will be over into Prima County by this time. He wasn't lettin' nothin' hold him! I reckon we-all had better drag it home."

Leather creaked, spurs jangled; there was a clatter of hoofs, some subdued laughter; several "So-longs" to Jeff. Then the sounds diminished, ceased, and a heavy silence settled.

The silence continued long—so long that Ellen was almost convinced that Jeff had gone away with the others. She found herself hoping he wouldn't go, for she was half afraid that her captor would return. Besides, despite the fact that this man Jeff and his men had hanged a horse thief she suspected that they were not outlaws but a band of men who had temporarily taken the law into their own hands. Their conversation seemed to have intimated as much. Also, there had been something in Jeff's voice that had appealed to her. Quietness, for one thing, self-control for another. Men who permitted their passions to rule them did not have voices like Jeff's. Also, whoever Jeff was, he was a diplomat. Most men, seeing a woman where they had not expected to see one, would have betrayed excitement. Jeff hadn't. There had not been a tremor in his voice when he had told his men that the room was unoccupied. It made no difference what Jeff's intentions were. He had saved her from embarrassment and she was thankful.

The silence continued. At least half an hour had passed before Ellen heard a sound from outside. Then she heard the bars being removed.

The door opened and Jeff stepped into the room.

Ellen still stood beside the window and the moonlight was shining full upon her. She stood very still as Jeff walked toward her. He stopped at a little distance and seemed to be gravely regarding her.

"Who are you and what are you doing here?" he asked.

There was an unexpected coldness in his voice; not a trace of the sympathy and concern she felt should be there. Suspicion, rather, mingling with the coldness.

"I am Ellen Ballinger. I would not be here if I had not been forced to come! Will you please take these ropes from my arms? They—they hurt!"

"The devil!"

He stepped forward. Evidently he had not observed the ropes. A hand went swiftly into a pocket and was withdrawn. A knife carefully applied severed her bonds and she moved her arms slowly and stifled a cry of pain as the blood surged through them.

She was still standing where the moonlight shone full upon her. Jeff was also in the mellow flood that entered the window. His arms were folded; his chin was resting upon the thumb and forefinger of his right hand. She felt he was interested in her merely as an intruder, and that he resented her being here.

While she looked at him her thoughts went to hardy adventurers whose pictures she had seen: vikings with their bold eyes, their clean-cut profiles, captains of sailing ships facing the hazards of storms, resolute explorers, leaders of forlorn expeditions. The indomitability of men who face death with a smile was in this man.

His hat was now shoved back and his black hair was tousled on his forehead. His eyes—which she thought were gray—were broodingly cynical in their depths but were flecked with lights of cold humour. His mouth was straight and hard, but in it somewhere was a hint of waywardness, of recklessness.

Ellen thought him handsome, but was certain he himself was not aware of his good looks. He exuded vitality, nervous energy, force. But all were sheathed by an easy deliberation of manner that must have been irritating and wrath-provoking to one in disagreement with him.

His skin was a rich bronze from his forehead to his chest. His woollen shirt, which was open at the throat, bulged slightly at the shoulders and the chest and sloped inward at his slim waist where a heavy cartridge belt encircled him. Suspended from the right hip, low, where its butt touched his wrist when his arm was hanging at his side, was a heavy revolver. On his legs were worn leather chaps and on his high-heeled, soft-topped boots were a pair of long-rowelled spurs which, Ellen decided, would be used without hesitation should the horse he happened to be riding prove recreant in an emergency.

A formidable and romantic figure.

Ellen had heard of his kind, but this was the first time she had met one of him face to face. At a distance yesterday she had observed some of the Hour Glass men, but though their trappings had interested her they had been so far away from her that she had not been able to judge what they were like. She had seen Jim Peters from the distance of a few feet, but Peters was at least sixty and what romance had been in him had evidently been ridden out of him. Peters was wrinkled and seamed and his legs were bowed from riding. Jim Peters had wonderful eyes, though. They were steady and serene, as if the things they had seen had bothered him very little.

Jeff's eyes were not like Jim Peters's. Jeff's eyes had the fire of youth—of youth's impudence and arrogance.

"You're Matt Ballinger's daughter, eh?" said Jeff, intently watching her. "You're off your range over here, ain't you? What were you doing over here?"

Jeff's voice was gruff, but Ellen was not frightened by it. Not in the least frightened. As a matter of fact, now that her arms were feeling better, she was rather amused over the whole adventure. For she had liked Jeff from the instant she had first seen his face, there in the moonlight. Moreover, although she was aware that he and his friends had hanged a man, she felt he was an advocate of law and order, and that she was safe. Her fears had been, and were, for the man who had picked her up and bound her arms. Now that he was no longer near she saw nothing to worry about.

"Yes," she said, answering his first question, "I am Matthew Ballinger's daughter. I am Ellen Ballinger. As a usual thing the Ballingers do not permit themselves to be barked at!"

She was expecting his start of surprise, and felt a pulse of vindictive amusement.

"If the Ballinger women are going to roam around in this country at night without company they can expect to be barked at," he told her, his voice snapping.

He hadn't been at all impressed, she perceived.

"Well, I shall not answer another question until you decide to be polite!" she declared.

"All right," he said shortly.

He turned swiftly, stepped to the door, went out, and closed the door behind him. Ellen could hear the fastenings slipping into place.

She was apprehensive for an instant, for she expected to hear him ride away. But after a while, when she heard no sound from outside and decided that she was not to lose him right away, she smiled knowingly and sought a comfortable position at the window.

For perhaps an hour there was no sound. Then she thought she heard him at the door and felt that he was coming in to her again. But he wasn't coming in; from the sound he made she decided that he was sitting on the door sill and that he had brushed against the door in changing his position.

Again she smiled, grimly. There were ways to make men do the things one wanted them to do. Even if they were great big gruff men like Jeff! All she had to do was to keep silent and after a while Jeff would become more amenable.

Her deduction was correct, for the second hour had not gone when she again heard a sound at the door. The door did not open, however, and she heard Jeff walking about.

Then his face appeared at the window, close to hers.

She did not move. And she would not meet his gaze, but stared past him.

"Well," he said gruffly, "are you willing to talk sense?"

She continued to gaze over his shoulder. He could not see that the victory had elated her.

"The Ballingers consider themselves mighty important people, I suppose?" he said.

"They know how to be polite, at any rate!" she declared.

"They know how to be stubborn, I reckon," he drawled.

Her chin went up and he laughed.

"You're a Ballinger, all right," he said. "I've seen Matt look like that. I expect you've got grit all right, but you ain't got much sense to be riding around this country at night."

"At least I don't ride around hanging people!" she retorted.

"So you heard that, eh?" he said. "I thought so."

His face seemed to lengthen a little. He smiled grimly.

"You heard the boys talking, eh?" he added. "Well, I reckon that as soon as you get where you're going you'll shoot off your gab about it?"

"You mean that you expect me to tell what I heard?"

He nodded.

"I certainly shall tell!" she declared. "What right have you to hang anybody without a trial?"

"I won't argue that," he said. "He's hung and no arguing will bring him back."

"But my telling will help the law to avenge him!"

"Yes, I reckon you telling what you heard might do that. But I expect you know that there was five men with me. They'd get away clean."

"You mean you wouldn't tell who they were?"

"That's a good guess."

"Then the law will punish you alone."

"I reckon it would, if I'd let it."

"You speak as though you are so great that the law cannot reach you!" She was incredulous and tremendously curious.

"The law!" he said, contempt in his voice. "A safe-guard for fools and weaklings. I make my own laws!"

For an instant Ellen was tempted to laugh, to tell him that he sounded like a boaster and a braggart. But the reflection that she had already overheard enough to convince her that he held the law in contempt sufficed to keep her silent.

She again scrutinized his face. With the moonlight shining upon him he looked more than ever like one of the wild adventurers of long ago, a self-sufficient and perverse spirit of the days when the strong imposed their wills upon the weak.

He had been looking straight at her when he had told her of his contempt for the law, and now his voice was strong with derision.

"Do you think I care a damn what you tell anybody? Tell them as fast as you can talk!"

"I shall!" she promised.

"You would. You're that kind."

"I'm—what?" she gasped.

"You're the kind of woman who talks without knowing what you are talking about. You hadn't sense enough to keep you from riding around in this country alone; and of course you won't have sense enough to use your brains in thinking why you shouldn't tell everything you hear."

"You're a brute!" she told him. Yet she was not as angry as she should have been. She didn't know why.

"We won't argue that," he said. "How did those ropes get around your arms?"

She had vowed she wouldn't tell him, but she did. And when she finished he was watching her steadily.

"You didn't see the man's face?"

"No," she answered, "but I heard his voice."

"You'd know his voice if you heard it again?"

"Oh, yes. I've been hearing it for several minutes. You are the man who brought me here, Mr. Jeff!"

She told the lie with a straight face, and watched him with level gaze as he stiffened and stared at her.

"Me!" he exclaimed in huge derision. "Hell, no! I'll hang a man quick enough for stealing horses, but I draw the line when it comes to fooling with women! I wasn't within a dozen miles of you when you were tied up!"

"Oh, you don't like women."

"Not well enough to try to abduct one."

"Are you afraid of women?"

"I reckon not. Do I act like I'm scared of you? I just don't want anything to do with women. I don't like them. They are too changeable and selfish. I reckon you think you are just about perfection. Anyway, you act like you think that. You get yourself in trouble because you want to have your own way, and when a stranger tries to get you out of it you hold your head up so high that you get a stiff neck. On top of that you accuse me of abducting you. Hell: Abduct you! What would I want to abduct you for?"

Ellen smiled.

"I can't answer that, of course," she said calmly. "All I know is that you *did* tie me up and bring me here. You are annoyed because you have discovered that I know you and your friends hanged a man. You don't want me to say anything about it."

"Well, I'll be damned!" he exclaimed disgustedly.

"You probably will be damned by a good many people when this story gets out," she said. "My father will be furious, of course, when he hears that you dragged me away and kept me in this place all night, after sending your men away. And the law will want to know about the man you murdered. So you see you are going to have a lot of explaining to do. And of course when I tell them the truth they will believe me."

His lips were in straight lines.

"Look here!" he said, his voice sharp and cold: "Do you sure think I tied you up and brought you here?"

"Why, of course," she answered. "What else is there for me to think? Something happens to my pony. I fall and am stunned. When I regain consciousness I find myself on a horse with a man. My arms tied and there is a handkerchief over my mouth. I cannot see the man who is on the horse with me, but I kick him and he threatens me. The voice is yours. Then you and your men come here. You send your men away and stay here with me. What am I to think? What will everyone think?"

The ancestors were wagging their heads at her, but she only smiled defiantly at them. For the longer she looked at Jeff the better she liked him. He was the first man she had met who looked good to her and she was determined to take him!

CHAPTER FOUR

The ancestors might be scandalized. Jeff might squirm.

Ellen did not care. She had started from the Hour Glass with the intention of marrying Jim Kellis. She couldn't marry a man who was already married, nor would she go back to the Hour Glass unmarried, to endure her father's amused glances.

She knew Matthew M. Ballinger. He'd smile at her. There would be no reproaches, no rebukes. But the Ballinger smile was singularly expressive. It could be bland and smooth and at the same time it could be eloquent with unspoken accusation and derision.

She would marry anybody rather than return to the Hour Glass in humiliation. Besides, Jeff wasn't "anybody"; he was "somebody." She knew character. Not for nothing had she calmly and coldly studied her male acquaintances.

No man, except Kellis, had ever appealed to her, and she realized at this moment that what she had felt for Kellis had been merely a sort of maternal sympathy for a weakling. She was rather glad she had found Kellis already married, for now that she had met Jeff she was aware that something startling had happened to her. For the first time in her life she discovered that she was interested in a man.

She wasn't in love with Jeff. Not that. Certainly not. Jeff merely interested her. He interested her because he was a new sort of being.

All the men she had known had been cut from the same pattern. They talked alike, dressed the same way, with some slight variation their manners were the same. She had never been able to detect a flash of individuality in any of them.

Jeff was intensely individual. He was a vital force. He was passionate, ruthless, vibrant with authority. Primitive. A glance into his moody, smouldering eyes had almost awed her. The fact that he had helped to hang a man aroused no emotion in her except that of a reluctant admiration for his daring.

He was not, she was certain, in the habit of hanging men. That is, he did not make a business of it. So far as she had been able to determine the man he and his men had executed had been a criminal who should have been lawfully killed, but had not because the law was reluctant or weak. Jeff and his friends had merely taken the law into their own hands. It was a primitive method, to be sure, but did that fact make the criminal less deserving of his fate? Weren't primitive emotions rampant in everybody? How often had she been angry enough to punish people! What is the cause of intolerance? What is behind the malicious impulse that makes people interfere in the lives of others? The primitive passion to punish for a fault, of course! Nothing less. Well, Jeff's primitiveness was not petty, since it deprived the culprit of life!

She felt the grimness of the tragedy; she was horrified, but her good sense told her that when the law failed there was justification in such executions. What was the difference between a chief witness and the executioner? She knew of respected men who had been chief witnesses.

She had not witnessed the tragedy and so she did not know what part Jeff had taken in it. She preferred not to know, because if she married Jeff she didn't want to be haunted by certain mental pictures.

"Well," said Jeff, watching her cynically, "I seem to have put my foot in it!"

"It was your own fault, you know. I didn't ask you to abduct me."

"Oh, no," he said, "you wouldn't do that. But you've got a mighty short memory for voices."

"Maybe I have. But I remember yours. And I won't forget that you cursed me!"

"I seem to have forgotten it," he said, his voice full of mockery.

"And I certainly won't forget that you threatened to slap my face," she added, maliciously, enjoying his rage.

"I must have thought you needed slapping!" he jeered. He looked closer at her. It appeared to her that for the first time he was studying her face. His gaze was critical; he seemed to be appraising her.

To her amazement she flushed. She could feel the blood surging hotly into her cheeks, up her neck, into her temples. She had not blushed in years, and this was a miracle which required explanation. The trouble was that at that instant she was not in a mood for analyzing her emotions. She was dismayed and her thoughts were incoherent.

The moonlight was white and her cheeks were crimson, so of course Jeff observed her embarrassment. Jeff had been skeptical, but the blush banished his last doubt.

"Hell!" was his thought, "the poor kid sure does think I'm the guy that abducted her! I'm in with both feet!"

"If you think I need slapping why don't you slap me?" she said, offering her cheek.

"I'll think it over," he answered gruffly. "The chances are that you need it."

He abruptly left the window and vanished from her sight.

She was tired now, and the bunks looked more inviting. Besides, although Jeff's final word enraged her, she was no longer afraid; so she walked to one of the bunks, stretched out on it and went to sleep.

The sunlight was flooding the room when she opened her eyes and sat up to gaze about.

The door was wide open and a cool, keen breeze was entering. She listened, but heard no sound. She swung around and sat on the edge of the bunk, wonderingly communing with herself, for she had awakened with a very definite sense of sheer delight in her existence. She had not experienced such a sensation since she had been a very young girl. A new and enchanting vista had been opened, and when she decided that Jeff loomed large in it she blushed again.

She got up quickly and walked to the door. Standing on the threshold she gazed outside.

Her pony was grazing contentedly in a grove directly in front of the door. She did not see another animal and she quickly decided that Jeff had deserted her. Very quietly and slowly she sat down on the threshold of the doorway and gazed with unseeing eyes into the dark green aisles of the forest.

Jeff had fled.

She felt like crying, but of course she wouldn't. No Ballinger ever yielded to tears when things went wrong. But she wondered if any of the Ballinger women had ever seen a man like Jeff!

She smiled wryly. Well, anyway, she hadn't wanted Jeff so badly. She had wanted him only because she had promised herself that she would marry the first man she met. After all, he wasn't gallant. But perhaps he had known she was lying. Darn him! She never wanted to see him again! She'd go back to the Hour Glass, pack her things and go back East!

"You're up, eh?"

Jeff was standing at a corner of the cabin. His voice had been gruff, unfriendly even, but it straightened her, brought her to her feet. She stood, her hands unconsciously clasped over her bosom, her eyes shining.

"Oh!" she exclaimed weakly, "then you didn't go!"

"Didn't go where?" he asked, staring at her.

"Why—why—I—I thought you'd left me!"

"Did, eh? Well, that would be just like you! What gave you that idea? Think I'm scared of you? Seems you must have been raised wrong."

Where was her independence? Ordinarily she would have overwhelmed him with her contempt, but somehow just now she was overjoyed to think that this particular man was here to talk to her. It made no difference what he was saying. At any rate he had not deserted her!

Then he said, more gently:

"You're hungry, I reckon. I've rustled some grub. It's in the mess house right around the corner here. Come along when you are ready."

Ten minutes later Ellen entered the door of a small building in the rear of the cabin to find Jeff pouring coffee into two cups that stood on a crude table. On a platter were some strips of crisp bacon and on a plate a mound of soda biscuits. There was no butter. But the biscuits were steaming and the coffee Jeff was pouring had a delicious aroma. Ellen was hungry, and when she saw that Jeff was not going to invite her to sit down she drew up a bench and dropped into it without invitation. The table was a long one and she felt very small sitting at it with Jeff opposite her.

She was strongly satisfied. The bacon was crisp, the coffee good, the biscuits light and flaky—and Jeff hadn't deserted her.

She had a qualm of misgiving. Where had Jeff learned to cook? She had never tasted such biscuits! The bacon was marvellous, and the coffee had been brewed by an expert. Was Jeff already married?

"You didn't find these biscuits already baked?" she asked.

"What got that idea into your head? I baked them myself," he answered brusquely, looking at her with level hostility.

"And the bacon! It is wonderful! And the coffee! Wherever did you learn to cook like that?"

"Just learned, I reckon."

"Your wife taught you, I suppose."

"Your supposing is away off."

That did not answer her question. It sounded like equivocation.

"Some wives teach their husbands to cook," she ventured.

"Mine didn't."

"Why?" Ellen almost held her breath.

"Look here," he said, glowering at her. "Get this straight. I ain't married, and I don't want to get married!"

Did he suspect her intentions? Was he warning her? Well, if he did not have a wife he was going to get one very soon, whether he wanted one or not! But before she took him as a husband she wanted to know something more about him. So now she pretended a great unconcern.

"Of course, living alone, you would have to do your own cooking—or go hungry," she said.

"Who told you I live alone?" he asked belligerently.

"Why—don't you? I got that impression. I suppose it was because of the way you go about things. Depending upon yourself, you know."

"I live with my father and mother," he told her.

He was so very young, after all! Young in spite of his tallness, his lithe muscles, his leonine head, his stern mouth and his glowering, moody eyes. She judged him to be twenty-eight or thirty, but she knew that his wilderness life had brought him none of the sophistication that makes people mentally old before their time. He was natural, sincere, and entirely without affectation. A novelty! Hers!

"Your father is one of the early settlers, I suppose?"

"He was one of the first in Cochise County."

"Oh. A cattleman?"

He nodded.

"I presume he finds it difficult to make a living, now that the country has so many big owners?"

"That's good!" he exclaimed. "My father is the biggest owner in the county."

She sipped her coffee to conceal her astonishment, for now she was almost positive that he was a son of Adam Hale, who owned the Diamond A. The Diamond A was the largest ranch in Cochise County. She had heard her father speaking of it; had overheard Jim Peters telling another man that Adam Hale practically ruled Cochise. The Hour Glass was a big ranch, but the Diamond A was bigger. Adam Hale must be a man of great importance. His son, of course, must also be a man of importance.

At any rate she was aware that Jeff was more interesting than ever. She knew now where he had got his air of authority; why he had gruffly told her that he made his own laws.

"Then your name must be Hale," she said.

He nodded.

"Is this cabin on your property?"

"It's a place we bought some years ago; we use it as a range camp."

They had finished with the food. Jeff sat with folded arms, gazing straight at his guest. He was perplexed, perhaps, but not perturbed. Perplexed because being innocent of the crime of abducting her he must devise some way of protecting her from the gossip that would inevitably follow the revelation that she had spent a night with him in a cabin on his father's property. He was aware that public opinion would be with the girl, that any explanation he might make would be rejected.

She would talk, of course. She had told him she would, and he believed her. He didn't like women of her type, but he had met courage in various forms and he knew she had it.

He could not understand how she could have made the mistake of thinking that he was her abductor, but if that was her belief he must accept it.

He could not consult his own feelings. He didn't even know if his feelings toward her were definite. She was beautiful, but he was convinced that she was headstrong and argumentative. She had opinions, a calm self-reliance that irritated him, a freedom of manner that aroused his disgust. She was of that strange breed of woman, who, emerging from the clouded atmosphere of the depths of inferiority, gazes with bright and ingenuous eyes at an amazed world and demands to be accepted as an equal, while blandly disregarding the fact that she is not equipped for equality.

She had plenty of spirit, he perceived that. Likewise, he surmised that so far she looked upon men as mere humans who had been placed in the world for the express purpose of being imposed upon.

Twice he had observed her blushing, and he had been amazed and baffled at the sight. That she had blushed because of him he could not presume to believe, for toward the man who had abducted her she could entertain only resentment. He was of the opinion that her blushes had been provoked by contemplation of her predicament. Yet he could not understand how a woman who would take such damn fool chances could have sensibilities that were susceptible to the emotion. She was a damn fool, he was certain. But whether she was or not he would have to do the right thing by her. But he was certain he would not enjoy the experience.

She made some sort of an appeal to him as she sat opposite him. She was now demure, shy, pensive. Around her was an atmosphere of alluring mystery, which always reaches out and envelops a man who is alone with an attractive woman. Jeff perceived that there was a delicacy about her that had previously escaped him, a persuasive feminine grace which he had not seen in women he had known—a helplessness so obvious that it smote him with the conviction that he was a great, overawing brute who was taking an unfair advantage.

He experienced his first pang of perturbation, of pity. He was exasperated by the emotion, so he abruptly got up and walked to the door, where he stood, frowning at the flashing green of the sunlit forest.

Her voice reached him. She was standing, also, and her voice had just the suspicion of a quaver in it:

"Will you please get my pony?"

He turned slowly and looked at her. The frown still wrinkled his brow.

"Where are you going?" he asked.

"Home, of course. Don't you think I shall have enough to explain without—without staying here longer?"

Jeff abruptly turned again to face the forest. He hadn't thought this situation could contain so much tragedy! Hell! He was sending this girl to face a father who might disown her; who at any rate would always be suspicious of her! And she hadn't done anything wrong. She had only been indiscreet in riding out alone.

He faced her again.

"Look here," he said. "I know Matt Ballinger. He would be suspicious of his great-aunt. You can't go back to the Hour Glass and tell him the truth."

"You mean I can't tell him that you abducted me? I shall, of course!"

"You can tell him what you damn please! He won't believe anything you tell him." He scowled at her, adding: "If you go back there you will only make a fool of yourself!"

"Oh, you think I have a choice of several places to go. Is that it?"

"You've a choice of two places that I know of," he returned, watching her intently; "you can go back to the Hour Glass or you can ride with me to Randall and get married."

He saw her cheeks grow pale; grimly watched how a stream of pink mounted the rounded column of her neck and spread to her face.

He felt that she did not appear to be greatly astonished at his proposal, though he should have known that a girl of her type wouldn't betray astonishment if she felt it. She faced him quietly and he observed that her eyes were very bright and that the stains in her cheeks took on a new shade—crimson. He was aware that she was more beautiful than ever. But he had no enthusiasm for his part in this affair. He didn't love her, and he probably never would love her. He'd marry her, though.

He spoke his thoughts, trying to make it easy for her to accept.

"It needn't be permanent. Likely it wouldn't be. As a matter of fact, it couldn't be. A girl like you couldn't stand it to be married to a man like me. You've been raised different and our ideas wouldn't jibe. But getting married will untangle this, and then you can go back East, stay for a while and apply for a divorce. You'll get it without any trouble. You don't even need to go to the house with me, if you don't want to."

She gazed straight at him. To his amazement the colour was still in her cheeks. There was defiance in her eyes.

"If I marry you I shall stay here and be your wife!" she declared. "At least for a time. If I married you and left you immediately father would understand. That ruse wouldn't fool him. I won't be laughed at! If you marry me you have got to pretend that you want me more than anything else in the world!"

"Well," he said cynically, "I reckon there's a lot of married men playing that game. It won't be hard, for I've been watching my friends."

"Well, you don't need to be offensive about it!"

"I'll do my best to be a proper married man," he said gravely.

CHAPTER FIVE

The trail was too narrow to permit the horses to travel side by side so Ellen followed Jeff. She was reminded of a picture she had seen in which an Indian squaw followed her lord and master through a painted desert. She and Jeff were not journeying through a desert but they were in a setting which was quite primitive.

They rode through a forest and crossed a shallow river which brought them into a country featured by low hills. After they got out of the hills they mounted a great upland which the horses climbed at a walk. There was a great deal of grass on the big slope, some huge rocks, clumps of yucca, here and there a fiery lance of ocatilla and stretches of low-growing mesquite. There were some stunted trees with thick, clublike branches. They looked prickly and when Ellen spoke to Jeff about them he told her they were a variety of cactus called choya. From a distance they were attractive and picturesque but upon closer inspection she found them repulsive. Their branches were armoured with close-growing scales.

Once they passed a forest of giant saguaro ranging in height to fifty or sixty feet. Their tall columns bore pale yellow flowers, and Ellen observed that there were small, circular holes in some of the columns. She saw small birds entering and leaving the holes. She did not ask Jeff any questions, for Jeff rode steadily ahead of her, tall and loose in the saddle, seemingly indifferent to her existence.

But when they reached the crest of the upland and Jeff halted to breathe his horse, Ellen turned, gazed backward, and gasped with amazement and delight. Jeff shifted in the saddle and watched her.

For more than two hours they had been travelling upward, and Ellen was now looking out and down over a wilderness domain of such magnitude as to seem endless.

A great, green world of space and silence basking in the white sunlight under a cloudless sky. At the foot of the big upland which they had just climbed was the shallow river they had crossed. It gleamed and shimmered where the sun struck it, reflecting shafts and beams of light that dazzled her eyes. She could trace its sinuous course until in the distance it narrowed to the proportions of a slender silver wire and then vanished altogether.

At the edge of the river immediately below her was the forest out of which she and Jeff had ridden. Yesterday and last night the forest had seemed very big to her, but now she observed that in comparison to the gigantic wilderness in which it was set it was very little more than a patch.

There were dozens of such forests visible to her. As a matter of fact the timber stretches seemed insignificant. They were overwhelmed by the vast reaches of level country adjoining them and circling them; they were dwarfed by mammoth systems of hills and valleys that rose and fell between them. Grim, rugged, and sombre cañons sank into the wilderness floor, great ragged gorges intersected; arroyos and barrancas could be traced as far as she could see. Far away, seeming to mark the northern boundary, stretched a purple haze that her gaze could not penetrate.

Ellen looked at Jeff. He appeared mildly amused.

"Big, eh?" he said. "One hundred and fifty miles wide, about two hundred and fifty long. Over beyond that stretch of timber down there is the Hour Glass. Your dad owns five thousand acres. You thought that was big. Well, down there, you'd have to hunt hard to find it. There's things down there that no man has ever seen. If you are going to stay in this country you'd better not try riding down there. There's only one trail."

He did not speak again, but sat patiently waiting until she turned her horse. Then he urged his own animal and rode slowly away from the crest over a level. She followed him, awed to silence by what she had seen.

They rode for another hour over the level in a southerly direction. Then Jeff headed his horse down a wash into a gorge so deep that part of the time Ellen's pony seemed to be sliding upon its haunches. But she had done a great deal of riding and she followed him closely, handling her animal well. Ellen thought that Jeff was furtively watching her.

Far down the gorge she followed him up another wash, and soon, behind her, she observed a great painted cliff which she suspected was the edge of the tableland they had been crossing when they had struck the gorge which had brought them to their present position. She shuddered when she thought of what might happen to a strange horseman riding the plateau at night.

They came after a while to where the land took a great downward sweep, and she observed below her another great valley. The floor of this valley seemed to be level except for some low hills that appeared here and there. The valley was green, and there was one big river running through it, with several branches joining it here and there. She saw a railroad down in the valley, its two lines of steel coming out of a gorge near where she and Jeff were riding and stretching away in a straight line into the oblivion of distance.

Near the centre of the valley were two rows of buildings forming what seemed to Ellen to be a town, Randall, possibly. She spoke to Jeff about the buildings.

"That's Randall," he answered. "That's where we'll find Jay Link, the justice of the peace who will marry us."

Jeff's voice expressed cold disinterest, and since he could not see her face Ellen smiled amusement. She was no longer worried. She had found her future husband. Moreover, she liked him; she wanted him; she intended to have him.

She said, softly: "You don't sound very enthusiastic."

He did not turn.

"Well," he said, "this is my first adventure of this kind. I'm trying hard to get adjusted to it."

"I have never been married before, either," she retorted. "But I think I am going to like it."

"H'm."

That was all the conversation. Thereafter he rode well ahead, not once looking back; and she followed, gazing with interest at the valley which was to be her future home.

However, as they reached the edge of town Jeff drew his horse down until he was riding beside her.

"We've got to make this look regular," he told her. "We've got to make it seem like the real thing."

"Well, it is, isn't it?"

"I reckon it's real enough, all right. Jay Link will marry us tight enough. But there's folks that know me, and they'll be watching. Maybe we'll have to do some lying. And I reckon that after Jay Link ties us up I'll have to kiss you to make it look straight. Can you stand that?"

"I'll do the best I can," she answered. She wondered if there was any eagerness behind his cold manner. She was amazed at her own feelings. He was the first man that she had ever wanted to kiss!

Randall was crude, unfinished, dingy. The two rows of buildings that stretched east and west with the railroad tracks between them were flimsy board structures that looked as though the first strong wind that struck them would demolish them. Their wooden walls had never been painted; their roofs were awry, their windows were small and grimy; most of them sagged—weak and maudlin.

The space between the rows was wide and unpaved. It was deeply rutted by wagon tracks, and dust lay in huge, soft windrows. Clouds erupted from the wheels of vehicles and volcanoes belched from the hoofs of horses. A fine film of the feathery alkali covered everything and floated like a veil between earth and sky, creating a yellow haze that moved slowly in the lazy breeze.

Randall was the first Western pioneer town that Ellen had so intimately viewed and she found herself more interested than shocked, although there were things in Randall to offend the sensibilities of any girl reared in an Eastern environment.

Randall's citizens were coatless; many of them hatless. Suspenders and blue denim overalls were there in profusion. A black-bearded man standing in front of a restaurant picking his teeth with the blade of a six inch clasp knife indicated the degree of refinement that might be expected in the town; while a teamster spouting lurid oaths gave her a distinct idea of the dialect she would meet.

However, she observed that when she and Jeff passed the teamster his profanity suddenly ceased. He stared at her in vast embarrassment and a hand went involuntarily to his hat, while the black-bearded man standing in front of the restaurant sheathed his knife, straightened, and pulled at his beard. By these signs she knew she was in a country where men predominated and that when a woman appeared she would be treated with respect.

The street was animated, and resonant with sounds that were new to her. Several prairie schooners were drawn up in a line upon the north side of the street. Evidently the occupants of these vehicles were resting, for they were draped about the wagons in clusters—men in stiff cowhide boots, jeans or overalls, woollen shirts and broad-brimmed hats; women in calico and bonnets; children barefoot, hatless. Dogs were barking, fighting. Open wagons, buckboards, and buggies were standing in front of various stores. Cow ponies, most of them ewe-necked, bearing heavy, pronged saddles with high cantles, were hitched to racks that were usually in front of saloons.

There were many saloons, and the atmosphere was heavy with the stale odours that issued from them. Beer kegs were mounted in front of many of the saloons, and about some of the doors men were congregated.

The scene was crude, but prophetic. These people were pioneers engaged in the business of establishing outposts, and Ellen felt no desire to laugh at them, for she was aware that not many generations ago the Ballingers had been likewise engaged.

She was conscious of the stares that followed Jeff and herself, though she was certain the stares were directed at her and not at Jeff. She knew that in Randall her riding outfit was conspicuous, but when she observed that Jeff was riding along, apparently serenely unaware of the attention they were attracting, she smiled with satisfaction. Jeff wasn't self-conscious, nor was he ashamed of her.

So far as she could perceive Jeff's manner hadn't changed at all. He was still what he had been from the instant she had first seen him—a deliberate, confident man, direct of speech and unaffected.

As they rode down the street she saw men nod toward him and speak to one another. She felt that several of them whispered, as if fearful that

Jeff would hear what they were saying. He nodded to some men, he smiled frostily at others, and Ellen observed that the men he nodded to were invariably men who were dressed as he was dressed; that his chilling smiles were directed at men who wore the heavy boots and the denim or jeans of the prairie schooners. Ellen became vaguely aware that there was animosity between Jeff and the rough-looking men of the prairie schooners, but she had no time or opportunity to speculate, for presently Jeff rode up to a hitching rack in front of a frame building that stood a little apart from the others, dismounted, looped his bridle rein over the rail, and looked steadily at her.

"We'll find Jay Link here, I reckon, Ellen," he said, gently.

She was amazed by the startling change in his manner and by his use of her name. And then she saw that there were several men standing near and she remembered his words: "We've got to make it seem like the real thing."

She smiled. The gentleness of his voice thrilled her, brought a blush to her cheeks. If only the gentleness were real. She hoped that in time it would be.

Her blushes were real enough, for as Jeff hitched her horse and came around to help her dismount, the men who were watching and listening smiled significantly, thinking her embarrassed.

She was embarrassed. For when presently they had entered the building and she was standing in the presence of a tall man of sixty with a drooping white mustache who was looking at her with a quizzical gaze out of experienced eyes, she knew that he was aware that she loved the man who was to be her husband.

She was silent as Jeff told Link what was wanted, and she tried to keep her gaze straight as Link said:

"Well, Jeff, I congratulate you. You've sure picked a prize!"

She wanted to see Jeff's face at this instant, and she had to use all her will power to keep her gaze downward. However, she could *feel* Jeff looking at her!

"Yes, I'm lucky," he told Link in a curiously steady voice.

"Ellen Ballinger!" exclaimed Link, a little later. "Not Matt Ballinger's girl!" At her somewhat amused nod he added: "Well, I'll be darned! How in thunder—— Why——" He paused and looked at Jeff.

"A thing that is—is!" said Jeff. "There's no need of doing any wild guessing, Jay. If you just hook us up we'll be obliged to you."

After the ceremony, with Jeff's ring on her finger, and Jeff's kiss upon her lips—a kiss which she felt had not a little passion in it despite the sternness of his eyes when they had been so close to hers—they stood for an instant at the door of Link's office.

Ellen was a trifle uncertain, but there was no diffidence or indecision in Jeff's manner.

"We'll have our wedding supper now," he said. "It will be dark soon and we've still got ten miles to ride." He turned and called to Link, asking the latter to take the horses to a livery stable for water and feed.

"We'll take an hour, Jay," he finished. "Tell Allen to bring them back to where he got them."

He slipped an arm through Ellen's and ushered her out to the street. She nestled close to him, enjoying the sensation, thrilling with the knowledge that she was married to him, no matter what might happen.

She knew that a year ago—a month ago—even yesterday—she could not have imagined herself marrying a wild man whom she had known only a few hours. She could not understand what had happened to her, nor was she aware that she cared. Yesterday seemed as far away as her previous ridiculous conviction that all men were worthless and unworthy, that they were vain and foolish creatures that one might play with and not commit oneself irretrievably. All her former philosophy of life was nebulous. It had not stood up under the stress of actual passion. A glance at Jeff had destroyed it.

The Ballinger pride—where was it?

She was delighted that it was not with her now. For the Ballinger pride could not have walked down the street of a crude Western town upon the arm of a Jefferson Hale; it could not have thrilled—as she did—to the feel of Jeff's muscular arm, nor could it have *hoped* that Jeff would ultimately grow to love her.

She did not see any of the people of the town who paused to stare at her. She was unconscious of all of them. Jeff alone was in her world.

"Well, I reckon Link didn't tumble," he said, glancing down at her face.

"I'm sure he didn't!" she replied, remembering the unexpected fervour of his kiss.

"H'm," he said.

Presently as they walked he looked down again. This time his lips were curved into a strange smile.

"How do you feel?" he asked.

"Why—all right, I think." She was puzzled.

"About being married," he explained. "I don't feel any different. There ain't much to it. Just a few words and a ring."

"I thought it was marvellous!" she declared.

"H'm." He looked closer at her. Was she mistaken, or did his arm tighten on hers.

"That ring is too big for your finger," he said. "While we're having supper I'll slip out and get another."

"That will be wonderful!"

"H'm."

He led her into a restaurant which looked inviting, and sought a table at a front window where, when Ellen was seated, she could peer into the street and see people passing in the semi-darkness.

Jeff sat opposite her. His felt hat, with a brim not as wide as some she had seen, was hanging upon a rack behind him. The imprint of the hatband was upon his hair, which was longer than it should have been, but not unsightly. On the contrary it was attractive. She had grown somewhat weary of seeing meticulously groomed men; she had never liked men who seemed to be always thinking of their personal appearance. She appreciated neatness in men but felt that their masculinity was somehow obscured by the trivial details of attire. A man's first duty to himself is to be masculine.

Jeff's hair seemed to proclaim the virility of its owner. It was wavy, glossy black; there was one wisp that hung negligently down over his left temple.

His forehead was high, and startlingly white in contrast to his bronzed face and neck. His mouth was not as stern as it had been; there was a half smile on his lips now, a wayward and reluctant good humour, perhaps a cynical tolerance. She could not tell. It seemed to her that his expression was conveying the thought: "Well, I'm licked, but perhaps it won't be as bad as I thought it would be."

"Well," he said gently, aloud, "here we are. I reckon this culinary department won't be able to provide the ingredients of a proper wedding supper, but we can't complain for we didn't notify them that we were coming."

His keen eyes were searching hers; she felt he sought for betraying expressions. He saw only lively interest and calm contentment, and was puzzled. She knew, for she saw his brows draw together.

He consulted a waitress who appeared at the table. Ellen had not seen him look at the girl and she was astonished to hear him address her by name.

"Sadie," he said, "what could you recommend?"

"The roast beef is good," replied Sadie. "And the chicken."

The girl was standing sideways, facing Jeff, and Ellen could see only her profile. But Ellen observed that her cheeks were flushed. Her voice was low.

"The roast beef, if you please," said Ellen in response to Jeff's glance of inquiry.

Ellen was aware that Sadie had turned and was looking at her. She met the girl's eyes, and smiled. Sadie did not smile. Her eyes flashed with cold hostility, her lips hardened.

"Two orders of roast beef, Sadie," said Jeff. He gazed gravely at Ellen. "The Elite isn't great on variety," he added. "We'll have to take whatever they've got ready. If you'd mention an entrée here they'd think you were getting personal. Salads have quit growing in this climate, and dessert is called pie."

"Cawfee?" asked Sadie. She was looking straight at Ellen now, and there was a challenge in her eyes.

"If you please," said Ellen.

Sadie abruptly departed and Ellen gazed out of the window toward the street. She could see very little beyond the window, and was not trying to see anything. She was embarrassed and indignant, for she felt that if there was or had been a romance between Sadie and Jeff he should not have brought her in here for their wedding supper. She rather thought, however, that Jeff was not a party to the romance, if there was one, although there was no doubt that Sadie was in love with him. She'd have something to say to Jeff about Sadie later on.

All through the meal Sadie silently attended them, and when she was not at the table she stood at a little distance, watching. She was facing Ellen, and although Ellen did not look directly at her she could see that the girl was rigid and hostile. Ellen knew that she was being inspected by jealous eyes, but she was pleased to discover that Jeff was obviously unaware of Sadie's scrutiny. This, apparently, was a one-sided courtship in which the girl was the aggressor. She didn't blame Sadie very much, though, for she had done the very thing that Sadie was doing. The only difference was that she had succeeded and Sadie had failed.

But now, while enjoying her triumph over Sadie, Ellen glanced out of the window to observe that a crowd seemed to have gathered in front of the restaurant. There was some sort of agitation outside, for she could hear the clatter of hoofs, the creaking of saddle leather, voices. Bronzed faces of many men were revealed in the light that shone out of the restaurant window; some of the faces were pressed against the glass.

Ellen looked at Jeff. He appeared to be unconscious of the commotion outside, for he was calmly eating. His thoughts must have been serious, for his face was grave. He was so absorbed that he did not hear her when she spoke to him.

"Jeff!" she said, again.

He straightened, looked at her. He must have detected the alarm in her manner, for he turned to the window and for the first time heard and saw the crowd outside.

"Something's up!" he said shortly.

He got up quickly, brushing his right hand against the stock of the heavy revolver at his hip as he reached with his left hand for his hat, which was hanging on a rack near him.

Ellen rose also, her alarm increasing as she heard the sound of many footsteps at the door. She was standing near Jeff when the door flew open and a dozen men crowded into the room. They were rough-looking men, arrayed in overalls, boots, woollen shirts, and broad-brimmed hats. They were not cowboys, but men of the prairie schooners, such as she had seen lounging in the street when she and Jeff had entered town. They were armed and their faces were grim. Their leader was a tall man of middle age who was dressed like Jeff—in cowboy regalia.

That they had entered the restaurant in search of Jeff was apparent from the way the leader's eyes lighted as his gaze went to him.

"You're here, eh?" he said. "Well, put up your hands! You're under arrest!"

CHAPTER SIX

For the first time in her life Ellen was breathing an atmosphere charged with the potentialities of tragedy, and to her amazement she found the scene grotesque, unreal, and its actors ridiculously inconsistent. She had thought that all tragedies must be brought about by a visible frenzy on the part of the chief actors, and that men meditating violence would be so wildly excited that their intentions might be plainly read. Tragedy threatened here, but the scene was not even dramatic.

The men who had entered were standing motionless and silent. Some other men, arrayed in the garb of cowboys, were pushing into the room from behind the others, but they did not appear to belong to the drama that was being enacted, for they spread out in the room and seemed to be merely interested onlookers.

The leader of the prairie schooner men was rigid. His face was expressionless, masklike. He wore a heavy revolver at his right hip, but his hands were hanging at his sides, empty. They were not even clenched. The men ranged behind him were likewise empty handed, and a stony calm seemed to have settled over their faces. The late comers, the cowboys, were also calm.

But it seemed to Ellen that of all the men in the room Jeff was the least perturbed. He had not reached his hat when the men had burst in, but now, with them all watching him, he placed the hat on his head, drew it well down over his forehead, folded his arms and smiled whimsically at the leader.

"Why, it's Bill Hazen!" he said. And then, distinctly in a cold tone that made every word a studied insult, he added: "What's eating you now, Bill?"

Hazen's lips writhed into a sneer of hate. The hard mask was destroyed and passion was revealed.

"I reckon you heard me!" he said. "You're under arrest!"

"Seems you're in a right smart hurry to arrest me, Bill; rushing in here like this with forty men behind you," said Jeff, his voice low, almost gentle.

"Some of these men belong to my posse," said Hazen. "An' I'm sure in a hurry. You come along!"

"I figure on coming to your office the first thing in the morning, Bill. To-night don't suit me at all. Important business."

"You're comin' right now!" declared Hazen. "Pass over that gun! You may be a big man in these parts but you're got to respect the law the same as everybody else!"

"Why, from the way horse thieves have been carrying on I didn't think there was any law here, Bill," said Jeff, still gently. "Since when have you taken hold?"

"That's none of your business, Hale!" declared Hazen. "As sheriff of this county I run things the way I want to run them!"

"You ain't running me, Bill," said Jeff. "And the kind of law you represent ain't running me, either. Whenever there's a law that don't operate, I make one that will!"

"That's what you done last night!" charged Hazen. "You an' some more of your critters was seen last night ridin' down into the Navajo basin. An' this mornin' word comes that Hank Kroll was strung up an' left swingin'! You an' your men done it! I'm takin' you into custody until I prove it on you!"

"Hazen," said Jeff, "I told you I had some important business to attend to to-night. I'm going to attend to it. You know where you can find me in the morning. Take your dry farmer posse out of here before somebody gets hurt!"

Ellen had stepped slowly away from the table, and she now stood where she could read Jeff's face. His voice was still low and gentle, but she could tell from the tightness of his lips that he had spoken his final word to Hazen.

And now to Ellen the scene was no longer grotesque, the actors no longer ridiculous. The silence that followed Jeff's words held the tension, the portent of imminent violence. Into that silence came no sound whatever. When Jeff had ceased speaking his head had gone forward a little. His body was rigid and his right hand had lifted a trifle, so that his elbow was slightly crooked.

Hazen had made the same movement. The men with Hazen, whom Jeff had contemptuously called "dry farmers," had not moved. But now expression had come into their faces. They were as tight-lipped as Jeff and passion gleamed in their eyes. The cowboys ranged about the room were grim-faced and silent, but a glance at them told Ellen that they were standing with Jeff. And apparently Hazen had also read their faces and was convinced that they were Jeff's friends, for he delayed making the motion that would bring death into the room.

Twice Ellen observed his muscles tremble on the verge of action; twice she saw his muscles relax. But she knew that ultimately he would act, for he represented the law and must accept the hazard of enforcing it. Also, his hatred of Jeff would drive him.

For an instant Ellen stood, wavering, uncertain, terrified. Then she became aware that she was standing directly in front of Hazen—between him and Jeff—and that she was speaking in a voice which she hardly recognized as her own. For she was seething with emotion, while her voice was cold, calm, and steady.

"Mr. Hazen," she said, "I think you are mistaken. For I happen to know that Jeff Hale spent last night in a Diamond A cabin that his men sometimes use as a camp."

"I know the place," said Hazen. His eyes, now gleaming with curiosity and suspicion, seemed to bore into hers. "That cabin is in the Navajo basin!" he added, triumphantly. "How do you know Jeff Hale was there?"

"He was there with me," she answered.

"Ha!" he exclaimed. "Do you mean to say that Jeff Hale spent all last night in that cabin with you—alone?"

"That is exactly what I mean!" Ellen declared, steadily.

Hazen's gaze wavered, returned to her again with definite incredulity and mockery.

"Well," he said, "that sounds like it's stretched. Who are you?"

"I am Ellen Ballinger."

Hazen's eyes bulged.

"Not Matt Ballinger's daughter!" he exclaimed, amazed.

"Yes," said Ellen.

And now Ellen became aware that Jeff was standing beside her and that his left arm was encircling her waist. She had lied to save him and to avert tragedy, and she knew that in this manner he was thanking her. With his touch she blushed and her gaze sought the floor at her feet. She heard voices buzzing around her, but she did not look up. And Jeff was speaking.

"Hazen," he said. "I wasn't intending to make any explanations to you, but since my wife has chosen to speak I reckon I can tag along. I've known Ellen Ballinger for quite some time. I met her last night and to-day we rode over here to get married. Jay Link was the officiating clergyman. It happened not more than an hour ago." He laughed and a dozen men laughed with him. "I reckon you can go now, sheriff. And unless you can pile up more evidence than you've got I won't even be around to see you in the morning. Good-night, boys."

His voice, now deep and persuasive, lingered in the silence which had fallen on the room. Ellen felt his hand leave her waist and gently grip her right arm. And then she was out in the street with Jeff walking beside her. A few minutes later they were bending over a tray of glittering rings and Jeff was fitting two of them to her fingers. One was a large solitaire, the other a wedding ring.

"This has got to be regular," he told her as he slipped the diamond on her finger.

CHAPTER SEVEN

They rode away from town, southward, through the valley. The lights of Randall were behind them and a heavy, windless darkness ahead.

This was not the sort of wedding journey Ellen had imagined she would take. She had always assumed that her wedding would be like others she had witnessed. There would be the church, the ushers, flowers, bridesmaids, and all the other stilted properties of the hymeneal ceremony. The honeymoon trip would follow and then the cogs of monotony would slip into place.

Rebellion against that sort of thing had made her skeptical of all marriages. She had watched her friends as they industriously laboured to take the romance out of their lives, and she had refused several men because she anticipated that they would not continue to be interesting. She would have married Kellis because while weak, he was different. But now she realized that she would not have respected Kellis. Marrying Kellis would have been a mistake. Perhaps she had made a mistake in marrying Jeff Hale, but she was certain that living with him would not be monotonous.

And she was aware that she had not married Jeff merely to spite her father. She had married Jeff because she wanted him; she had fallen in love with him at sight.

She felt no pang of regret or remorse over her methods. The wild and primitive passion for possession had seized her and she had yielded to it because she could not resist it. She had tricked him, had lied to him and for him. She possessed him legally, but she knew that he did not love her, that he had married her merely to protect her.

They had been riding for nearly half an hour when a faint, luminous glow appeared upon the eastern horizon, and presently the moon's brilliant disk swam in a clear, velvety blue sky.

Jeff's conversation since leaving Randall had been monosyllabic. The tenderness he had shown her in town had been replaced by obvious indifference. She knew of no reason why he should continue the sham of gentleness, since she knew it had been assumed for the benefit of anyone who might have been observing them, but still she was disappointed.

She wanted to talk to him, but there seemed to be nothing to say. The ordinary trivialities of conversation would sound ridiculous. Worse; the uttering of them would perhaps convince Jeff that she was frivolous. And never in her life had she felt more serious than now.

The moon rose and bathed them in its radiance. The silver flood poured into the valley, tinted the slopes and the rimming mountains and disclosed a sinuous trail leading southward to a group of buildings.

Jeff was riding a little distance ahead of Ellen. She felt she had to speak to him.

"Jeff!" she said as she urged her pony beside him.

He turned his head and she saw that his face was grave.

"Well?" he answered.

"You are taking me home, aren't you—to your father's house?"

"Yes."

"Your mother will be there?"

"Sure."

"Do you think she will suspect that—the truth?"

"She won't know anything about it if she isn't told."

"You won't tell her?"

"No. I told you I was seeing this thing through."

"Thank you!"

Jeff detected the fervent note in her voice and smiled faintly, mockingly.

"What's wrong?" he asked. "Getting panicky?"

"Do you think they will ask questions?"

"They are not that kind of folks," answered Jeff. "They'll know just what I tell them. And they'll believe what I tell them."

"And what are you going to tell them, please?"

"That I met you before—when I was East to school."

"Oh! Were you?" She paused, amazed. She had got the impression that he had never been away from the West.

"Where?" she questioned.

"Yale. Expelled for insubordination after one term."

Yes; that would be the fate of one who boasted that he made his own laws. Very clearly she could imagine him defying the faculty, his eyes blazing his contempt of their arbitrary rules.

"It will be easy, you see," he added. "I'll tell them as little as possible, for I don't want to lie any more than I have to."

She closed her eyes and prayed that he might never discover she had lied to him!

The leaven of a new philosophy had been working in her. It was slowly wrecking her previous convictions and bringing new perceptions of conduct. For example, life had amused her, for she had been able to detect its absurdities. She hadn't seen anything inspiring in it. Women arrayed themselves in expensive garments to impress other women, to hold their places in the little cliques they had formed, to attract attention, to please their husbands or to draw other men to them. Some of them lied and cheated. Very few that she knew were happy. Some pretended to be happy, but they weren't. They were playing a game in which there was no goal.

Ellen was not amused by what she had glimpsed of life since leaving the Hour Glass. It seemed to her right now that life had a very definite meaning; that there was a scheme in which every man and woman must play a serious part.

Her mood now was solemn. As she rode down a long, gradual slope in the moonlight she decided that the world wasn't exclusively a playground; it was a place in which men and women were supposed to work at tasks which required all the intelligence and the courage given them by their Creator.

Before her stretched an arid flat upon which little whirlwinds of dust curled and danced in the moonlight. Scattered here and there were hummocks of prickly pear. Clusters of greasewood appeared, fringing alkali beds that spread gray and dull between grass levels. She followed Jeff through a prairie-dog town where the inhabitants squealed in shrill protest against their intrusion, and she observed that for many miles the character of the country was the same as that through which they were passing. A grim land, vast and sombre at night, hinting of mystery, challenging the life that entered it.

She felt that the land was challenging her, that it was whispering to her, reminding her of wasted years, of misdirected endeavour, of purposeless quests. She felt it was trying to tell her that men and women were not as important as they thought they were, that there was a mighty and mysterious power which could, at a stroke, destroy all the petty structures of man's devising. There was a titanic undercurrent of laughter in the whisper.

She divined that there were men who absorbed something from nature; men whose minds were in tune with the infinite, who unconsciously caught something of the ruthlessness and the irony of nature's whims.

Jeff Hale was that kind of man. Looking at him the first time she had wondered. But now she knew. He was a product of the country, and he was as wild and ruthless and as primitive as the grim land that surrounded him. "Whenever there's a law that don't operate, I make one that will!" he had told Sheriff Hazen. Jeff Hale would make laws and enforce them!

Yet she was disturbed about Jeff. He didn't love her. She wanted him as a husband but she didn't want him until he could love her as she loved him. She had gone into this affair cold-bloodedly, with a fixed determination to acquire a man, and she was now apprehensive that the man she had chosen would demand the rights that the marriage ceremony gave him.

As they topped a slight rise and she saw a cluster of white adobe buildings in a grove of giant cottonwood trees, she was assailed with sudden
panic and wheeled her pony around, meditating flight. But evidently Jeff
had been watching her, for he was at her side in an instant. The moonlight
shone full upon him and she saw now that his face was set in stern lines.

"No," he said, "it's too late to do any running. If you'd go back now
you'd be laughed out of the country. You've got to go through with it. And
you've got to pretend that you like it. Mother's got sharp eyes."

They rode on again, in silence.

The Diamond A buildings were low and rambling. A big ranch house
was the centre of the group, but there was a great deal of space between the
various buildings and giant trees were everywhere. A wall of adobe about
five feet high spanned a small stream of water that doubled away from the
group of buildings. The wall was rectangular, inclosing a space of several
acres, and Ellen recognized the inclosure as a corral. The buildings and the
corral wall were white and smooth in the moonlight, reminding the girl of
Spanish mission units. They seemed as quiet and peaceful.

There were several lights visible, dull, flickering through various windows of the ranch house and illuminating a patio garden. Evidently Jeff's
parents were at home, but if they were they did not appear while Jeff helped
Ellen to dismount and turned the animals into the corral. She watched Jeff
as he carried the saddles into a low building which she surmised was a
stable; caught her breath now in amazement at her own foolhardiness in
deliberately contriving this strange situation, and stood, trembling a little
as Jeff approached her.

"Well," he said, "the bride and groom will now present themselves."

He took her by an arm and they moved toward the ranch house. As
they approached the house Ellen observed that the door providing entrance
to the main house from a broad, low-ceilinged veranda, was open. A faint
light was issuing through it and disclosing a portion of the room—a big living room. This house, Ellen could see, was not unlike the Hour Glass ranch
house. There would be the big living room with a door opening into a patio;
a dining room, a large kitchen. The sleeping quarters would surround the
patio, and the patio would be shaded by trees. There would be a garden in
the patio and a flagged walk. Over it all would be the indescribable aroma
of pepper trees, desert flowers, and leaf mould.

Guided by Jeff she went reluctantly to the door. Then she was standing
on the threshold with Jeff beside her.

She saw Jeff's mother first. She was sitting in an easy chair near a big
centre table and the light from a shaded kerosene lamp shone mellowly
upon her. At the instant Ellen observed her she was gazing at the door, and

some needlework which she held in her hands dropped into her lap as her eyes brightened and widened in astonishment.

She smiled at Ellen, rose, placed the needlework upon the table and moved toward her son and his companion. At a little distance, just far enough away from them to betray the doubt and wonder that she must have felt, she stopped, bowed to Ellen and then looked inquiringly at her son.

"Mother," said Jeff, "this lady is my wife."

The Ballingers would have been frigid until explanations had been made. Perhaps, afterward, there would have lingered the chill of damaged pride. But before Ellen knew what was happening she was in Mrs. Hale's arms. There had been no explanations; Ellen's name had not even been mentioned.

In this unquestioning reception to a wife brought in without previous announcement was respect for Jeff Hale's judgment.

Jeff's father was standing.

"Well!" he said, his face beaming. "Jeff's wife, eh? You're mighty welcome!"

In Adam Hale Ellen saw Jeff as he would appear at sixty. Their features were identical. The elder Hale's skin was more deeply wrinkled, and the mellowness of age was upon him, but still the resemblance was startling. Even Adam Hale's hair, white as Spanish-dagger blossoms, was as unruly as Jeff's black locks.

And then Jeff and his father were standing in the open doorway, while Mrs. Hale with gentle tact had taken Ellen into another room, where they stood in a stream of light from the living room, and where their voices could not be heard by the men.

What confidences were asked or given in there none knew.

CHAPTER EIGHT

Mrs. Hale had shown Ellen to her room and had then discreetly retired, leaving the girl in possession. As Jeff had predicted there had been no questions asked. Jeff's parents evidently permitted Jeff to attend to his own affairs.

The room into which the bride had been taken was one that opened from the patio. It was simply but neatly furnished. The bed was large, its coverings white, its pillows soft and inviting. And Ellen was tired.

A big dresser with a tall mirror stood against a side wall. A kerosene lamp stood in front of the glass and as Ellen sat on the edge of the bed she could see her reflection in the lamplight. It was the first time since leaving the Hour Glass that she had been able to get a good view of herself and she was rather astonished to find that her colour was good and her eyes bright.

Jeff must have found her good to look at for he was watching her.

He stood in the door that opened into the patio. His hands were shoved deep into his pockets.

"Well," he said, "it wasn't difficult, was it? It must have seemed sudden to them, for I had never told them that I was contemplating marriage. They took it like thoroughbreds, didn't they?"

"They are wonderful people!" Ellen declared.

"Straight-thinking folks. They'll assume anything is regular. Mother is going to like you."

Ellen was wishing that everything had been "regular" but of course she couldn't tell him that, knowing he did not love her.

"Did they ask any questions?"

"No. I told you they wouldn't." He gazed straight at her. "You see," he added, "it works this way. If you ask a man a question and he doesn't want to tell you what he knows he'll lie or evade. My folks know that if there was anything I wanted to tell them I'd tell it. They won't ask questions that I'd have to lie about."

"Then of course you think they believe you are silent because to explain you would have to lie."

"They are not as subtle as your conclusion. They have faith." He was frankly studying her, and she was convinced that his interest was entirely unromantic. "You like to twist things about," he added. "Don't you think there are people who say exactly what they mean?"

"People are not always truthful. There are times when diplomatic evasion is necessary. Suppose I had told the sheriff that you were away from me long enough last night to hang the man you call Hank Kroll?"

"Well, why didn't you?"

"I did not tell him because I wanted to avert a tragedy."

"You had threatened to tell," he reminded her.

"That was before we were married. I lied to keep my husband out of trouble."

He was plainly skeptical. His gaze was searching.

"What difference could our being married make to you?" he said. "It's only temporary. You know that. There was no courtship, no romance in it. It was merely a form without the spirit."

"Well then," she said, "we will concede that I did not lie to protect the man I had married. Suppose we say that I did it because I didn't want my people to know I had married a man accused of hanging another man."

"That's more like it—more like you; more like the conception I have of you. That's probably the reason you did it. It must have been the reason, for your husband didn't mean anything to you. You see, you hadn't even got acquainted with him."

He was still thoughtfully watching her, and there was no change in the uncompromising steadiness of his gaze. No sign of admiration, no hint of passion, was noticeable. She was convinced that if he felt any emotion whatever it was that of curiosity, merely. She was a new type of individual which chance had turned over to him and he was examining her at leisure without hope of discovering anything about her that might interest him.

"Well," he added when she did not speak, "I suppose you will be going back to the Hour Glass to-morrow?"

"No!" she answered, emphatically.

His brows lifted.

"The next day?"

"No!"

"When?"

"I don't know."

"That's indefinite." He smiled. "That's good, for me. It gives me more time to think up a plausible explanation for our separation. If you could make it a week I could tell the folks that you couldn't stand the climate or the lonesomeness. Almost any excuse would do—after you'd been here a week."

How could she tell him that she wanted to stay with him as other women stayed with their husbands? How could she tell him that she wanted him to love her as she loved him; and how could she make him understand that until he did love her she could not accept him as her husband?

Obviously their marriage meant nothing to him. But it meant a great deal to her and she intended to stay at the Diamond A to attend to it and cultivate it until it blossomed into a wonderful romance. For she felt that she could win him. If she could stay here with him he could begin after a while to see that she was desirable.

Other men had wanted her, and her glass had told her that she was attractive. She knew of course that in Jeff's eyes she was over-sophisticated; she knew her self-reliance was visible to him, and that it had irked him, and she knew that he considered her deficient in intelligence. She remembered his voice and his words when he had frankly expressed his opinion of her: "You hadn't sense enough to keep you from riding around in this country alone; and of course you won't have sense enough to use your brains in thinking why you shouldn't tell everything you hear."

She remembered that she had called him a brute for that, and she also remembered that she hadn't been so very angry. That, she supposed, was because she knew there had been a great deal of truth in what he had said.

She sat on the edge of the bed gazing at her hands, which were folded in her lap. She was strangely humble and subdued—for a Ballinger. Her pride, which had always sustained her, had deserted her. Perhaps it had gone back to her ancestors, where it belonged. For pride seemed out of place in this bedroom. There seemed to be no space for it.

"Do you wish me to leave that soon?" she asked, looking up at him.

"No," he answered, "stay as long as you like. And when you leave be sure I'm not around. I'd find it hard to pretend I was shocked." He smiled, bowed to her, somewhat ironically she thought; said good-night shortly and vanished into the semi-darkness of the patio.

CHAPTER NINE

Being married to a man who did not want her and who wasn't even interested in her as a woman, Ellen had no expectation of enjoying life at the Diamond A. And yet she did enjoy herself. And she did it without Jeff, for when she awakened on the morning following her arrival Jeff had gone, leaving her no word.

She wasn't surprised or offended. There had been a time when she would have been conscious of both emotions, a time when, with her chin in the air and an expression of disdain in her eyes, she would have effaced herself.

She could not do that to Jeff. She did not even think of doing it. In deep humility of spirit she merely smiled when she discovered Jeff's absence, gazed with contemplative eyes at the distant hills and thought of the time—to come—when Jeff would burn the trails in his eagerness to reach her. The inner voice of prophecy was strong in her.

The restlessness which had harassed her in the old days no longer caused her to yearn, fretfully, for undiscovered pleasures. She did not miss her old friends, and she began to wonder if her father had not been right when he had deprecated the self-sufficiency of the younger generation.

As the days went and Jeff did not return she calmly explored the ranch buildings, the river, and the wide, pleasant valley which nestled between the rugged hills. And in all her explorations Jeff was ever in her thoughts. She could imagine him roping his horse in the corral, saddling it, riding the level and the various slopes. In all the rooms of the ranch house she could visualize him in the various stages of his growth, from infancy until the day she had met him. And it seemed to her that if she had known him sooner she might not have acquired some of the mannerisms that, she knew, had offended him.

She was not aware that Mrs. Hale had been quietly watching her and the knowledge did not come to her until one day Mrs. Hale smiled and said:

"My dear, I think women are all alike. Women who are in love, I mean. I acted the same way——"

"Why——!"

"It makes you glow, my dear. Jeff is very fortunate to have found a girl like you. Are you aware that you have been studying that picture for fully fifteen minutes!"

The photograph, unostentatiously framed, was upon a shelf near which Ellen had been standing while talking with Mrs. Hale.

"That was taken just before he was expelled from college," Mrs. Hale informed her. She shook her head. "They found him difficult," she finished.

"I think he cannot be driven," said Ellen.

"You have discovered that already? Well, it is a fact, dear. And as few people will use persuasion, Jeff is continually fighting. Just now he's fighting the dry farmers who have come into this country in droves. They are taking our land, deliberately claiming it. They are aided by Wade Dallman, a man who makes land stealing his profession, and by another man, named Ballinger."

"Ballinger," said Ellen steadily. "Do you happen to know his first name?"

"Matthew," returned Mrs. Hale. She looked at Ellen, seemed to divine that she had been indiscreet, and added: "Why, have I said something I should not have said?"

"No indeed," returned Ellen, "we like to hear the truth about our parents—especially when they have been posing as angels. Matthew Ballinger is my father. Of course Jeff did not tell you."

Mrs. Hale was pink with embarrassment, but she said quietly:

"Jeff should have told me. And I do hope there is a mistake!"

"I should not be surprised if father is mixed up in it," said Ellen. "Would you please tell me exactly what has been going on?"

"There isn't a great deal to it, as I understand it," answered Mrs. Hale. "We came here thirty years ago and Adam preëmpted the land upon which our buildings now stand. It was a section, or six hundred and forty acres. Adam got his grant in about three years and the papers were on file at the General Land Office in the capital. So far as we know there was no error in the title. But strange things have been going on in the Land Office, it is said. A great deal of land has been stolen from the original grantees, by forging certificates and signatures, by fraudulent transfers, by duplicate patents, by forging field notes of the survey, by counterfeiting deeds, and by using lying affidavits. I am repeating what I have heard Adam say, for I know nothing about it. We thought our title was secure. But recently we discovered there was a flaw. It seems that the original certificate is missing from the files, and that there is no memorandum or date on the wrapper to show that it had ever been issued. If the certificate is not found our title to the land is invalid."

"You have searched for it, of course?"

"Everywhere."

"Please go on," suggested Ellen. "I am finding this very interesting."

"There isn't much more," said Mrs. Hale. "It seems that Wade Dallman or—or—"

"Matthew M. Ballinger," supplied Ellen. "Please don't spare him if you think him guilty," she added grimly. "He has a great deal to answer for!"

"Well, somebody discovered that the certificate was missing, and Wade Dallman and Matthew Ballinger have filed claims to the land. So far Matthew Ballinger seems to have done nothing more than file, but Wade Dallman has been selling land from the grant to the dry farmers that have been coming here. It seems that Dallman thinks he is certain to receive the grant." She smiled at Ellen. "That is all, my dear."

"H'm. That is all, eh?" said Ellen.

"Of course," added Mrs. Hale, "we own other land. About twenty thousand acres, I think, and a great deal of it adjoins the town site of Randall. But the strip they are fighting about runs straight down the valley for some miles. It is narrow, but it takes in the river and quite a stretch of the level land near it. I understand there is talk of running a railroad through the valley, and perhaps that is why the land is wanted."

That was exactly why, Ellen decided. Her father was interested in railroads. No Ballinger woman had ever chased after a man, but a man of the Ballinger family wasn't above chasing after railroad land, and stooping to questionable methods to obtain it. Ellen's thoughts at this moment were treasonable for she experienced a thrill of delight over the knowledge that in her father's attempt to gain possession of the Hale land he had inadvertently opposed himself to a fighter. A fighter, moreover, who could not be bullied, coerced or driven; a fighter who believed that laws were made to protect the weak. Jeff did not love her, but she was his wife and she would fight for him.

Jeff had been away from the ranch house for about two weeks when one morning Ellen opened her eyes in her patio bedroom tingling with the conviction that Jeff had returned. She had been dreaming about him and now, having awakened, she heard his voice.

"Coming!" he said.

His voice came from the bedroom adjoining hers. During his absence she had entered it and had curiously examined everything in it. It was a man's room. Its walls were adorned with skins of wild animals, guns, revolvers, cartridge belts, powder horns of ancient make, deer heads. On the floor were bear skins, a buffalo robe. The bear heads, with their polished fangs, grinned at her. Here and there were mementos of his college days—pennants and photographs. One picture had received her attention because there was a pretty girl in it. She had frowned at this picture.

She got up now, knowing that Jeff had answered Mrs. Hale's call to breakfast. Ellen could detect the odour of frying bacon, the aroma of coffee. The acrid smoke of a wood fire reached her.

There was something about ranch life that was strangely satisfying. She missed her morning tub, but had found a wonderful substitute in the river, around a bend under some willows and aspen where a shade stretched in the late afternoon. Her wardrobe was meagre, consisting of the riding suit she had worn when she left the Hour Glass and some necessary garments given to her by Mrs. Hale, among which were several calico house dresses. Since these were becoming she selected one to wear this morning.

In front of her glass in the bedroom she deliberately arrayed herself in the borrowed dress. Half a dozen times she rearranged her hair until it created the effect she desired. She was aware that in her riding habit she must have appeared somewhat masculine to Jeff, and the clothing would inevitably accentuate the air of sophistication that, she knew, had aroused Jeff's contempt. If she were ever to win Jeff's love it would be through the lure of femininity. Her hair was a brown, wavy mass of smooth coils and seductively curving wisps when she finally left the room in response to Mrs. Hale's call.

She sat opposite Jeff at the big table and was aware that he was furtively watching her. He said little, however, confining himself to the ordinary amenities of the occasion, but once Ellen met his gaze fairly and was pleased to discover a sort of reluctant admiration in his eyes. And once, she was certain, he opened his lips to speak about her changed appearance, but closed them again and smiled.

He did not speak to her when he left the room with his father, but she knew she had scored. And once again, while she was helping Mrs. Hale with the dishes, the latter told her she was "glowing." "You're like a blossom that has just opened," Mrs. Hale added.

A Mexican girl relieved Mrs. Hale of much of the house work, so there was nothing for Ellen to do after breakfast. She had hoped that Jeff would seek her, but though she lingered in the patio garden for some time Jeff did not appear. After a while she walked through the ranch-house yard to the river.

She stood under the willows at the brink of the swimming pool for a time, meditating. She was astonished that Jeff's hostility toward her was not more bitter. Considering what her father had done to the Hales Jeff's attitude toward her was exactly what it should be. In fact, he had given her better treatment than she deserved. He had not mentioned her father, and she could understand that he had not meant to mention him. Very likely she would have heard nothing about the title dispute if Mrs. Hale had not mentioned it.

The Hales—all of them—were wonderful.

The pool beside which she was standing was about a hundred yards from the adobe fence which formed the southern line of the corral, and from the stream the land rose gently to a level. On the level in a small clump of trees were several low buildings which she knew were for the use of the Diamond A cowboys. They were now unoccupied, for the cowboys were out on the ranges with the cattle. Over the top of the corral fence she could see the roofs of the ranch house and the other buildings, but there was no sign of Jeff or his father. Jeff had left again, she supposed. He was giving her an opportunity to desert him. He had told her that he did not wish to pretend to be shocked. She wondered what Jeff's mother had told him. Nothing, of course. They would not interfere in Jeff's affairs.

Ellen was at the pool for an hour or more and was so deeply engrossed that she did not observe that a horseman had ridden close to her and was sitting motionless in the saddle, watching her.

She was startled for an instant, then resentful and angry. She stood rigid, facing the rider.

"I do not know who you are," she said, "but I can assure you that your manners could be improved upon!"

"It's likely they could," returned the rider, grinning impudently; "But my manners suit me, just as they are."

The man was tall, lithe, and slender, and not bad-looking. However, there was a sly gleam in his eyes which seemed to hint of designing thoughts, a queer, downward quirk to the corners of his mouth which seemed to indicate a fixed habit of insolence.

Just how long he had been there watching her Ellen did not know, but he appeared to be at ease and not in the least perturbed over the indignation she was exhibiting.

But while Ellen was angry she was also puzzled. For the man's voice had a familiar sound. Somewhere she had heard it. But she was not interested enough to attempt to urge her memory.

"Please go!" she said coldly; "I do not wish to be disturbed!"

She turned her back to him.

He laughed, dismounted, appeared in front of her, leaning forward so that he might peer into her eyes. He was grinning.

"You're Matt Ballinger's daughter, ain't you? Sure. There's no mistake about that. And a couple of weeks ago you married Jeff Hale, over in Randall. I saw the record. Folks are talking about it happening so sudden. They're wondering. I've been wondering myself. I've been wondering if Matt Ballinger sent you over here to marry Jeff Hale so's to sort of sew up his interest in the Hale property. Keep it in the family, eh? Well, if that's Matt's game he won't get away with it!"

Ellen was watching the man with a new interest, with a new contempt.

"You must be Wade Dallman," she said.

"I'm Wade Dallman," he answered.

"I thought so. No one except a man like Wade Dallman would entertain a suspicion so absurd!"

"No?" he said, derisively. "Maybe a man like Jeff Hale might entertain such a suspicion—if he knew just how you happened to be in that shack in the Navajo Basin the night before you were married to him?"

"Why—how——" she gasped.

He laughed.

"Thought you was the only one that could think things out, eh?" he said. "Thought you and Matt Ballinger was the only ones that knowed how Matt Ballinger does things, eh?" he jeered.

Where Jeff came from Ellen never knew, because he did not tell her and she did not see him approach. But suddenly he appeared behind Dallman, so quickly that Ellen had a fleeting impression that he had come up behind Dallman's horse. There seemed to be no passion in him, yet Ellen observed that his lips were tight and that the muscles of his neck were at a tension.

He seized Dallman by a shoulder and swung him around so that the man faced him.

"Dallman," he said, "I told you that if you ever came around here again I would use a bullwhip on you! Do you reckon I was just trying to bluff you?"

Whatever Dallman had thought when the threat had been uttered he was aware now that the chastisement impended, for his cheeks grayed and his body quivered. Then suddenly he cursed and reached for the gun at his hip.

The arm was seized, twisted. Dallman screamed in agony and dropped the gun into the sand as he went to his knees and writhed there, holding the injured arm.

Jeff kicked the gun into the river. His eyes were alight with a cold fire as he stepped back a pace and looked at Dallman. He did not appear to see Ellen. He drew a bullwhip from a hip pocket, shook out its heavy lash and spoke to Dallman.

"Get up, Dallman!" he said.

Dallman wavered to his feet. He threw himself bodily at Jeff in a desperate attempt to clinch with him before the sting of the lash could catch him, but as he came close with his hands grasping, Jeff changed the whip from his right hand to his left and his right fist thudded heavily against Dallman's jaw.

Dallman staggered, swayed and fell to his knees. For a moment he stayed in that position, glaring his hatred.

In that moment Ellen cried, imploringly:

"Oh Jeff! Don't!"

Jeff did not look at her; he kept his gaze upon Dallman, who glared back at him. But he spoke to her and his voice was calm, sane, though derisive.

"Go to the house, please. I promised Dallman this, Matthew Ballinger the same. I intend to keep both promises!"

Ellen did not obey Jeff's command. Whether she was paralyzed by the horror of Dallman's impending punishment or by Jeff's threat of similar treatment of her father, Ellen did not know. She was aware only of a terrible nausea which seemed to spread to every nerve of her body, and she was conscious of only one impulse, which was to shut out all sound and vision. So she closed her eyes and placed her fingers in her ears. And when Dallman's screams still were audible she began to run toward the ranch house.

Strangely, however, her recreant memory was flashing an intelligible message. Now, of all times, it was telling her that it recognized Dallman, telling her that he was the man who had carried her to the cabin in the Navajo Basin, where Jeff had found her!

CHAPTER TEN

Jeff had been away again for another two weeks. For a second time Ellen knew he had absented himself for the purpose of permitting her to desert him without creating a scene that would apprise his parents of how matters stood between them, for when he came upon her in the patio, on his way to his room, he started, looked keenly at her and confronted her.

"You're still here," he said, and she perceived that he seemed slightly puzzled.

She was arrayed in one of Mrs. Hale's house dresses and was confident that she looked her best.

"Don't you want me here?" she asked.

"You are my wife," he answered.

"That isn't an answer," she declared. "If you don't want me here I shall go!"

"I never evade my obligations," he said. "You can stay as long as you want to stay."

He smiled, though there was hostility in his eyes. It seemed to her that there was also suspicion and perhaps grim amusement. He hated her father and he suspected deceit from her because of the relationship. He was loyal to his parents and expected her to be loyal to hers. A simple philosophy.

But of course he didn't know that she would not be loyal to her father when she knew a crime was being committed. He did not know enough about her to decide whether or not she was in sympathy with her father's deeds. And perhaps he would never know her. He didn't seem to care. She thought of his promise to whip her father as he had whipped Dallman. Telling her of that promise was his way of warning her that he wanted nothing to do with the Ballingers, herself included.

"I am going to stay here until you discover that I am not the kind of girl that you think I am!" she declared. "I want you to know that I am not trying to steal your land!"

"Nobody will steal it," he said. He looked at her with queer intentness as though studying her. He said quietly: "Your father has been inquiring about you. He sent Jim Peters to Randall to search for you. Jim told various people that you were lost. They are reported to have had a posse out searching for you. Jim finally discovered what had happened and I presume that by this time your father knows you are married."

"Isn't it odd that father's men did not come here to verify the report of my marriage?" Ellen asked.

"It's not very odd," returned Jeff. "I told Ballinger that if I ever caught him on the Diamond A I would use a bullwhip on him. It is likely that he considers that the promise applies to his men."

"Would you really whip him?"

"Certainly."

"Why haven't you whipped me? I am his daughter, I am on your land, and you seem to dislike me as much as you do my father and Dallman!"

"I haven't decided that you are concerned in the plot to steal the land."

"Oh, you haven't! Well, the evidence points that way, doesn't it? I am a Ballinger. I managed to have myself abducted by you, and I arranged matters so that you would have to marry me."

"You couldn't have foreseen where I would be on that night," he said. "I've thought about that."

"Oh, you have!" she said. "Well, that's encouraging!"

He ignored the sarcasm. There was a sombre shadow in his eyes.

"What was Dallman saying to you?" he asked.

"He was saying just what you are thinking—that my father arranged to have you marry me so that part of the Diamond A land might come into the Ballinger family."

He shook his head.

"You don't know what I think. But there's this much to be said: If you hadn't threatened to tell what you knew about the hanging of Hank Kroll, and about your thinking I had abducted you, the marriage wouldn't have taken place. If you had had sense enough to promise to keep those things to yourself you wouldn't have got yourself into this fix."

"Oh, you think it is a slight thing for a girl to be abducted?"

"I don't know a damned thing about it!" he declared. "How can a man tell what a woman thinks, or if she ever thinks! A man meets a woman. When he meets her he is free as air, and the first thing he knows he's tangled up so bad that he don't know whether he's going or coming. A man wants to do the right thing, but after he gets tangled up with a woman he don't know right from wrong."

She could not restrain a smile. She had what she wanted, anyway, even if he was dissatisfied.

"I didn't ask you to marry me, you know. You did the proposing."

"I'm not kicking about that," he said. His brows were wrinkled and the shadows in his eyes were deeper. "Any man would have married you, and I reckon you'd have married any man right then."

Jealousy!

Just a throb. The first exhibited sign of interest.

She wisely turned her head so that he might not observe the flash of triumph that lighted her eyes. She must be careful now.

Then she looked straight at him, to observe that he was still frowning.

"Would you have married *any* woman?" she asked.

"Yes," he answered slowly. "I had to, just to be a man. But it was different with you. If you didn't like the man you could refuse to marry him."

"How do you know?" she said, smiling mockingly. "I married you without liking you. And I don't know that I like you now. You aren't ideal, by any means. You have a terrible temper, you go around whipping people that offend you; you hang men without giving them a fair trial, you think laws are safeguards for fools and weaklings, and you think all women are liars and cheats. Could you expect a woman to like a man of that type?"

It was obvious that no other woman had ever talked to him as Ellen was talking. It was doubtful that his mother had ever even reproved him. In fact Ellen had gained the impression that he had been spoiled by lack of governing influences. He was a wild product of a wild country and whoever tamed him would bear scars of the battle.

"Well," he said, "we are even. I married you without liking you. It seems to have all the prime disagreements of a first class divorce case. Whenever you are ready to go back to the Hour Glass I'll take you."

He turned and began to walk away from her. She had been wondering how she could get to the Hour Glass to bring back her personal belongings.

She calmly halted him with a word:

"Jeff!"

He paused, turned.

"To-morrow morning, if you please," she said.

"What?" he asked. She perceived that he was frowning.

"You may take me to the Hour Glass in the morning, if you please," she said. "I have been wanting to go."

"H'm," he said. "You decided in something of a hurry, didn't you?"

"Oh, no. I have been thinking of going for quite some time."

"Well, why didn't you go?"

"You weren't here to take me," she said quietly. "Don't you remember what you told me about gadding around the country alone?"

His frown deepened. His gaze was sombre.

"All right," he said suddenly; "be ready at six."

He turned again, walked stiffly across the patio and vanished through the doorway of his room.

Ellen watched him out of sight. Then she turned, entered the living room, and sank into a big chair facing a shelf upon which reposed a photograph. She was sitting there smiling at the picture when Mrs. Hale entered and observed her.

"Ellen," she said, shaking a reproving finger. "I shall have to tell Jeff how you sit here and smile at his picture: I don't believe he knows how much you love him!"

"Does any man?" asked Ellen.

"No," declared Mrs. Hale, "they don't. And you can't tell them. They're all alike. There's only one way to convince them, and that is to show them."

Ellen smiled at the picture, nodding wisely.

CHAPTER ELEVEN

When they rode away from the ranch house the next morning Ellen divined that Jeff's morose mood had lasted through the night. He hadn't said a word to her at breakfast, and he did not speak as they rode into the great, green valley.

Ellen talked whenever the impulse seized her. Jeff's answers and forced comments were monosyllabic and gruff. He would not look directly at her but she observed that when she appeared to be interested in objects ahead of her his surreptitious glances were long and frequent. He appeared to be studying her again—moodily, sullenly. As Ellen was aware that she was not more mysterious than other women she decided that he was finding her more interesting than he wished her to be, and that having invited her to leave him he was now reluctant to see her go. Of course she was only visiting the Hour Glass to bring back some necessary clothing, but he thought she was not going to return.

Ellen intended to permit him to go on thinking that. She had got a delicious thrill out of his flash of jealousy the day before and she was now enjoying the knowledge that at last he was finding her desirable.

Of course she did not anticipate sudden surrender from him. He would never give himself to any woman without first convincing himself that she was the sort of woman he wanted. He would take a long time in his appraisement of her but his surrender would be complete or his rejection final.

Just now she knew he was resisting. He hadn't liked her at first. He was only just now discovering that he was interested in her and he was setting his reason and his prejudices against his emotions, with the result that he was uncertain and irritable.

The trail they were taking would not lead them into Randall, but a few miles southeastward of the town, and Jeff rode beside her as silently as if he were alone. She observed that his furtive glances at her were growing more frequent and she suspected that he had thoughts that would presently be expressed. She was not surprised when he spoke.

"You were mighty sudden in making up your mind to leave!" he said.

"Oh, no," she answered without looking at him. "I have been contemplating this trip for quite a while." She had, for she had needed other clothing.

He evidently considered her manner frivolous for he glowered at her.

"I can't make you out," he said.

"Can't you? Well, I'm sorry I'm such a puzzle to you. But you haven't paid much attention to me, have you?"

"H'm. You're used to having people pay attention to you, I reckon. You're not satisfied to be a little in the background."

"Why," she said, laughing, "we are quarrelling just like people who have been married for years! Can't you think of other disagreeable things to say?"

"Plenty of them," he returned, frowning at her. "One is that you have been brought up wrong. You've been travelling with a fast crowd. You think life is a farce comedy, that there is nothing to do but have a good time and try to put fool theories into practice."

"Won't you explain?" she said.

"Glad to. Have you done anything in a serious way?"

"I married you. Wasn't that serious?"

"It's the most serious thing you've done, I expect. But it isn't serious to you or you wouldn't be joking about it."

"Being married to you is no joke, Jeff," she said, smiling.

He frowned.

"That's like you," he charged. "It proves what I've said—that you can't be serious. You're insolent and impudent. You go to a university to be educated and when you come out you are merely fresh and arrogant. You think you know a great deal when you know nothing. You miss the big things in life."

"Just what are the big things, Jeff?"

"The big things are love, duty, and achievement."

"Ah! You place love first!" she said, glancing at him. "Do you love anybody?"

"No!"

"Not even your father and mother?"

"That's different."

"Oh, then there are different kinds of love! The kind of love you mean is the love that a woman should have for her husband—or a husband for his wife. Is that it?"

"Of course."

"And you do not love your wife?"

"Look here," he said, "you're impudent! When the time comes I expect I'll do my share of loving. But I don't intend to love anybody until I want to."

"I see," she said, "your kind of love is the kind that comes when you beckon to it."

He nodded.

"You don't see anything!" he charged. "Your conclusions are absurd!"

"Don't you believe in love at first sight?"

"No," he stated, heavily. "You can't love anybody without first knowing that person's character, and you can't read character at a glance."

"Oh. Then beauty doesn't appeal to you? And character is everything. I had never thought of that before. But it seems to me that beautiful women have more suitors than homely women. And have you ever noticed how women run after a handsome man? Do you think those people are studying character?"

Jeff did not answer. He was frowning.

They rode up the slope of the big valley and reached the crest from where they saw the silent, rugged country basking in the sunlight below them.

Jeff halted his horse and wheeled him so that he faced the valley out of which they had just climbed.

"Look down there, please," Jeff directed.

Ellen looked. About ten miles out in the valley were the Diamond A ranch buildings. Ellen could see them very clearly. There was the river, gleaming in the sunlight, there was Randall with a yellow dust cloud veiling its crude structures; scattered here and there were shacks belonging to the dry farmers who had bought or preëmpted land and were eking a precarious existence from it. However, the valley was so big that all the buildings together were insignificant dots upon the vast bosom of nature.

"Can you imagine what that valley was when my father and mother took up the Diamond A land?" asked Jeff. "They were the first settlers. For a great many years Mother lived there with Father. Their nearest neighbour was more than a hundred miles away. There wasn't a doctor within three hundred miles. They had to freight their supplies from Laskar. That was three hundred miles. There was only Father and Mother, and Mother would be alone for weeks at a time. There were hostile Indians and roving outlaws. Can you imagine how lonesome that was for a woman?"

Ellen shuddered.

"She is a wonderful woman!" was Ellen's tribute. "How she must have loved your father!"

"Well," he said drily, "I reckon it was something more than looks that kept them together. Father wasn't what people would call handsome. What he had is called character. He took his part in life seriously; he meant business. He had his mind set upon building himself a home in this wilderness, and he did it. Mother stayed with him.

"Mother wasn't exceptional, nor was Father. What they did has been done, and is being done, all over the West. It was done in the East, the North, and the South. You know that."

"The Ballingers did the same in the East," Ellen said, straightening.

"Well," said Jeff, "do you think a woman of to-day—a woman of your East—would go through that with a man?"

"Certainly, if she loved him."

He was gravely watching her.

"She couldn't do it if she loved him only because his hair was black, or wavy, or because he had an engaging eye?" he suggested.

"No. I think he would have to be kind and considerate and brave. Certainly he would have to be all of that, and perhaps something more. He most assuredly would not possess a temper," she concluded.

"And his wife would not be impudent," said Jeff. "Nor could she put on airs that she had brought straight from a university. Such a marriage would not last."

Ellen looked at the far horizon.

"We are temperamentally unsuited to each other," she said, lowly.

"H'm," answered Jeff, musingly, with a note of irritation in his voice.

"I could never cease being impudent, because in my husband's opinion frankness is impudence."

"H'm."

"And I would always be 'fresh' while my mind was young."

"H'm."

"And I want my husband to be handsome."

Jeff frowned.

"And he should have to govern his temper and be very much in love with me."

Jeff moved uneasily.

"Therefore since we disagree so completely, we should cease this profitless discussion and be on our way," she added.

They went on again, into a virgin wilderness. And as they rode side by side Ellen cast glances at Jeff and perceived that his lips were set and his face stern. He was handsome, he was brave, and she had no doubt that to the woman he finally loved he would be kind and considerate. Also, she suspected that toward one he loved he would exhibit no temper.

They rode down the great slope into the Navajo basin about eight o'clock. Before long they were watering their horses at the river in front of the cabin in which Ellen had been imprisoned by Wade Dallman, and where she had fooled Jeff into believing she was convinced that he had abducted her.

And not yet did she regret fooling him. She had him, and she intended to keep him. And she knew why his mother had spent thirty years in the wilderness with his father, and why she had endured lonesomeness and danger for him. She knew more about it than Jeff knew, for Jeff did not love.

She was interested in the trail that led northward through the forest, for it had been over that trail that Dallman had taken her, after he had found her unconscious beside her horse. She recognized the hill where she had fallen, but all signs were obliterated, and they passed the place in silence.

Jeff avoided a trail that led to Jim Kellis's cabin, though Ellen saw the building from a distance, and remarked:

"There's a house."

Jeff laughed and told her that a man named Kellis lived there.

"Tin horn," he added.

When she asked him what the term meant he told her that Kellis was a petty gambler. Ellen had not told Jeff that she knew Kellis, and now she was glad that she hadn't told him.

Jeff followed the trail that Ellen had taken to reach the Kellis cabin, but Ellen's feelings on this trip were different. She knew that she had learned a great deal. Coming, she had been confident and carefree; returning, she was deeply in love and acutely conscious of the seriousness of life. She had discovered that life is serious enough when there is a goal to be attained.

Curiously, her feelings toward her father had changed. Somewhere in this wild land she had lost her resentment. She perceived that she had been just what her father had declared her to be, heedless and self-sufficient, headstrong and arrogant. In one month she had mellowed into maturity, with maturity's wisdom, its calmness and conservatism.

She had found her man, she was married, and yet her former wild desire to confront her father and confound him with the evidence of her achievement had changed to a quiet timidity. She no longer blamed her father for her own shortcomings; she understood that he had merely been wiser than she.

Emerging from the timber, they crossed a big pasture and rode down along its fence to the ranch house. Ballinger was seated in a chair on the wide gallery. He was smoking a pipe and when he observed her he drew the pipe from his lips and sent a long spiral of smoke upward. And when Ellen and Jeff rode up to the edge of the gallery, Ballinger slowly got out of the chair, walked to the edge of the gallery and greeted them, bowing formally.

Matthew M. Ballinger was sixty. He was tall; his hair was white, wavy, and abundant; he had keen, humorous gray eyes, his chin was pugnacious and his head was set on his broad shoulders in a manner that hinted of independence. In his expression at this minute was none of that derision that Ellen had anticipated and dreaded. He seemed to Ellen to be the perfect father—kindly, considerate, suave, and sympathetic. Ellen wondered if he had not always been that; wondered if her own judgment had not been warped. However, she was amazed and delighted, and for the first time in years Ballinger witnessed the miracle of his own daughter blushing at sight of him.

"Mr. and Mrs. Jefferson Hale are welcome," he said. "Won't you get down and visit?"

The man who had threatened to whip Ballinger was coldly polite in the presence of his enemy and his wife.

"I am forced to decline your invitation, sir," he said. "I came merely to escort my wife. Good-day, sir."

He would have dismounted to help Ellen off, but she was out of the saddle before he could move, and was standing facing him when he had answered Ballinger. And now he swept his broad brimmed hat from his head and bowed to her from the saddle, his gaze holding hers and seeming to tell her that he understood that this was to be the end and that he had some regrets in the matter. But before she could read his expression clearly he had wheeled his horse and was riding away, tall and erect in the saddle.

Ellen watched him until he vanished among the trees, watched him, knowing that her father was regarding her quizzically, and finally turned, her colour betraying her.

Ballinger smiled. And Ballinger's smile, when guileless, was wholesome and winning.

CHAPTER TWELVE

The Hour Glass was a modern ranch. Its buildings were of the Spanish type, with low walls, wide eaves, and gently sloping tiled roofs. There was the ranch house itself, distinguished by its huge red-brown sandstone courtyard and the roughly rounded pillars of its colonnade; the garden with its palm trees, prickly pear hedges, and vine-laden trellises, white pergolas and flag walks. There was a tennis court, a swimming pool, great stables.

The atmosphere of the ranch suggested wealth and efficiency. It was operated without visible effort, smoothly, like a well-oiled machine. Like a gentleman's country estate.

Ellen spent two days in the ranch house. Two restless, lonely days. There was nobody there but her father, herself, and the servants. Ballinger was not in the house often, and when he was he spent his time at his desk in the big library, reading or writing. The big rooms with their polished floors, their gloomy recesses and nooks; the great dining room with a table which would seat forty; the colonnaded courtyard with its vacant chairs, oppressed her. Wherever she went it was the same. The house was magnificent, luxurious, spacious, but it was not a home. It lacked something. It lacked the intimate relationship that should exist between members of a family. Every time Ellen stood in one of the big, silent rooms she visioned Jeff's parents in the living room of the Diamond A ranch house—Adam Hale in a big chair reading a newspaper, Mrs. Hale sitting in a chair beside a centre table, contentedly sewing. No formality there!

Ellen had intended to stay at the Hour Glass for a week at least, which would give Jeff time to miss her. She had a feeling that before the week passed Jeff would ride over to see her.

But the evening of the second day found Ellen more restless than ever, and she began to pack. She filled two trunks and several bags, and on the morning of the third day she appeared at breakfast arrayed in her riding garments.

"Riding?" asked Ballinger.

"I am going back to the Diamond A," Ellen answered.

"Jeff coming for you?"

"Jeff thought I would stay longer," said Ellen.

Ballinger smiled.

He had treated her with unusual consideration. He had not questioned her, nor had he acted as though he expected her to explain her action in marrying Jeff Hale. And, strangely, the Ballinger smile of derision—which she had expected—had not once appeared on his lips. More than once in the two days she had spent with him Ellen had wondered if she had not been to blame for her parent's former attitude toward her. Perhaps, as he had told her, she had been too insistent upon having her own way. At any rate the father who now took leave of her was new and interesting.

"You are going to stay at Hale's?" he asked.

"For the present."

"No honeymoon trip?"

"We don't care for that."

He smiled at her.

"You have changed, Ellen," he said. "You seem to have developed a new, a more attractive, personality. You are growing to be very much like your mother. No wonder Jeff Hale loves you!"

"Aren't all husbands supposed to love their wives?" she asked.

"I could name some who don't. Jeff does or he wouldn't have come here with you after threatening to horsewhip me." He chuckled. "Did you know that?"

"Yes. But I think he did not mean that, father."

"He whipped Dallman," he reminded her.

"Don't you think Dallman deserved it?"

"Do you?"

"Yes. Dallman had been warned to stay away from the Diamond A."

"Then I think that if you are to see me again you had better come here. I don't care to tempt your wild man."

"He isn't a wild man, Father! You'd be astonished to see how gentle he can be!"

"Dallman's evidence is all to the contrary." There was a glint in Ballinger's eyes. "And there's his record in college. Ever hear it?"

"It wasn't scandal, Father."

"No. Just hellishness. Wouldn't conform to rules. They had to expel him or the place would have been turned into an Indian war village. Oh, yes; he's gentle!"

"Why do you want that piece of Diamond A land, Father?"

"That's business, Ellen. It was open, and I filed on it. Anybody had that right."

"You won't do as Dallman is doing, Father?"

"Hardly. Dallman is a land shark. I'll do nothing but wait. If the title is awarded to me I'll take it, of course."

"How did you know the certificate was missing?"

"It was Jim Kellis who told me about that. He'd been over to the land office looking over the records and discovered that there was no certificate on file and no record of one ever having been filed."

"It would appear that Jeff Hale and Kellis are not on friendly terms. If they were it seems Kellis would have gone directly to Jeff with his information."

"Kellis and Jeff have had trouble," said Ballinger. "Kellis is a worthless fellow."

"And you permitted me to go——"

"I wouldn't have sent this Ellen!" interrupted Ballinger. "The girl I sent on that wild goose chase was insolent and stubborn. She needed a lesson. But she didn't go alone, for Jim Peters kept her in sight all the way. I made one mistake, though. I told Peters to follow you to Kellis's cabin, and back here. I thought you'd head straight home as soon as you found out about Kellis. Peters waited a mile or so back on the Hour Glass trail for you. And when it grew dark and you didn't come he went to the Kellis cabin to find you. He found that you'd gone toward Randall. He felt that he had no right to spy upon you further so he came back here. The next day, toward evening, I sent a party of the boys out to search for you. They came back the following day and reported that you had married Jeff Hale, in Randall.

"I had an impression that you never had any idea of marrying Kellis and that you and Hale had an agreement to meet and marry. That shows how little fathers know about their daughters." He shook a finger at her. "I supposed I was disciplining you, and you had your mind made up to marry Hale."

She nodded.

Yes, she had been determined to marry Jeff, but the determination hadn't been taken until she had met him in the cabin. What would her father say if he knew the truth? What would Jeff do if he discovered that she had lied to him? The Ellen of a month ago would have been amused; the Ellen of to-day was subdued and worried and wistful.

Ballinger followed her to the edge of the courtyard and helped her upon the horse that the stableman had brought up. She told him about the trunks and bags she had packed and asked him to send them the next day to the Diamond A. At the edge of the forest she turned and waved at her father, who still watched her.

CHAPTER THIRTEEN

Ellen rode into Randall at three in the afternoon. Since she wanted to make several trifling purchases she had reached town early enough to do her shopping and still ride the ten miles to the Diamond A before dark.

Randall was in the throes of its midafternoon activity when she rode down the street, and apparently no one paid her special attention. She remembered that on the night of her marriage Jeff had sent the horses to a man named "Allen," and so now she rode along looking for that name on one of the numerous signs. She saw it after a while, at a little distance down the street from the jeweller's shop where Jeff had selected her ring, but before observing the sign she had seen something else which set her heart to throbbing abnormally.

Jeff's horse was hitched to a rail in front of the Elite restaurant!

The animal was his favourite, and she would have recognized it anywhere. A big, rangy, glossy black with a patch of white on its forehead and another just above the fetlock on the left foreleg.

Ellen grimly fought the sudden surge of jealousy that seized her and calmly rode to the door of the livery stable, dismounted, and gave her horse into the care of the man who came forward.

The man gave her a curious glance but she was convinced that he did not know her.

"Feed and water him, please," she directed.

"What's the name, ma'am?" asked the liveryman. But though Ellen heard she did not answer. She had already selected a store across the street, from where she could see the front door of the Elite, and she entered.

She made some purchases. The man who waited on her was talkative, but he received answers that silenced him.

Ellen was not familiar with the emotions that seethed in her. She did not know whether she was hurt or angry. The torturing suspicions of jealousy had never before attacked her.

She could not stay in the store longer, for the storekeeper was watching her curiously; so she stepped out into the street again, pausing for an instant on the sidewalk, undecided. Just ahead of her she observed a sign which was suspended above the sidewalk, bearing the words: "The Randall House." Instantly deciding, she walked rapidly down the street, entered the doorway below the sign and approached the clerk.

Only one man was in the lobby and he was huddled in a chair reading. He did not look up from his paper.

The hotel was small but seemed respectable. Ellen asked for a front room and the clerk himself ushered her upstairs after she had signed the register as Ellen Hale. She thought the clerk looked at her curiously several times, and thinking that he was speculating upon her presence at the hotel unaccompanied by her husband she told him that possibly Jeff would join her later. That would keep the clerk from talking and thereby spreading the news that she was in town. She didn't want Jeff to know she was in Randall, but she would not stoop to signing a fictitious name to the register.

The clerk paused in the act of closing the door.

"Jeff made it hot for Wade Dallman, didn't he?" he said.

"What do you mean?"

"Whipping him that way. Dallman wasn't for letting it get out, but it seems a man named Seifert was riding in the valley that day and saw Jeff whipping Dallman. Dallman was cut up considerable. He's boiling mad. I'd tell Jeff to keep his eyes open. Dallman's bad when he's stirred up!"

"Thank you," said Ellen. "But I think Jeff is not afraid of Dallman."

"Afraid!" laughed the clerk. "Not him! But you know what I mean, ma'am. It ain't that Dallman will go gunning for Jeff right out. He knows better than that! He won't do that unless he's stung bad, though folks tell me that he's right clever with a gun when he's cornered. But Dallman's slick and he's got friends who are just as slick as he is. Bill Hazen, for instance."

"Are Hazen and Dallman friends?" asked Ellen, astonished.

"Well, they ain't parading that they are," answered the clerk. "But there's people that have seen them with their heads together pretty often, and I reckon if they was enemies they wouldn't have nothing confidential to talk about."

"Does Jeff know they are friends?"

"Sure! That's what stirs Jeff and his ranch-owner friends up so much. Look, ma'am. You don't know what's happening in this section of the country, do you? Well, you wouldn't. Well, Dallman's a land shark and everybody knows it. He's stolen land enough to start a State. And he'll steal more. He ain't got no scruples at all, for he sells land that he ain't got any title to. Then he goes over to the land office and juggles the records. Well, Bill Hazen knows what Dallman is, and yet he throws in with him against the ranch owners. There was that hanging. Hank Kroll and his gang of horse thieves have been stealing stock from all the ranch owners. There's folks that think Hazen and Dallman are making things easy for Hank Kroll's men. However, nobody's saying that very loud and I wouldn't want you to repeat it. Jeff's friends have caught some of the thieves but Hazen always let them go. Some of the ranchers have been shot up by the thieves. Well, about a month ago Hazen found Hank Kroll swinging from a tree in the Navajo Basin. But shucks, you know that, for it was you proved an alibi for Jeff. Well, Hazen ain't got over that. Swears he knows Jeff done it and that he'll get him some day!"

Ellen did not answer and the clerk closed the door and departed. Ellen locked the door, glanced at the room, which was clean and plainly furnished, then walked to one of the curtained windows and gazed down into the street.

The Elite restaurant was almost directly across from the hotel. Jeff's horse was still at the hitching rail, but it seemed that Jeff himself was not in the restaurant, for the tables were all vacant. Sadie was there, however. She was standing just inside the front door, arrayed in a gingham dress, a stiffly starched white apron, and a white cap which sat jauntily on her head. And Sadie seemed to be looking straight at the hotel door!

For an instant Ellen was convinced that Sadie had seen her enter the hotel and was watching for her to come out, but presently she observed that Sadie's gaze was roving as if it were following the progress of someone who was walking along the street. And then Ellen saw Jeff come into sight on the sidewalk directly in front of the hotel.

Jeff crossed the street, passed around the hitching rail in front of the Elite and entered the restaurant doorway. There, for several minutes, he stood and talked with Sadie. Then he turned from the girl, stepped down to the sidewalk, and stood motionless for a time. Presently he was joined by two other men—evidently friends, for there was no mistaking their pleasure over the meeting. They were ranchers. Ellen watched them as they walked down the street together. She lost sight of them when they mingled with a crowd far down on the other side of the street.

While the meeting between Jeff and Sadie suggested intimacy it did not definitely prove anything serious in their relationship. But that fear had been in Ellen's mind when she had entered the hotel, and even now she was conscious of a cold and furious resentment.

Yet it was with a feeling of guilt, of shame almost, that she turned from the window. The impulse which had led her to enter the hotel for the purpose of spying upon Jeff and Sadie had seemed justifiable at the moment, but now she knew that the action was undignified, contemptible. She had always managed to deserve her own good opinion of herself, but now she was in danger of losing it. She suddenly decided that she would leave the hotel and ride at once to the Diamond A. If Jeff wanted the girl in the restaurant he could have her.

She started toward the door, hesitated, and glanced out of the window. Twilight had come. There were still her purchases to be attended to. By the time she did her shopping it would be dark. She didn't know the trail to the Diamond A well enough to ride it at night and so she decided that she would remain at the hotel overnight and go to the Diamond A the following morning.

She locked the door of her room, walked down the stairs, crossed the lobby and stood for an instant in the hotel doorway. There were not so many people on the street now. Twilight was merging with darkness. Many windows were glowing with light. A hush had enveloped the town. The houses seemed to huddle together as though seeking protection from the monstrous blackness that was slowly settling over them and pressing in upon them from all directions. Randall was brave enough in the daylight but it was strangely humble and subdued at night.

She glanced across the street at the Elite, to discover that Jeff's horse was no longer at the hitching rail. He had probably ridden away while she had been preparing to leave the hotel. Sadie was inside the restaurant carrying a tray between the now well-filled tables.

Ellen walked down the street a little distance and entered a store. She was inside for perhaps an hour and when she again stepped out on the sidewalk the darkness was intense. While she had been in the store the merchants had closed their establishments for the night. While she stood on the sidewalk the man who had just waited on her extinguished the lights and emerged. He locked the door, stepped down to the sidewalk, and almost collided with Ellen.

"Shucks," he said, apologetically, "I didn't see you." He started away, paused, and added: "You're a stranger here, ain't you, ma'am? Well, if I was you I wouldn't hang around long. Do you want me to see you where you're goin'?"

"Thank you," Ellen answered, "I'll manage. It isn't far."

The man grunted and vanished into the darkness. Ellen could hear his step on the board walk for a time. She turned and began to walk back the way she had come.

She now realized that she had walked quite a distance to reach the store. There were no lights anywhere near her. Far away, seemingly, she could see the illuminated windows of the Elite and at other points were the dimly glowing windows of saloons.

She had never encountered darkness so impenetrable. She could not see a foot ahead of her. Twice in walking less than a hundred feet she stepped off the walk and floundered in the dust of the street. Then a little farther along she stepped off the other side of the walk, bumped into what she thought was a corner of a building, and fell to her knees. When she got up she could see no lights anywhere, and in something of a panic, stretching her hands out in front of her to protect herself in case she should collide with another building, she began to search for the sidewalk.

In falling she had lost her sense of direction, but she kept moving, hoping to see a light. Presently, when the feeling of panic left her, she stood still and attempted to penetrate the wall of blackness that surrounded her.

She turned clear around, slowly. There was no light anywhere. Even the stars were obscured by the veil of dust that perpetually swam over the town. She was on a stretch of level ground, she decided, for her feet had encountered no obstructions or depressions of any kind. She knew of course that she had strayed from the street or the lights of the saloons would be visible to her. She also knew that she was south of the street because she had been walking on that side when she had collided with the building. But the knowledge was of no use to her because she had lost her sense of direction.

She was calm now, and grimly amused over her predicament. Of course she wasn't lost, and of course she was not far from the street, for she hadn't been away from the street for more than ten minutes and she couldn't have walked very far in that time. Moreover, she had probably been travelling in a circle. All she had to do was to keep on moving and presently she would see a light. She had undoubtedly got into a vacant space which was surrounded by buildings, and if she could find the opening through which she had entered she would have no trouble in reaching the hotel.

She moved on again, carefully, feeling with the toes of her riding boots for pitfalls and obstructions, stretching her hands out in front of her so that she would not strike her head if she ran into anything.

It seemed to her that she was confined in a windless void. There was no sound, no motion. Silence, dead, heavy and oppressive, enveloped her. If she could have heard a voice on the street, the rumbling of the wheels of a passing vehicle, the hoofbeats of a horse, music—anything—she would have directed her steps in that direction. But the town was dead. The coming of darkness ended all activity.

She was still moving carefully when she heard a noise. It was a dull, sodden thud. That was all. No other sound followed, though for several minutes she stood motionless, listening. She was about to go forward again when the sound was repeated and this time her heart thumped heavily, for she recognized the thudding noise as the impatient stomping of a horse. She was now evidently near a stable, and if she could find it she could follow along it to the door, and by finding the door she could determine the direction of the house, for invariably stables were built behind houses.

She again heard the thudding sound and this time located it as being almost directly ahead of her, so she moved toward it, still slowly and carefully, and at last felt her outstretched hands come in contact with its wall. And now, triumphantly, she began to feel along the wall.

She had reached a corner and was preparing to go around it when a match flared a little distance from her and she saw two men sitting on the ground beside the wall. If she had kept on going she would have stumbled over them!

One man was lighting a pipe. The flickering light that he held over the bowl disclosed his features and the face of the man sitting beside him. The man who held the pipe was Bill Hazen and the man sitting beside him was Wade Dallman!

Ellen was startled but not frightened. It was quite evident that she had surprised the two men in the midst of one of their secret conferences. They would not dare harm her even if they discovered her.

But she did not intend to let them know of her presence and so she drew back and flattened herself against the wall of the building until the flame of the match went out. Then she stood there silently, listening.

For a time there came no sound from the men. The scent of Bill Hazen's tobacco floated around the corner of the stable and assailed Ellen's nostrils. The smoke was strong, and once or twice Ellen was in danger of sneezing. But she fought off the impulse and presently heard Hazen's voice.

"Well, they'll run into a snag to-night!" he said.

"Why to-night?" asked Dallman.

"If you'd have been in town to-day you'd known," replied Hazen. "Jeff Hale got to town early this mornin'. Him an' Slim Patton an' Cherokee an' Jim Withington have been together. An' just about dusk Hale rode out of town. Sure as them fellows meet in town there's a raid that night."

"That means they'll raid Bohnert's place," said Dallman. "Bohnert got a warning from somebody three or four days ago."

"I know that," said Hazen. "Bohnert found it tacked to a post in front of his house. I've tried to identify the writing, but I can't do it. It ain't Jeff Hale's nor Patton's nor Cherokee's nor Withington's. There's a gang of them fellows and it might have been any of them that wrote the notice Bohnert found. Bohnert ain't on Hale's land, is he?"

"No; he's on that strip of Miller's, that I sold him three months ago. There was a mistake in the field notes and I found it."

"Ha, ha!" laughed Hazen. "If there's anything wrong with a survey you'll find it, and if there ain't anything wrong you'll make somethin' wrong. You're a slick sucker, Wade!" he finished, admiringly.

"I aim to get what's coming to me," said Dallman. He shifted his position; Ellen could hear his shoulders brushing against the boards of the wall. "These moss-backs don't know anything; they ain't got any right to hold any land at all. They've never done anything but run cattle on it. Anyway, that piece that Bohnert's on belongs to me, now, and those fellows have no right to run him off. You say they'll run into a snag if they try it to-night. What you done?"

"Plenty!" declared Hazen. "I sent four deputies over to hide in Bohnert's stable. They've got rifles. I told them to blast into any gang that tries to raid Bohnert. They're to shoot first and ask questions afterward. I told them to make sure of getting Hale. He's the ringleader, and if they get him it's likely the rest will scatter and quit."

"You aiming to take a hand in it?"

"I ain't going near Bohnert's, if that's what you mean. I don't want to go riding around and mebbe flush them. But I figure I'll get close enough to hear what's happening."

"Well, if they get Jeff Hale I'll be satisfied," said Dallman.

"Sure, you would be!" laughed Hazen. "What did you let him whip you that way for? Why didn't you shoot him?"

Dallman cursed.

"I didn't see him coming," he said. "I was talking to that slut he married and didn't see him sneaking up behind me."

"It's too bad Hale flushed you out of that cabin in the Navajo that night or you'd have spoiled Ballinger's scheme to get hold of that Hale land."

"I might have known she wouldn't be hanging around there just by accident," said Dallman, disgustedly. "Her and Ballinger must have knowed Hale would be at the cabin that night. She was heading straight there to meet him. After Hale's gang quit chasing me I cached my horse and sneaked back there. Jeff Hale and the Ballinger hussy was standing by the window of the room where I'd left her. They was chinning and quarrelling, I wasn't close enough to hear what was being said. But anyways, she stayed there all night with him. I'd have snuck their horses off if I'd have had a chance. I figure she met him when he was East to school, and when Ballinger wanted the land he brought her out here to marry him. Ballinger would do that; he'd do anything to have his way about a thing. Well, they're hooked up all right, and now let's see what good it will do them!"

Dallman, of course, was merely guessing. His voice lacked the ring of conviction. He hadn't guessed the truth and his reasoning was absurd. Yet he was vindictive and unscrupulous and perhaps dangerous.

Ellen did not listen further. Carefully she moved along the stable wall, again seeking egress from the blackness that inclosed her. Her lips were set tightly together and a fierce hatred gripped her. Never had she hated anybody as she hated Dallman! She had been nauseated by the spectacle of Jeff beating Dallman with the bullwhip, and for a time she had not been able to think of the scene without a shudder. But if there had been a bullwhip in her hands now——

She saw a light gleaming through the blackness somewhere in front of her, and she ran toward it.

CHAPTER FOURTEEN

When Ellen reached the street she discovered that she was within a few hundred feet of the hotel. She had been running, and for a few minutes she stood on the sidewalk attempting to regain her breath and her composure. She brushed the dust from her clothing, made certain that her hat was on straight, tucked in some wisps of hair that had been neglected, and by the time she entered the doorway of the hotel she felt that she had subdued her excitement.

At least the clerk appeared to observe nothing unusual in her manner as she stopped at the desk and smiled at him.

"Man called while you were out," said the clerk. He was leaning over the desk and his gaze seemed to be slightly derisive. "Jim Kellis," he added; "said he'd be in later."

The news was a shock to her; it enraged her. Her contempt for Jim Kellis was as great as her amazement that she had ever wasted time in talking to the man. She had almost forgotten that she had ever known him. Certainly she never wanted to see him again!

She ignored the clerk's reference to her caller and asked him if there was a man named Bohnert in the valley. She tried not to appear eager, for she did not wish to arouse the clerk's curiosity.

"Bohnert?" he said. "Why, yes. Sure. Ain't it strange, now? It just happened that Bohnert was in here the other day. Usually I don't ask a man what his name is, but I saw that this fellow was a newcomer, sort of, and so I asked him. Sure. Bohnert. One of those dry farmers. A Dutchman or a German. A Dutchman, most likely. I couldn't decide which because I never could catch onto their lingo. And I never could see any difference between a Dutchman and a German, myself. He's just as likely to be one as the other. Names don't mean a lot. There was a fellow in here the other day——"

"Oh," said Ellen in a burst of impatience, "I don't care anything about his nationality, I merely wish to know where he lives!"

"Sure. I know where he lives. That's funny, too, isn't it? We got to talking. Usually I don't engage people in conversation, but this day maybe I felt a little lonesome. Some days there ain't much doing and time sort of drags along. You take to-night, for instance. There ain't been a soul——"

"But where does Bohnert live?" asked Ellen, ruthlessly interrupting.

"I'm coming to that," returned the clerk, smiling fatuously. "As I was saying, I don't talk much. But this day I felt like talking, and so I asked this man—this er—Bohnert, a lot of questions. He's a new man out here, I believe I told you. A dry farmer. Well, we got to talking about dry farming, and that's how I came to ask him where his place was. Seems he——"

"Where is his place, please?" interrupted Ellen.

"Why it's just down the valley a ways. About seven miles, I think he said. Not right straight down the valley, but a mile or so east of it. You go straight down the valley for about five miles, and then you strike a creek. Red Creek, I think he said it was. Well, there's a trail leading along it. He said if I ever wanted to visit him I should turn east just after I passed a saguaro forest, and once on that trail I couldn't miss it."

"Thank you," said Ellen.

She crossed the street to the livery stable, asked for her horse, and was presently riding down the street to the edge of town. She rode slowly—for she observed the hotel clerk and the liveryman watching her—until she was certain the darkness concealed her, and then she wheeled her horse and sent him southward, straight down the valley.

She could not see the trail, but trusted to the instinct of the animal under her and to the conviction that she was following the trail Jeff had taken when he had escorted her to his father's house on the night of their marriage.

The darkness did not seem to be as dense as when she had lost herself by stepping off the sidewalk. She could see some stars and there was a luminous haze, faintly blue. No doubt the horse could see better than she, for he loped steadily forward without guidance.

Ellen had no idea of how to find Bohnert's place, nor did she know what she should do once she reached there. She could not go boldly to the door of Bohnert's house and tell him what she had overheard, nor could she let herself be seen by the deputies in the stable. Her only hope of averting the tragedy that was sure to follow the arrival of Jeff and his men was to intercept them while they were on their way to Bohnert's. And there would be no possibility of intercepting them in the darkness unless she chanced to be near enough to them to call to them.

She did not know just what happened when such men as Jeff and his friends made a raid. She assumed a raid meant violence of some sort, and from the conversation between Dallman and Hazen she understood that Bohnert was to be driven off the place he had bought from Dallman. She was certain, now, that Jeff was morally right, although she also suspected that Dallman was adroit enough to have the law on his side in all his transactions. But whether Jeff was right or wrong she didn't want him killed.

She drew a deep breath of gratitude when she became aware that the stars were paling and that the haze above her was growing brighter. And when a yellow, effulgent glow appeared on the eastern horizon and spread with incredible swiftness up the great arch of blue she felt a new reverence for nature. The magic night light disclosed the trail, the river beside which she had been riding, trees hitherto unseen, and presently, as the disk of silver swam clear of a mountain peak, the entire valley was revealed to her.

She brought the horse to a halt and scrutinized the glowing levels, the great slopes, the high ridges. She saw no moving object and so she settled herself more firmly in the saddle and gave the horse the rein. The animal ran lightly, easily, his hoofs drumming with a thunderous rhythm that filled her with a strange exaltation.

She met and passed the saguaro forest with its weird and grotesque desert sentinels, and saw beyond it a faint and narrow beaten path that swerved eastward in long undulations beside a small stream of water. The stream was Red Creek, if the hotel clerk's information was correct, and so she took the trail and straightened the horse out for a final run.

She was now on the giant upland east of the centre of the valley and she felt the horse slowing its stride. She did not urge the animal, for though she was impatient to reach Jeff she judged that he and his men would not appear at Bohnert's place until later, around midnight, perhaps.

About a mile up the creek the land in the vicinity of the stream began to narrow and after a while Ellen found she was riding through a gorge. On both sides of the gorge rose mountainous walls and buttes, and for a time the trail ran through a wild mass of virgin timber and brush. She held her breath while riding through this section, for down here the moonlight did not penetrate and the darkness was solemn and oppressive. But the gorge widened presently and when she reached its end she saw stretching before her a moonlit flat.

About half a mile ahead of her was a house with a glimmer of light flickering through a window. She brought the horse to a halt and sat rigid in the saddle, wondering if the house were Bohnert's.

She could not be certain of that. If she had taken the right trail there could be little doubt that the house was Bohnert's. But if she had been wrongly directed and the house was not Bohnert's she would miss Jeff and his friends and——

A mental picture of Jeff being shot down by the deputies' rifles flashed vividly for an instant, bringing incoherence of thought that frightened her. She hoped she was not going to become panic-stricken in this crisis, and she sat there fighting for clarity of vision and calmness. Calmness would not come. She found she was trembling in a frenzy of apprehension, and when after a while the torture of inaction assailed her she determinedly sent the horse scurrying down the trail toward the house. She meant to go straight to the stable to see if Hazen's deputies were there. While she was riding she could manufacture some sort of an excuse to explain her presence at Bohnert's. No matter what explanation she made they would have to accept it. They would not dare to harm her.

The flat was not very wide. She could see the entire length and breadth of it. No horsemen were visible. The trail she was riding was straight through the centre and the moonlight was now so bright that she could be seen by anyone who might be concealed in the wooded slopes surrounding her. Jeff and his men might be hidden somewhere close at hand, waiting a convenient time to raid Bohnert's place, but if Jeff and his men were around they either did not see her or were disregarding her.

When she drew nearer she observed that Bohnert's house faced the creek. It was a small house containing, she estimated, not more than three rooms. It was built of logs, but had a shingled roof and a small porch. The light she had seen was in the kitchen, and it was still burning as she passed at a little distance and rode toward the stable—a small building situated about three or four hundred feet from the house.

There were several giant cottonwood trees between the stable and the house, a great many pines and fir balsam and junipers and small pecans surrounding the stable, so the moonlight did not strike her as she rode close to the building and dismounted.

She heard no sound. She led her horse close to a small juniper, tied it and turned to be smothered in the strong grasp of a man who had suddenly materialized from the darkness in the timber. His sinewy arms were holding her so tightly that she could not move, and her face was buried in his shoulder so deeply that her startled gasp was almost inaudible.

The man laughed lowly, mockingly, still holding her so tightly that she could only wriggle impotently. But she did kick at his legs in an effort to force him to release her.

"You're caught," he laughed. "Go easy. No use of kicking!"

Jeff!

Her heart fluttered wildly for an instant, and for an instant she was rigid, straining to free herself so that she might attempt to see his face. Then she relaxed, sobbed once convulsively, and was still.

Jeff must have felt her weight, for he loosened his grasp, pushed her back a little and peered intently at her, seeking her face in the shadows. She felt his arms stiffen, heard his voice, a hoarse whisper:

"Hell! It's Ellen!"

He pushed her farther away and held her at arm's length, rigidly, almost savagely, she thought. He was amazed, incredulous, for his voice betrayed him.

"You!" he said, "You!" His voice changed instantly to mockery. "I thought you'd be on your way East by this time!"

There was a note of elation in the mockery. She detected it and exulted. He could not see the light in her eyes.

"No," she said, forcing calmness. "Oh, no. On the contrary you observe that I am gadding about the country alone, as usual."

He released her and stood motionless, peering at her, trying to see her face.

"Seems you've got that habit," he said gruffly. "But I can't understand why you have gadded in this direction!"

"Yes," she said, "I believe there are times when you don't understand very well. I don't believe you ever will understand."

"What are you driving at?"

She laughed, knowing that he ought to understand that her gadding to the Bohnert place could not be accidental. She wondered if he really did believe that she was in the habit of wandering aimlessly about the country?

"I presume it isn't much—to you," she said. "But you see, I got into Randall this afternoon. Just after dark I went out to do some shopping. I got lost and wandered around among the buildings in the town's back yard for quite a while. While I was lost I overheard Hazen and Dallman talking about you. They were saying they had a trap laid for you. Four deputies in the Bohnert stable, who were to shoot you on sight. I just thought I would ride over here and try to warn you. That is all."

"You rode all that distance alone?" he said, his voice tense.

"Why, yes. There was no one to send. I have no friends in Randall."

"H'm," said Jeff. "Shucks." He laughed lowly and spoke to her again. "Would you like to see how Hazen's kind of law has fared to-night?"

She felt one of his hands gripping her arm and she was led around a corner, through a door and into the stable.

Half a dozen men, their faces masked with handkerchiefs, were inside. Some were standing, others were lounging on a pile of straw in a corner. But all were facing Ellen; she could see their eyes glittering in the light from a lantern that stood on the dirt floor near them. Ellen gazed wonderingly at Jeff and he placed an admonishing finger to his lips. Then he quickly covered his own face with a handkerchief, drew still another from a pocket of his shirt and covered Ellen's face so that merely her eyes and a little of her forehead were visible under her hat.

And now, peering deeper into the shadows beyond the light, Ellen saw four other men. They were in a stall. They were facing the manger and their backs were toward her, but she divined they were Hazen's deputies. Four rifles were on the floor behind them; in a corner on some straw were several heavy Colt revolvers and two long-bladed knives. Ellen observed that the men were bound together. Their hands were tied behind them, and their necks were encircled by four loops made in a single rope, so that one man could not walk without taking the others with him.

The atmosphere of the stable seemed to be heavy with a grim humour. Nobody laughed; there was not the slightest sound, and yet Ellen's impression was that the eyes which were regarding her were gleaming with an emotion akin to mirth, or at least with appreciation of the grim comedy that was being enacted.

Comedy it must be, of course, or Jeff would not have brought her into the stable to exhibit his captives. But she well knew that Hazen had planned a tragedy. Jeff and his friends had averted it and were now enjoying their victory. How had they captured the deputies? A smiling devil lurked in Jeff's eyes as he watched her. What other mischief was he meditating?

Jeff made a sign to one of his friends and the six instantly moved toward the men in the stall. Jeff gently ushered Ellen through the door which she had entered, and standing outside in the shadows of the trees removed the handkerchief from her face. He merely pulled his own down so that it encircled his neck.

"Hazen's deputies are not so bloodthirsty now," he said.

"You knew they were here! You must have known!" she said.

"Sure."

"Then I rode over here for nothing."

"Well," he said, "you couldn't help it that we knew. Your intentions were the best. We thank you, of course. But you shouldn't have come. This is a man's country, you know, and if a man isn't able to take care of himself he'd better not stay here."

There was a sound that seemed to come from the other side of the stable. A door banged open. There came a shuffling noise, cursing. Then from the shadows around the stable the four captives appeared, walking away from the building in single file, the connecting rope still looped around their necks. Jeff's friends were walking behind them and the cavalcade moved slowly eastward, out into the moonlight beyond the trees.

"What are they going to do with those men?" asked Ellen, dreading.

"They won't do as much to them as they'd have done to us if they'd had their way," answered Jeff. "They're hoofing it back to Randall. The trail they're taking will cover ten miles. One of the boys will ride behind them until they come in sight of town, so they won't try to break loose. Hazen will appreciate that."

"What have you done to Bohnert?" she questioned.

"Bohnert! Why, Bohnert went away to-night. He found that Wade Dallman had sold him something that Dallman didn't have any right to sell. He admitted he had made a mistake in not heeding a warning he'd got to the effect that the land is owned by someone who don't want to sell it just now, and so he decided that he wouldn't object to the real owner taking possession."

"There wasn't any violence?"

"No. Bohnert was sensible. He was mighty eager to oblige."

"There is a light in the house," she reminded.

"Yes. We left that burning so that in case Hazen came snooping around he'd think nothing had happened. But there'll be more light pretty soon."

Ellen gasped.

"Do you mean that you are going to burn the buildings?" she asked.

"Sure. If we'd leave them here Dallman would soon sell them to another dry farmer. We've got to remove temptation from Dallman's path."

"Isn't it rather ridiculous for big, strong men to go about in the darkness setting fire to buildings?" she said, scornfully.

"We've got to have some pleasure," he mocked.

"Oh, then you take pleasure in these—er—depredations?"

"Look here," he said, "you're deliberately trying to ride me. This isn't boys' play, though it may seem like that to you. But I think you know a damned sight better than to think that. We're fighting for what belongs to us. Do you think Hazen put those deputies in the stable just to play hide-and-go-seek with us?"

He turned and faced the house. Ellen heard a crackling sound and faced about also, to see tongues of flame shooting up inside the kitchen. The faces of several men were revealed by the flames. The faces were lean, bronzed, grim, but not villainous. Through the windows of the house Ellen could see gargantuan shadows cast upon the walls by the men's bodies as they busied themselves setting their fires. Taller shadows flitted here and there upon the ground outside the house. At a distance, in a clearing, Ellen could see the deputies filing away, distinct in the moonlight, followed by a rider with a rifle resting in the crook of an arm. No; this was not a boys' game. The shadow of death was here.

The flames were now roaring. Ellen turned to see Jeff watching her.

"Well," he said, "that's about all. The show is over. It isn't likely that the light from this fire will be seen in Randall, for there's a high ridge between and quite a stretch of timber. But it's just as well to be on the safe side. Hop on your horse. I'll take you back to Randall."

Ellen mounted and rode away with him. Twice before they reached the gorge where the fire would be hidden from them Ellen looked back. Now the stable was also burning. She glanced at Jeff. He was staring straight ahead, and his face was expressionless. She had hoped to place him in her debt and had not succeeded. She wondered if he really thanked her for what she had tried to do for him. She could not tell. But of one thing she was certain. When he had recognized her there in the shadows of the stable there had been something in his voice that closely resembled delight. She was not prepared to definitely decide, but it was something—something which would not have been there if he disliked her. A tremor of satisfaction ran over her.

CHAPTER FIFTEEN

When they rode through the gorge the blazing buildings were no longer visible. After riding a mile upon the gently sloping plain west of the gorge Ellen glanced backward and saw the sky glowing crimson. Jeff did not turn. He seemed unconcerned over what had happened, indifferent to Ellen's feelings. With his hat pulled well down over his eyes he appeared to be intently scanning the country in front of him. Ellen did not speak to him until they reached the saguaro forest where, if he intended riding to the Diamond A, their trails would diverge. He had told her that he would escort her to Randall, but Randall wasn't far and she wasn't afraid to ride alone. She was reluctant to have him run the chance of meeting Hazen and Dallman to-night, for by this time they would probably have seen the glow in the sky and would naturally have interpreted it correctly.

"Thank you," she said, then, "and good-night."

He did not answer, did not seem to hear her. But when she swung her horse northward to follow the trail that led down the valley toward town, he followed, his horse a step behind.

She drew her animal down, wheeled it so that she faced him, and spoke sharply, for she was tortured with apprehension over the possibility, the certainty, of his meeting Hazen and Dallman if he persisted in his determination to go to Randall.

"Do you understand?" she said. "I wish you to leave me! I do not want you to go to town with me!"

"I heard you. But I'm going to town just the same. You've no business gadding around this country alone."

"You said that before!" she reminded him.

"Sure. You've gadded before. Somebody ought to tell you every time you do it. It seems you haven't sense enough to think for yourself."

"Well, I didn't marry you to have you do my thinking!"

"Somebody's got to do it. You don't."

"You wouldn't be complimented if you knew what my thoughts are at this minute!" she declared, scornfully.

"I can get along without them," he said. "If you were doing any thinking to amount to anything you'd be in bed in town."

"I think I told you I rode to Bohnert's to warn you!" she said, exasperated.

"If you hadn't been in town you wouldn't have known anything about Bohnert's. Randall's no place for a decent woman to be gadding about, alone."

"I wasn't gadding, if you please! I went to Randall to do some shopping!"

"Isn't there a man at the Hour Glass that can ride a horse?" he asked. "Don't your father know that it isn't safe for you to ride through the Navajo basin?"

"I could have had company if I had wished!" she declared.

"But you didn't want company, of course," he said. "You're not that kind of girl. Any time you want to do anything you just go ahead and do it. You're independent. You're one of those nothing-can-happen-to-me kind—the kind that something always happens to."

"Nothing has happened to me yet!" she said.

"Sure not. Only you got married."

"Oh, that!" she said.

"It's nothing to you, I reckon," he said. "To you and your crowd marriage doesn't mean anything. They get married fast and get unmarried faster. There's no sentiment about it. Their idea of love is that it's some sort of disease which attacks the weak. To express any kind of emotion is disgraceful. Affection and passion should have icebergs of indifference between them. Nobody tells white, clever, diplomatic lies anymore to save one's feelings. Everybody's frank. But the trouble is they have nothing left to be frank about."

"How do you know so much about my friends?"

"I don't particularly know about your friends. But when I was——"

They had ridden down a slope into a big swale which was fringed by trees and carpeted in the centre with tall saccaton grass. On a little bench eastward, where the trail ran, the grass was shorter and there was a heavy growth of brush. The moonlight shone brightly upon the trail, disclosing two riders who were coming toward them.

Jeff brought his horse to a halt, brushed a hand over the stock of the gun at his right hip and then rode on again. Ellen drew her horse down until it was following Jeff's.

They met the riders directly in the patch of moonlight, and Ellen caught her breath sharply when she recognized the riders as Dallman and Hazen.

Hazen and Dallman had halted their horses fairly on the trail, and they sat motionless in their saddles, Dallman behind Hazen. As Ellen and Jeff continued to ride toward the two Ellen was certain that Hazen turned his head slightly and spoke to Dallman.

Jeff was about to pass when Hazen spoke sharply:

"Hold on a minute, Hale! I want to talk to you!"

Jeff halted, wheeling his horse so that he faced the sheriff and the land shark.

"Well?" he said.

"There ain't nothin' well about it, Hale!" answered Hazen, his voice high with rage. "Not a damn thing! I'm an officer of the law an' I'm here to tell you that I don't like the way you've got of sneerin' at me every time I ask you a question or speak to you. I'm entitled to respect an' I'm goin' to have it!"

"You'll get respect when you deserve it, Hazen," said Jeff. "Is that what you stopped me for?"

"It ain't! I stopped you for another reason! I want to know what you an' that female are doin' on this trail at midnight."

Hazen's voice was almost a shout. It was evident that he had seen the flame in the sky, knew what it portended, and was aware of the futility of attempting to capture the raiders. No doubt he felt that something had gone wrong with his plans to entrap Jeff and his friends.

Jeff laughed.

"Look around you, Hazen," he said: "and use your brain, if you have one. This is a public trail and it is on the Diamond A range. You must be drunk or crazy." He laughed again, but there was an ominous note in his voice which sent a chill of trepidation over Ellen, for she suspected that Hazen was deliberately seeking trouble and that Jeff was willing to meet him half way in his search for it. Jeff's laughter had been particularly irritating.

"I don't care a damn where we are, Hale!" shouted Hazen. "I've got a right to stop anybody, anywhere, an' inquire about their business. An' right now I'm askin' you what you're doin' galivantin' around the country at midnight, when decent folks ought to be home in bed! I'm askin', an' I'm goin' to have an answer, or I'll take you an' your female back to town an' lock you up! I'm askin' you again. What you doin' an' where have you been?"

"I'm not answering fool questions to-night, Hazen."

"By God! I will make you!" yelled Hazen. He waved a hand to Dallman, behind him. "Dallman," he said, "this man is under arrest! If he moves a quarter of an inch, or lifts a finger, shoot him for resistin' arrest! Now tell me where you've been!"

Ellen was not more than a dozen feet from Dallman and she had observed that from the instant Jeff had halted his horse Dallman had had him covered with his rifle. The weapon was lying in the crook of the man's left arm, its muzzle was pointed directly at Jeff's chest, and Dallman's right forefinger was on the trigger.

Dallman's eyes were glittering with hate and his lips were pressed so tightly together that even in the semi-gloom behind Hazen Ellen could see that they were white with passion. Also, it was apparent to her that this challenge was a mere pretext for the killing they meditated. They intended to goad Jeff to resistance. They knew he would not permit himself to suffer the indignity of arrest.

Ellen deliberately urged her horse forward and halted it so that she sat in the saddle between Jeff and Dallman. She calmly smiled into the faces of the sheriff and his friend, though she was cold and rigid with fright.

"Why this is ridiculous, gentlemen!" she said. "I am sure that Mr. Hale and myself have no secrets that we wish to conceal from the law. There is nothing mysterious about our being here. You see, I was in Randall to-day to make some purchases. I rented a room at the Randall Hotel, and when I left there about dusk I forgot to bring the things I bought. I had ridden clear to the Diamond A before I remembered that I had left them lying on the desk at the hotel. They are things that I need very badly, and so I asked Jeff to ride to town with me to get them. There is no crime in that, is there, gentlemen?"

Hazen's eyes were dark with rage over Ellen's interference.

"You got your gab in again, eh?" he sneered. "Once before you horned in when I had the goods on Hale. Now you're tryin' it again. I know you was in town, because I seen you. But you come into town from Navajo Basin an' not from the Diamond A!"

"Certainly I came from the Navajo Basin," answered Ellen, serenely. "I had been over to the Hour Glass to visit my father and stopped at Randall on my way back to the Diamond A."

Hazen's lips were in a pout. He glared his disbelief.

"Was Jeff Hale at the Diamond A when you got there?"

"No. He rode in about an hour later."

"What time did you get there?"

"Do you mean to the Diamond A? About an hour after dusk."

"How long did you stay there?"

"Why, until about half an hour ago, I think. Certainly not longer, for we have been riding steadily, and I think we have come about four miles."

"So you've got an alibi for him again," said Hazen. "Seems you're always around when somethin' happens."

"My place is with my husband, of course," she answered.

Hazen grunted, and glared.

"Do you know anybody named Bohnert?" he asked.

"It seems I have heard the name."

"Humph! Do you know where Bohnert lives?"

"Not exactly. I think it is somewhere in the valley."

"Bohnert's place is about eight miles from the Diamond A. Jeff Hale left Randall about dusk. You say you got to the Diamond A about dusk an' that Hale got there about an hour after you did. Are you sure he didn't get there later than that?"

"Positive. Why, we were sitting on a bench in the patio when the moon came up!"

"Humph! Did you see anything in the sky besides the moon while you've been ridin' toward town?"

"We saw a crimson light, over to the east."

"You speak to Jeff Hale about the light?"

"Oh, yes."

"What did he say?"

"He said it looked like a fire."

"Did he mention where he thought it was?"

"Why, we had just seen it. We were talking about it when we saw you."

"You're a damned liar!" charged Hazen. "You're lyin' to save Jeff Hale's hide!"

Dallman cursed, jumped his horse toward Jeff's. Ellen screamed as Dallman's rifle went off, the red lance from its muzzle tracing a line about a foot above the pommel of Jeff's saddle. But Jeff was no longer in the saddle. To Ellen's startled senses he had seemed to flit from it like a shadow at about the instant the weapon in Dallman's hands was discharged; and so swiftly that she could not follow his movements he was under the neck of his horse and at Dallman's saddle skirts. There was a heaving, writhing blur in which were the bodies of the two men and the plunging horse, then another lance flame streaked, downward this time, and in the flash Ellen saw Jeff, gripping the barrel of the weapon, twist it from Dallman's grasp. Dallman toppled, lost his balance as Jeff swung the rifle in a short, vicious half circle. Ellen heard the swish, the dull, heavy thud as the stock struck Dallman's head.

Dallman fell into the grass.

Hazen was cursing and trying to wheel his horse in an effort to snap a shot at Jeff with the revolver he had drawn. He might have succeeded but for the plunging of his horse and Ellen's seemingly awkward handling of the animal she was riding. Twice Hazen might have shot Jeff, but each time he was balked by Ellen looming between him and his target.

He saw Dallman go down, and the shot he finally succeeded in snapping at Jeff missed as his horse reared. He had no chance to shoot again, for Jeff was at his stirrup swinging the rifle he had wrenched from Dallman. Ellen heard the stock of the weapon strike Hazen. He toppled backward out of the saddle and fell heavily into the deep grass.

Jeff's horse stood where he had left it, but the horses belonging to Hazen and Dallman had moved off a little distance and were now grazing. A silence which seemed ominous to Ellen had succeeded the brief but violent battle. The two forms in the grass were motionless. Hazen was lying flat on his back, his arms and legs flung wide, while Dallman was lying upon his right shoulder and was strangely huddled, like a man sleeping in the cold without coverings. Ellen was certain that both men were dead, and the feeling of nausea that swept over her was so overpowering that she sat for a time tightly gripping the pommel of the saddle to keep from fainting.

A solemn hush had settled over the big swale. The grazing horses made no sound; the two men lying so significantly relaxed in the grass were horribly pale in the moonlight; Jeff, standing rigid, his feet spread far apart, his arms hanging stiffly at his sides, was leaning a little forward, gazing down at Hazen, who was nearest him. Somehow to Ellen at this instant Jeff seemed to have grown to gigantic proportions. That of course was an illusion resulting from his victory over odds, for the conqueror captures the imagination.

Ellen sat motionless, watching Jeff. The nausea and the faintness were leaving her and reason was slowly subduing the feeling of panic which had seized her. She knew that in attacking the men Jeff had merely defended himself. She could not blame him for that.

Jeff turned and looked up at her and she perceived that there was a heavy calmness in his manner.

"You can go along to Randall, now," he said. "It isn't far and I reckon nobody will bother you. I'm going to stay here until these jaspers wake up. I've something to say to them."

"They aren't—dead?" she gasped, hopefully.

"Far from it," he answered. "They'll be plenty active after a while."

"How do you know they are not dead?"

"Well, I had hold of the rifle. I know how hard I hit them. I felt like busting them wide open, but didn't. You get along!"

"No!" she said. "I am going to stay here until you go with me!"

"Suit yourself."

Jeff walked to Hazen, unbuckled his cartridge belt and the gun belt with the holster attached, and threw them into some brush that fringed the grass beside the trail. Hazen's gun was not in the holster, for it had dropped from his hand when Jeff had hit him with the stock of the rifle. Jeff found the weapon in the grass near where Hazen had fallen and tossed it after the cartridge belt. Then he walked over to Dallman. He threw Dallman's cartridge belt and pistol after Hazen's, then caught the horses and tethered them. Returning to a point near Ellen he sank to the ground and stretched himself comfortably out, facing the silent forms of his enemies.

"If you're not going to town you may as well get down and rest," he said. "It may be quite a while before I will be able to do that talking."

He did not offer to help her dismount and was apparently indifferent as to whether she stayed or went. He was examining Dallman's rifle when Ellen slipped out of the saddle and went toward him.

"I reckon you know I had to do it," he said, pointing to Dallman and Hazen.

"Why, yes; I think you had that right. It was obvious they meant to kill you."

"You saw that, eh? Well, I didn't want to throw my gun on them. Killing Hazen would require a lot of explaining. And Dallman's a deputy."

He became silent and stared at Hazen; Ellen observed that his brows drew together.

"Some people just can't be straight," he said presently as if speaking to his unconscious enemy. "They're naturally crooked. There's a mental kink in them that doesn't get straightened out. An accident of birth, I reckon, or maybe inherited tendencies. Who knows about that? Who cares? When we get around to caring we'll be stepping along. But until that time we'll have to keep on knocking hell out of people with kinks in their brains. That's the only way we can handle them."

It was a stern philosophy, and Jeff had been merciless in administering it. He had certainly "knocked hell" out of his enemies.

She sat down on the grass near him. He did not look at her but kept staring at the forms of the two men. The revelation of his ruthlessness in action awed her. Four times since she had known him he had shown her that the fight he was waging was a serious business to him: when he and his friends had hanged Hank Kroll, when he had whipped Dallman, when Bohnert's house had been fired and Bohnert driven off, and now when he had knocked Hazen and Dallman off their horses. Certainly, if Jeff did not make his own laws he dealt justice with a rigid arm!

She was so absorbed in her thoughts that she did not observe that Jeff had turned his head and was ironically smiling at her. And when she did see him his gaze was so intent that she reddened.

"I'm thanking you," he said. "If it hadn't been for you I reckon they'd have got me. That's twice your lying has helped me. You're mighty good at it. When you were telling Hazen about how I was sitting beside you on a bench at the Diamond A about the time the fire at Bohnert's was started I almost believed it myself. What's your idea of lying? Are you afraid of taking the consequences of telling the truth?"

"You know I lied to prevent those men from killing you!" she said, defiantly. "And perhaps I also did it to show you that there still are people who will tell white lies when telling them will keep others out of trouble!"

"So the things I said about your crowd stirred you, eh?" he retorted. "Well, you sure are a mighty fine liar."

His lips curved with contempt and she knew he believed that cowardice had prompted the prevarications that twice had flowed so glibly from her lips. And she knew that his abhorrence of all liars was so great that if he discovered that she had won him through lying to him he would never look at her again. And now, dropping her gaze from his, she prayed that he might never discover the original lie.

Hazen stirred and sat up. He was weak and dizzy and braced himself by placing his hands on the ground beside him. There were no marks on his face or head, but he rubbed a spot just above his right ear and blinked owlishly at Jeff and Ellen, who watched him.

Jeff had not changed position, and he said nothing as Hazen stared about him in stupid bewilderment. Dallman was regaining consciousness; he floundered about and finally gained a sitting posture. Like Hazen, Dallman was bewildered. He turned his head from side to side and appeared to be having some difficulty in remembering what had happened to him.

Jeff did not move. Ellen was conscious of no emotion except that of curiosity. It was strange to see the three men sitting there in the bright moonlight—two of them staring foolishly, the third cold and unsympathetic, imperturbably watching. What was Jeff going to say to them?

Hazen was recovering more quickly than Dallman, for he was first to speak.

"Hale, eh?" he said. "Busted me with the stock of a rifle."

He stared downward as if embarrassed.

Dallman grunted and tried to get up, but Jeff's voice sent him to a sitting position once again.

"Keep sitting, boys!" he said sharply. "Don't try to get up until you are certain you remember what happened to you. I've lifted your guns."

The men were silent. Jeff sat erect, drew his long-barrelled Colt and calmly inspected it. Ellen drew a long breath of apprehension. Did Jeff mean to shoot the men?

It was evident Hazen and Dallman thought so, for they stiffened and stared at Jeff with peculiarly mingled expressions of incredulity and dismay. But both were silent.

"I reckon I ought to turn my gun loose on you both and leave you to the coyotes," said Jeff. "I'm yearning to do that. Not because you'd framed up to kill me or because I'm afraid you'll keep on making trouble for me. Some day I'm going to kill you anyway—the next time you crowd me. I'd decided about that before I met you here on the trail. If you get out of this I'll throw my gun on you the next time you interfere with me. Maybe you won't get out of this. We'll see. Get up!"

The men obeyed. They stood, rigid, motionless, facing Jeff. Jeff also got up, the heavy revolver dangling from his right hand.

"Calling a man a liar is one thing," said Jeff. "Calling Jeff Hale's wife a liar is another thing. We're getting this straight. One of you did the talking but both of you thought it. I'm not making any suggestions, but I'm curious."

Hazen looked at Ellen.

"Mrs. Hale," he said, "I'm apologizin'. If you say Jeff Hale was sittin' on a bench with you, I believe it."

"It's curious what a crack on the head with a rifle stock will do to a man's brain," mocked Jeff. "Hazen, I've never seen you more sensible. How about you, Dallman? You didn't talk but I reckon you were thinking. Express yourself!"

"I never doubted the lady," said Dallman.

"That's handsome," declared Jeff. "It's plain you boys like to live. How much longer you're going to live depends upon how long you can keep your noses out of my business. Hop! Go and see the pretty fire!"

Hazen and Dallman went eagerly to their horses, mounted and rode away. They did not even look back, and they left their weapons where Jeff had thrown them. It was quite evident to Ellen that they knew of the deadly earnestness behind Jeff's grim banter. And it was equally evident to Ellen that though Jeff disliked a liar, and knew her to be one, he did not wish others to share his knowledge. Would he shield her in this manner if he did not care for her?

Jeff's manner told her nothing. He rode with her to the door of the livery stable in Randall, sat silently on his horse and bowed to her as she crossed the street to go to her hotel. He watched her until she entered, then he wheeled his horse and rode slowly down the street.

CHAPTER SIXTEEN

The sun streaming in the front windows awakened Ellen. She got up and standing behind the curtains glanced down into the street.

Randall was humming with activity, and already the dust from passing vehicles was swimming over the roofs of the buildings. Some of it was drifting into Ellen's room through the open windows and though the morning was hot she lowered the sash. Then she washed her face and hands, dressed, combed her hair in front of the glass in the dresser, and went downstairs to inquire about breakfast. The clerk was not at the desk and the lobby was deserted. She could not see any signs of a dining room, so she walked to the door, stepped down into the street, and strode vigorously down the sidewalk.

Not until she had gone several hundred feet did she think of her first adventure of the preceding night and then, her curiosity awakened, she moved more slowly, trying to remember where she had strayed from the sidewalk. She found the store in which she had made her purchases, and after carefully scrutinizing the section she decided that she must have wandered into an open space between two buildings just a little distance down the street from where she had stood when the proprietor of the store had spoken to her. Some frame sheds were scattered about the open space, forming the sides of an irregular square, and at a little distance was another and larger shed which was used as a stable, and which, she decided, was where she had overheard Dallman and Hazen talking.

The space was small, but last night it had seemed like a great plain on the edge of an abyss. How different it appeared with the friendly sunlight shining down!

She was hungry. Obeying a sudden impulse she crossed the street, walked down a little distance until she reached the Elite, opened the door, entered and took a chair at one of the tables. She did not look up when she felt a waitress standing near her, but she knew the waitress was Sadie. And when she gave her order to the girl Ellen looked up and met her steadily hostile gaze with a smile.

The girl was pretty but there was a glint of recklessness lurking in her eyes, something wayward and subtle which she did not bother to conceal.

"Is Jeff in town with you?" she asked boldly when Ellen was ready to leave.

"Do you mean Mr. Hale?" said Ellen quietly.

"He's Jeff to me," stated Sadie, shortly.

Ellen was unmoved by this insolence. She smiled.

"He isn't in town, now," she said. "I came to town from the Hour Glass yesterday to buy some things I needed. Last night about dusk I rode to the Diamond A, and Jeff rode back to town with me. We reached here shortly after midnight. I think Jeff went to join some of his men, somewhere on the range."

Sadie laughed and narrowed her eyes at Ellen.

"Bohnert's place was raided and burned last night," she said.

"Was it Bohnert's? Jeff said he thought it was. We saw the light in the sky while we were riding toward town."

Sadie gave her a sharp glance, then laughed again.

"There was plenty of excitement in town this morning," she said. "Four of Hazen's deputies walked into town roped together by their necks. They all had their hands tied behind them. A crowd of those dry farmers collected around them and freed them. There was some loud talking and a lot of threatening. Hazen was there. He was wild. They can't swear who tied them up that way, but Jeff's name was mentioned. But if you were riding with Jeff last night, of course that makes him innocent." She deliberately winked at Ellen.

Of course, loving Jeff, Sadie sympathized with him. But the wink was conclusive evidence of an intimacy between Jeff and Sadie which had reached the confidential stage. Ellen resented the girl's boldness.

"Thank you," she said, coldly.

"Gawd," laughed Sadie, "ain't you the icicle!"

Ellen reached the sidewalk with Sadie's laugh following her. She had turned to walk the little distance which would take her opposite the hotel when someone seized her right arm. She wheeled, indignantly, to confront a slender man of medium height whose face seemed familiar. The man smiled, and then she knew him.

Jim Kellis!

A different Jim Kellis, though. Jeff's words, "tin horn," accurately described him.

He looked cheap. He had lost weight, and dissipation had brought queer, drooping lines into his face, lines of weakness. His eyes, never steady, had become furtive. A satyric slyness had got into them. His lower lip, always full, had dropped a little, and the upper one had taken on a queer, set quirk. His frontier clothing fitted him badly and his broad-brimmed hat sat on his head at a rakish angle.

Ellen repressed a shudder of loathing. She said "Hello, Jim" in a voice which was entirely without expression, and attempted to slip out of his grip. But he held on tightly, almost possessively, and grinned apologetically at her.

"What luck!" he said. "Heard you were here!"

"Yes, Jim," said Ellen, "your wife told you. I stopped there one day."

"Say!" he said, frowning. "I don't know how it happened, but I married her. Lonesome, I suppose. Can't explain it any other way. God! I was lonesome. 'Shamed, too. 'Shamed to write to you and tell you the truth. Always hoped you'd marry me, but didn't think I had much of a chance. You wouldn't promise, you know. Couldn't pin you down to a thing. We said a lot of things to each other—remember? Worst of it was you couldn't tell when you was in earnest. Our crowd was always like that. Kidding. Joshing. Didn't know where I stood. Anyhow I pulled a scurvy trick in not letting you know. But your father knew. Didn't he tell you?"

"Yes; he told me," she lied. "I never loved you, Jim, so you didn't hurt me after all. I'm glad I met you, Jim."

She would have moved away, but his grip held her.

"Look here," he said. "You can't go this way, you know. There's some things I've got to say to you. Explanations, and all that sort of thing, you know. Give a fellow a chance, Ellen."

His face had come close to hers and she detected the fumes of whiskey on his breath. She grew rigid.

"Not now, Jim," she said coldly, "some other time, perhaps."

She pulled away from him, crossed the street, and entered the door of the hotel. Looking back over her shoulder as she passed through the lobby she saw Jim standing on the sidewalk where she had left him. He had watched her enter the hotel.

There was also another watcher. Sadie stood in the open doorway of the Elite.

Ellen went up to her room and sat on the edge of the bed. She was furiously angry. Why on earth couldn't Kellis have met her elsewhere—anywhere but where he had met her?

Ugh! What a beast the man had become! The skin of her arm crawled; she brushed it with a hand in an effort to erase the memory of his touch. And she had once felt a maternal interest in the man! What a perverted faculty of judgment must have been hers! How infallible she had once considered herself! Jim Kellis!

"Oh!" she breathed aloud. "I once thought he was a man! I must have been crazy! Ugh! I hope I never see him again."

But inside an hour Kellis appeared again to her. She heard a soft knock on her door and when she opened it a trifle to peer out Kellis abruptly pushed it open, walked in, and closed it behind him.

Kellis had taken more drinks. He visibly swayed as he stood against the door, looking at her. He was grinning slyly, and he spoke softly, as though keeping a tryst.

"Slipped in without the guy downstairs seeing me," he said. "We won't be disturbed."

She was white with a realization of her helplessness. A scream would bring help, but what of the resulting disturbance, the curiosity, the questioning, the gossip, the stares, the incredulous smiles.

"You want that talk, I suppose," she said, smiling stiffly. "We can't talk here, you know, it is too hot and stuffy. Let us go down to the lobby."

"Nix!" he said. "That's too public! What's the matter?" he added impudently, "we used to talk in private, didn't we? Lots o' times. What's the matter with you? Getting prudish?"

"I am married now, Jim," she told him, keeping her voice low.

He laughed unpleasantly.

"Don't you think I know that?" he asked. "It's no secret, is it? Everybody knows it. Everybody's talking about it. Everybody's wondering how you got acquainted with Jeff Hale. You didn't know him East—I'll swear to that, for I used to know all the fellows that even looked at you. You didn't have time to get acquainted with him between the time you left the Hour Glass that night and the time you and him got to Randall and got married. Kind of sudden, wasn't it? Something mighty mysterious about that marriage, Ellen!"

He wagged his head at her.

"Well, that ain't my business. What I'm wanting to do is to explain why I got married."

"I don't care to hear any explanations, Jim," she said. "I wouldn't have married you, anyway. I wouldn't even have stopped at your place that day if I hadn't wanted to be neighbourly. And if you don't leave this room instantly I shall never speak to you again!"

"Riding a high horse, eh?" he mocked. "Well, ride him. You're Mrs. Jeff Hale, now, and you don't want to talk to common people! Well, the Hales ain't so much, or the Ballingers either, for that matter. Crooks and bullies, that's what! Jeff Hale thinks he's a prize fighter, or something. He's bigger than me or he wouldn't have hit me that time!" He leered at her. "You didn't hear about that, eh?" he went on. "Just for nothing at all he hit me! Anybody'll tell you that! He and that Sadie Nokes was in the Elite talking and I said something to her that he didn't like. Just as though she's a lady! Why hell, everybody talks to her. She's—she's a—a——"

"Don't you dare to speak that word, Jim Kellis!"

"You know what she is without my telling you," he grinned. "Well, then I don't have to tell. And you know Jeff hangs around her! That's the kind of a man you married! Hit me for butting in when he was talking with a strumpet! Hit me so hard I didn't know anything for a week! Busted me wide open!" He stared at her for an instant and then dropped his chin to his chest as if suddenly overcome with emotion.

"Hit me!" he said, his voice muffled. "But old Abe Lincoln knows that I'm going to get even with him. When the time comes to settle that land deal Old Abe Lincoln is just going to keep on saying nothing."

His sudden maudlin raving terrified her. What would she do if he fell over in a stupor? She decided that if he did succumb to the unconsciousness that seemed to be stealing over him she would drag him outside the door and lock it, trusting that if he was found later it would be thought that he had wandered aimlessly into the hall. He had said that no one had seen him enter the hotel.

But Kellis did not fall. He had sagged against the door with his head drooping and his arms hanging limply at his sides, but his eyes were open and he was muttering unintelligibly. Apparently he realized his condition and was fighting off the stupor which had seized him, for his limp arms stiffened and he raised his head to stare at Ellen. He must have drunk a great deal between the time Ellen had met him on the street and when he had entered the room, and was just beginning to become affected by it, for now his eyes had a dazed and foolish expression, seeming to reflect the growing conviction that his muscles would not obey him.

"I'm drunk," he mumbled. "Shouldn't have come, maybe, eh? But had to explain. Lonesome. What th' hell do I care about Jeff Hale? Answer that! Knocked me down! Knocked me down! And you married him! And you're riding a high horse, eh? I ain't good enough now, eh? Was once, wasn't I? Old Abe Lincoln will fix him. Owns that land, does he? Old Abe Lincoln ain't talking!"

Why was Kellis mentioning Lincoln's name in his drunken mutterings? What mental vagary was associating Lincoln with the Hale land? Obviously Lincoln could not talk because he had died a great many years ago. Did Kellis know another man who bore the martyred president's name? Or had the man's muddled brain grotesquely linked the past with the present?

Ellen was alert. Kellis's mention of the Hale lands had penetrated her consciousness like an electric shock and brought the instant conviction that Kellis knew something about the missing land certificate.

She moved closer to Kellis.

"Why doesn't Lincoln talk, Jim?" she asked.

Kellis stiffened himself and looked at her blankly. As he continued to stare the blankness slowly gave way to heavy derision. He seemed to awaken mentally, and he laughed, loudly and mockingly.

"You'd like to know, eh? You'd like to know why Lincoln don't talk? Some other people would like to know, too!"

He lurched away from the wall and staggered to one of the windows. He threw the curtains aside, gazed down into the street, and then sank heavily into a chair. He sat there for a little while, while Ellen stood near the door watching him, then he slowly relaxed and seemed to sink into a doze.

He was drunk, but not drunk enough to remain unconscious while Ellen could drag him to the door and into the hall. She knew that if she attempted such a thing he would awaken and make a scene. So she did the only thing that was left to do. She gathered her few belongings together, opened the door, left it open so that anyone finding Kellis in the room would think he had mistakenly entered, descended to the desk, paid her bill and hurried across the street to the livery stable to get her horse.

Two hours later she was at the Diamond A, where she was greeted affectionately by Mrs. Hale. Her trunks and bags had come from the Hour Glass and had been placed in her room.

But she discovered that Jeff had not been home since the morning he had left to escort her to her father's ranch.

CHAPTER SEVENTEEN

Adam Hale liked Ellen. The stalwart, white-haired pioneer was her escort upon many rides she had taken during Jeff's latest absence. As Jeff had predicted she had not been asked any questions, but she had observed that Adam listened very attentively every time she mentioned her father.

"He's a big man," said Adam. "He's always lookin' ahead."

Ellen and Adam were at a corner of the corral fence. Ellen had walked out there and had been standing there shading her eyes with her hands against the bright glare of the sun when Adam had joined her. As usual, she had been scanning the empty distance for signs of a rider. This was the second week and Jeff had not yet come.

"Yes, he has vision," answered Ellen. "He can see a railroad running through the valley—through your land. It is land that he would like to own."

Adam regarded her steadily.

"I reckon he'd like to own it, all right. But Matt Ballinger ain't stealing anything. He don't know anything about that missing certificate."

"You are confident," she said.

"I know men," was his answer. "Matt's got a right to file on that land if he wants to. Anybody has. If he don't know who stole the certificate he's honest."

"I think he doesn't know who stole it," said Ellen. "I think if he did know he would tell you about it. You are right. Is Wade Dallman honest?"

"Dallman would steal anything!"

Hale's fine old eyes were troubled as he laid a hand on Ellen's shoulder and looked gravely into her eyes.

"There's somethin' I've got to tell you," he said. "You love Jeff an' you're Jeff's wife. You've got a right to know. Jeff's a little wild. I reckon you already know that. You see, Jeff was brought up in a wild atmosphere. When he was a kid things were different out here. A man couldn't run to a town an' bring the law to him every time anything went wrong. Mostly all differences was settled with a gun. It was a pretty tough section an' things went wrong mighty often. Jeff was old enough to take that all in. By the time he was fifteen he could throw a gun with the best of them, an' he got wild. He ran with a bad crowd. He's got a bad temper an' he's reckless an' impulsive. By the time he was eighteen he'd shot two gamblers, an' a sheriff over in Yavapai."

"Killed them!"

"No. But it wasn't his fault that they lived. He had intentions, all right. One of Jeff's shortcomin's is that he's got nothin' but contempt for the law. He'd ought to have been born a generation or two ago. But now the law is all over the country, and Jeff has still got his contempt. I'm afraid he'll go too far.

"I packed him East to school just to get him away from the bad gang he was running with. First to St. Louis an' then to Yale. He didn't do so bad at St. Louis, but he didn't last long at college. Ma'am, I heard that he just raised the devil there. I wouldn't tell you this if you wasn't his wife. I want you to know just what you've got to contend with.

"I'll help you all I can because I know that if Jeff's in love with you he'll finally settle down. I'm afraid he'll do somethin' wrong before he does. What is happenin' right now shows his temper. This land deal. There's no use fightin' it with a gun. Any settlement that's finally made will be made by the courts. But Jeff won't have it that way. He's fightin' just like we used to fight out here. He's determined to settle it with a gun. He's runnin' with men that I know are outlaws. He's their leader. They'll do anything he says. They've burned more than a dozen of these dry farmers out an' the farmers are organizin' against him. Some night there'll be a battle and somebody will be killed. I can't talk to Jeff. He just looks at me an' grins."

"Do you know any of the men—the outlaws—who are helping him?"

"I've seen two of them with him—Dell Hart and Jess Givens."

"I shouldn't worry," said Ellen. She remembered Jeff's cold composure on the night he had knocked Dallman and Hazen from their horses, and it seemed to her that Jeff would not kill except upon great provocation. She thought that Jeff's gestures toward the law were more derisive than criminal.

"The crisis is comin'," Adam went on. "The first of the month the land office is goin' to make a decision about the ownership of the section in dispute. Dallman will get it, for he's a crook and he knows how to influence folks. Dallman will go ahead an' try to settle it. He'll have Bill Hazen an' the law behind him. Jeff won't give in, an' there'll be the devil to pay! This thing wouldn't have happened if the certificate hadn't got lost."

"Mr. Hale, do you know anyone in this vicinity named Lincoln?" asked Ellen.

Hale shook his head.

"There never has been anyone of that name here. But folks have been comin' in an' maybe there's a Lincoln here now."

If there was a Lincoln in the country around Randall, Ellen meant to find him. A man named Lincoln, she was positive, knew something about the missing certificate and perhaps if he could be found he could be made to talk, notwithstanding Kellis's declaration that he wouldn't. If she could find him she might bribe him to talk, to reveal what he knew.

She had decided that she would not take anyone into her confidence, and so she asked no more questions of Adam. Anyway, the question of who finally obtained title to the land was not as important to her as Jeff's future. Despite her knowledge of Jeff's character, Adam's revelation had distinctly shocked her.

She rode into Randall the following day and spent her time roaming from store to store, ostensibly to shop, but in reality to discover if she could find anyone who knew a man named Lincoln.

Nobody knew anyone of that name. But she was certain that if there had not been a Lincoln in or around Randall, Kellis would not have mentioned him.

However, her quest had no result except to stiffen her determination. She felt that if she could find the missing certificate and restore the title of the land to Jeff's father, the fight between Dallman and Hazen on one side and Jeff and his friends on the other, would cease. The motive that actuated Dallman was greed, of course, and he would draw off if he knew the land could not be stolen.

Ellen spent as much time in Randall as she dared, but did not succeed in finding anyone who knew of a man named Lincoln. She even slyly questioned Link, the justice who had performed the marriage ceremony. She had hoped that perhaps Kellis in his drunken mutterings had intended to say "Link," But she discovered that Link had no secret which he shared with Kellis. She drew out of him the statement that he didn't like Kellis. He added that he would never have "any truck" with "a tin horn like him."

She was returning at dusk from one of her trips to town, and had reached a turn in the valley which brought her within view of the Diamond A buildings, when she heard the sound of hoofs behind her and turned swiftly in the saddle to see Jeff riding toward her out of the deepening shadows.

Her heart thumped with delight, but she brought her horse to a halt and faced him, calmly smiling.

He rode close to her. It was still light enough to permit her to see his face. He rode so close to her that she caught the gleam of his eyes. She had never seen them so sombrely lustrous; had never seen his lips as tightly compressed.

She knew something had aroused him. He was suppressing passion.

"What were you doing in a hotel room with Jim Kellis?" he said, grimly.

"I was not in a room with him!" she declared.

"Lying again," he mocked. "You were seen. Kellis was found drunk, in your room!"

"I—I couldn't help it. I was there. I had met him on the street and thought I had dismissed him. He forced his way into the room and I couldn't get him to leave. He was drunk and couldn't understand."

"You're a fool," he said, speaking through the light lines of his lips, "but you are not the kind of woman who keeps appointments with men in hotel rooms. If you wanted to give me grounds for divorce you needn't have troubled yourself. I don't think what some people might think. I know you better than that. But why did you select Jim Kellis? He is my enemy."

She told him the truth about Kellis—how she had once thought she had loved him. She ended by telling him that since she had seen Kellis again she loathed him. But she did not tell him about Kellis's reference to Lincoln and the Hale land.

When she finished she observed that some of the cold rigidity had gone from his lips, and that the dark fire in his eyes had lightened a little.

"Who told you Jim Kellis was in my room?" she asked.

"I have friends in town."

"Sadie Nokes is one of them, isn't she?"

He laughed, peered closer at her, observed her flaming cheeks and her eyes, which were flashing scorn at him. He seemed incredulous, amazed, and she knew that he had interpreted her scorn as jealousy.

"Sadie Nokes!" he said, his voice once more normal. "Why, shucks; Sadie! Why I reckon Sadie's a female Jim Kellis! Both have loving dispositions. But I don't love Sadie any more than you love Jim Kellis!"

"No," she said steadily, "you don't love anybody. I think you have no regard for the feelings of others. If you had you would show it. Don't you know that you are worrying your father and mother by associating with the kind of men who are helping you to fight Dallman?"

"What do you know about my friends?"

"I know enough about them to understand that they are not the sort of companions you should choose! You ought to be ashamed of yourself!"

"What's the cause of your sudden interest in my affairs?" he said. "Are you trying to get me to lay off Dallman so that he and your father can get the land?"

"My father wouldn't enter into any such an agreement with Dallman, and you know it. You are just trying to be mean. And why are you changing your opinion? It wasn't long ago that you told me I had married into the Hale family so that the Ballingers would have a claim to the land."

He laughed.

"Maybe I did have that idea at first. You gave it to me by your eagerness to marry me. There was another way, you know. If you had promised not to talk about Kroll the marriage would not have occurred."

"You proposed it!"

She abruptly wheeled her horse and sent him down the trail toward the Diamond A buildings. She had been hurt by his insolence and suspicions but, strangely, she was not angry. She merely pitied him. He was not entirely responsible for the wild and primitive traits that had developed in him. The country was to blame for that—the country, environment, and perhaps inherited passions which had descended to him from his parents, who may have had them but had succeeded in suppressing them.

Ellen had meditated much about Jeff. His face was always before her. She had spent many nights lying fully awake, recalling expressions she had seen, carefully and painstakingly tracing them, identifying them, interpreting them. She loved him and wanted to understand him. And she did not gloss his faults with the veneer of indifference. Pitilessly she dragged them forth. He had a strain of brutality in him. That had been proved by his whipping of Dallman. But she remembered that she had also felt like whipping Dallman when she had stood in the darkness beside the stable and had overheard him refer to her as a "slut." So she didn't hold that against Jeff.

Jeff hadn't any other bad traits. She knew how he must appear to other men; she could readily understand why they feared and respected him. They were aware that he was dangerous when provoked or aroused, that he feared no one, and that he made no threats or promises that he did not mean to keep.

He had one glaring fault—indifference to the opinions of others. His own word was final. That was his vitality and confidence. He was a natural leader of men. He had contempt for all weaknesses, just as he was contemptuous of all liars—herself included. It had made no difference to him that she had lied in his defense. He could defend himself. A liar was a liar no matter what he lied about.

And there was no subtlety in him. He could mask his feelings but could not assume spurious ones. His speech was straight, frank, pointed; he dealt in no obscure or double meanings. "The law was made for fools and weaklings," came as quickly as: "What were you doing in a hotel room with Jim Kellis?"

He was man in a raw state; wonderful material to work on, to shape, to polish. He belonged to her and she would fight to keep him, would endure much.

But his distrust of her stung her. He could not dispossess himself of the idea that her motive in marrying him had been for the purpose of attempting to secure title to the Hale land, and yet he had nothing valid upon which to base his suspicion. Obviously he had never considered that she might have fallen in love with him, for he had told her that one fell in love with character, and character could not be read at a glance.

She hadn't told him of her suspicion that Kellis knew something about the missing certificate. She wouldn't tell him. She intended to try to recover the certificate herself, and then she would show him that she didn't want his land. And she would never let him see that she loved him. After she had proved that she hadn't married him for the land she would leave him. Then he would understand why she had married him. He would come to her then, and she would refuse him.

Her lips were set tightly as she rode ahead of him.

He could joke about Sadie Nokes, but he thought a great deal of the girl or he wouldn't be hanging around her as much as he did. He was jealous of Kellis, but of course she mustn't be jealous of Sadie Nokes! Wasn't that just like a man!

Jeff was suddenly riding beside her. She turned her head away and would not look at him.

"Riding alone again, eh?" he said. "Seems you'll never get any sense!"

Ellen gave no indication that she heard him.

"Forget something at the Diamond A?"

"No!" Sharply.

"What are you going back for?"

"Because it's my home."

"Your home, eh? Thought you left it about two weeks ago!"

"I went to father's to get some things. I only stayed there two days. I came back here the day after I went to Bohnert's to warn you."

"You didn't mean to make your visit permanent?"

"Of course not."

"Why didn't you tell me that?"

"You didn't ask. You showed very little interest in my movements."

She was an enigma. He couldn't understand her. She had gone away. She had come back. He could understand why she had gone away. She hadn't wanted to be married. Now she wanted to continue in the married state. There must be a reason. He thought he had it!

"Ballinger sent you back, eh?"

Ellen laughed disdainfully, though she felt like slapping him because he wouldn't, or couldn't understand.

"That explanation is as good as another," she said.

"Well," he returned, "until you've got a better one I reckon you'll have to play a lone hand!" He pulled up sharply, called a curt "So-long!" and sent his horse plunging into the night.

Ellen brought her own horse to a halt and stared after him. She saw him for a little while and then the darkness swallowed him. She rode on. Desolation seemed to creep in upon her and a strange, haunting sadness oppressed her.

CHAPTER EIGHTEEN

The turbulence of spirit which Adam Hale feared would one day incite Jeff to reckless violence had finally gripped him. When he sent his horse against the long, eastern slope of the valley the mighty wrath which he had succeeded in repressing was sweeping through him slowly and resistlessly. He fought it no longer. A dozen times in the past year he had felt a savage urge to kill Dallman and Hazen, but against that yearning he had arrayed his reason. Now his passions were driving him.

He couldn't fight his enemies their way, so he would force them to fight his way. With the help of dishonest servants of the land office Dallman would take possession of six hundred and forty acres of land that Adam Hale had held for thirty years. Through a mysterious combination of circumstances a marriage had taken place with the object of wheedling still more land out of the control of the Hale family.

He could understand Dallman's methods, but the Ballinger attack had been so insidious that he had not known it was being made. Because of the treachery of the Ballingers he hated them—father and daughter. When he reflected how easily Ellen had deceived him he was disgusted. Mentally he reviewed the drama. First, her presence in the cabin. Of course she had been brought there by the man he and his friends had pursued. There was only one detail which was not yet clear to him, and that was how they—the Ballingers—had known that he would be in the vicinity of the cabin that night. That explained, the last pricking doubt would be removed. For the rest of it had obviously been prearranged. The ropes which bound Ellen's arms he had later examined, to find that they had been cut from a hackamore which had been rolled in a slicker behind the saddle on the horse Ellen had ridden that night. And when one day he had ridden to the cabin to seek for further evidence, he had found the handkerchief with which she had been gagged, to discover that it was silk, with a small "B" worked in one of its corners. He knew that Matt Ballinger sometimes wore silk handkerchiefs, and that nobody else in the section would wear them.

He was convinced that she had deliberately lied to him when she had told him that she recognized his voice as that of the man who had abducted her. Of course she would lie. That had been part of their plan to enmesh him. How many times she had lied to him since he did not know. She had lied for him in the Elite, on the night Hazen had threatened to arrest him;

she had lied again for him on the night they had met Hazen and Dallman, after Bohnert's place had been fired. Those lies had been uttered to keep him alive so that the Ballingers might later use him. A dead husband would not be of use to them. He was more than half convinced that she and Dallman had been discussing some secret on the day he had used the whip on Dallman. He had seen them standing close together; had heard Dallman laughing; had observed Ellen's face redden as Dallman had spoken to her. He hadn't hesitated to listen, and at the moment he hadn't cared what they were saying to each other. But now he felt that the meeting had had some significance. It might even indicate that Dallman and Ballinger were working together.

But the thing he couldn't get out of his mind was her clever acting in the cabin, her haughtiness, assumed to impress him; her threat to reveal what had happened to Hank Kroll. Of course, being his wife, she would keep silent! And she had kept silent. But she had had marriage in mind all the time. "You probably will be damned by a good many people when this story gets out," she had told him. "My father will be furious, of course, when he hears that you dragged me away and kept me in this place all night, after sending your men away!"

If that hadn't been a hint that marriage would be acceptable he didn't know a hint when he heard one. And now he could see that it had influenced him, for from that instant he had begun to pity her.

Moreover, he knew that in spite of it all he loved her. He had loved her from the instant he had seen her standing in the cabin, the moonlight from the window shining on her face. He hadn't wanted to love her, for he knew she was brazen and shameless. But he couldn't help it. There had been times when he had fought to resist the impulse to take her in his arms and crush her to him while telling her that he loved her in spite of her duplicity. He had conquered that wild impulse as he had conquered his yearning to kill Dallman and Hazen.

He gained the level above the valley and when the moon rose he was riding steadily eastward. From the brow of a distant hill he saw Bohnert's place and he thought of the tumult which had raged in him on the night of the fire he had momentarily held Ellen in his arms. Grimly he rode on.

About midnight he rode to the door of a ranch house. Before he could knock half a dozen men were moving toward him from the direction of the stable. Gillman, the owner of the ranch and his chief confederate in many raids, was foremost.

Gillman motioned for him to approach, so he rode over and pulled his horse to a halt near them. The faces of the men were visible to him and he was amazed to find that none of the men would look directly at him, though he greeted them variously, by name. They stood, strangely silent. One was kicking a hummock of earth, one stood with folded arms staring into distance, another appeared to be dejectedly studying the earth at his feet. Ed Davis, who had been with him on many a lark in the old days, was not facing him at all, but stood motionless with his back turned. Sam Tilton, possessing a waggish, vitriolic tongue, did not make a sound. Gillman alone seemed to act naturally.

But there was something wrong with Gillman, too. He seemed embarrassed. His face was long and solemn.

"What's happened to you jaspers?" inquired Jeff. "We ought to be riding."

"We ain't goin', Jeff," said Gillman. He folded his arms uneasily; unfolded them, stuck his hands into his pockets, removed them and placed them behind him.

"What's wrong?" asked Jeff. "Hazen got another plant?"

"It ain't that," answered Gillman. "The fact is, we—me an' the boys—have decided that there ain't no use raidin' any more. The farmers is comin' in faster than we can chase them out. Seems there's a regular movement. It's like tryin' to sweep the ocean back with a broom. Seems like our day's over. I hear this thing is happening all over."

"We've got a right to keep them off our land, Gillman!"

"That's just it. We keep them off our land an' they take up land right next to us. The government owns most of it an' is parcelling it out. There ain't none of us owns land enough to ranch cattle on. Pretty soon they'll be makin' us put up fences. You can't stop them fellows from comin'. A whole wagon train of them came in to-day. They pitched tents along the north fork. They fill up the whole basin. Must be twenty families. The wagon boss said they was another train followin'. What chance we got with them comin' in like that? We're through, Jeff."

Jeff looked at them. He knew how hard it had been for Gillman to tell him. He had half expected this to happen, and he was positive that theirs was not a sudden decision. They had discussed it thoroughly, and despite their friendliness they would not go further with him.

This meant that hereafter he would have to do his fighting alone. Morally, they were with him. They were still his friends. But they had foreseen the end of their era and would no longer fight against the inevitable.

"It ain't that we're scared, Jeff!" added Gillman, looking up and meeting Jeff's gaze fairly. "It's just that there ain't no use fightin' it any longer. We're licked, an' we might as well admit it. You're licked, too, but I reckon you'll never say so."

Jeff straightened in the saddle.

"All right, boys," he said, "you know your business best. So-long!" he waved a hand to them and rode northward.

CHAPTER NINETEEN

At dawn Jeff was in sight of the Hour Glass. He had camped at the Hale cabin in the Navajo basin, but the sleep that he sought there would not come.

He knew that Gillman had told him the truth. Gillman had merely expressed a conviction that he, himself, had felt from the beginning of his war with Dallman—that the raiding of the farmers was a futile method of waging the war and that in the end it would have to be fought out between Dallman and himself personally.

That method meant a killing. Jeff had sought to avoid violence of that particular kind. Three times in his life he had drawn a gun, and three times he had experienced a passion which he knew was a heritage. It had been in his blood from the day he had handled a revolver the first time, and it had stayed with him all his days—a lurking yearning to provoke other men to fight.

The yearning had amazed him. It was not a desire to kill. Three times he might have killed men, but he had been careful not to do so. He had merely wounded them. And in those three combats he had not felt the slightest tremor of fear or of rage. He had been calm and alert, merely. Coldly calculating his chances, absolutely without rancour, but with that curious yearning to quicken his muscles and his brain, he had deliberately avoided shooting the men to death.

His father had talked to him. And his mother. They had thought him wild, had warned him about what they had been pleased to call his ungovernable temper. But he knew he was able to control himself, that not once in his life had he felt the passion of a wanton rage.

But he was close to it as he rode across the pasture toward the Hour Glass ranch house. He was convinced that Ballinger and Ellen as well as Dallman and Hazen, were his enemies. He hadn't decided how he would fight Ellen and her father; he couldn't decide that until he solved the mystery of his marriage. But toward Hazen and Dallman his intentions had become definite. He had warned them on the night he had knocked them out of their saddles with the rifle.

The sun was rising as he rode out of the pasture toward the colonnaded courtyard of the ranch house, and when he observed Ballinger walking slowly between the columns he reined his horse toward him.

Ballinger recognized him and waved a hand to him.

Jeff did not answer the greeting. When he reached the edge of the court-yard he slid off his horse, trailed the reins and confronted the other man.

"Well," said Ballinger pleasantly, "you are early! Shall I call anyone to take care of your horse?"

"No," answered Jeff, "thank you."

Ballinger knew men, and he was aware that something had gone wrong with Jeff. The sombre eyes which were steadily regarding him reflected distrust, suspicion, and hostility. It is true that Jeff's voice was low and that his manner was gravely polite, yet in the atmosphere about him was the chill of enmity.

These things Ballinger observed, yet he maintained his own quietly pleasant attitude.

"Ellen isn't with you?" he asked.

"Ellen is at the Diamond A."

"Then——"

"You talk too fast, Ballinger," said Jeff. "I didn't come here to answer questions but to ask some. The first one is this: What are you going to do about filing on the Hale land?"

"Nothing," replied Ballinger. "I have withdrawn my papers."

"Why did you withdraw them?"

"Out of consideration for my daughter and my daughter's husband."

"But you still want to run your railroad through there."

"I'd like to, certainly." Ballinger smiled, adding: "And if Dallman doesn't get the title to the land I believe we could arrange a deal for a right of way that would be most advantageous for the Hales and the Ballingers."

"I thought that was in your mind," said Jeff. His suspicions were confirmed. His lips curved in contempt.

"Whose idea was it—yours or Ellen's?" he asked.

"What idea?"

"The idea of having Ellen marry me so that the deal you are figuring on could be arranged." He smiled ironically as Ballinger stiffened. He thought Ballinger a mighty good actor, for he was making a splendid effort at pretending amazement.

"I don't know yet how it was worked," Jeff went on. "I can't figure out how you and Ellen knew I would be at the Navajo cabin that night."

"What cabin? Explain yourself, man; I don't know what you are talking about!"

"Your mind's a bit hazy on it now, eh?" mocked Jeff. "Well, maybe I can freshen it up a little. There was that handkerchief with the letter 'B' worked in a corner of it. A silk handkerchief. You've got one on like it, now. Then there was the rope her hands were tied with. I found the rest of it in her slicker. I'm admitting it was pretty slick. I hadn't advertised I would be there. I thought nobody knew I had thought of going there. The men with me knew, but no one else could know. Yet when I went into the cabin she was there, waiting for me, bound and delivered."

Ballinger was staring at him. Watching intently, Jeff was more than half convinced that the man's amazement and bewilderment were real. Ballinger could hardly assume the pallor that suddenly whitened his face, nor could he at will counterfeit the horror that shone in his eyes, replacing the bewilderment.

Jeff smiled derisively.

"I'm not insane, Ballinger," he said. "Though I admit that there have been times when I thought I would be—trying to figure this thing out."

"If you are not crazy you must be talking about something that I have no knowledge of!" declared Ballinger. "Or you are trying to tell me something that you think I have knowledge of. At any rate I don't know what you are talking about. Are you trying to tell me something about Ellen?"

"You're getting more intelligent every minute," said Jeff. "Give you time and you'll remember the whole deal. I'll try to help you along. Do you know what Ellen rode into the Navajo basin for?"

The mockery in Jeff's voice angered Ballinger.

"Yes," he said, "she rode over to marry Jim Kellis!"

Jeff's muscles seemed to stiffen, but his gaze was cynical.

"That don't quite get over, Ballinger," he mocked. "She couldn't marry a man who was already married."

"She didn't know Kellis was married," exclaimed Ballinger. "She and Kellis had been writing to each other, and Kellis had not mentioned his wife."

"You knew Kellis had a wife."

"Of course. I suppose I'll have to explain. It is evident Ellen hasn't. I don't think it's any of your business. Hale, but something has happened to you and I suppose I've got to do what I can to clear it up—even to revealing secrets that perhaps Ellen doesn't want you to know!

"Ellen got unbearably impudent and arrogant. I presume you have found that out. I wanted to take it out of her, and when she told that she intended to ride over to marry Kellis I let her go, thinking the shock of finding he was already married would do her good."

"Did you send anybody with her?"

"She wouldn't permit that. But I had Jim Peters follow her. Peters came back and told me he had seen her enter the Kellis cabin. He waited some distance away for her to go back toward the Hour Glass. She didn't come, and as Peters had no orders to follow her anywhere else he rode back here and reported. I sent Peters and some other men out the next day to look for her and they reported that she had married you at Randall."

Jeff might have been convinced but for the fact that the rope and the handkerchief indicated that Ellen had been taken to the cabin by someone who knew her. The silk monogrammed handkerchief did not belong to Ellen but to Ballinger, for Ellen had worn a smaller one. She would not wear two and the one that had been tied over her mouth was a duplicate of the one Ballinger was wearing around his neck at this minute. And if there had been a rope and a silk handkerchief in the slicker on Ellen's pony that night, what had they been placed there for? Jeff had never heard of anybody carrying a forty-foot rope in a slicker. He was now almost convinced that Jim Peters had played the rôle of abductor. Peters, perhaps, had done more than merely follow Ellen that night.

Jeff looked straight at Ballinger.

"That's pretty thin," he said. "You're not as good a liar as your daughter."

"Hale!"

Ballinger's face was white with anger, but there was a deeper passion in Jeff's eyes, a slumbering, sombre light that awed him, that caused him to catch his breath and hold it.

"There never was any chance of you putting it over, Ballinger," he said. "The night I found her in the cabin with her hands tied behind her, I was fooled. I was fooled until after I married her. When I opened the door and found her standing there with the moonlight shining on her something happened to me. I didn't know what it was until a long time afterward. What happened to me there made me believe her lies. It made me marry her. It wasn't the fact that she'd overheard the boys and myself talking about hanging Hank Kroll that influenced me to marry her. I didn't care a damn about that. Why hell! I pitied her. And I must have loved her to make such a fool of myself!"

"Hale, what in thunder are you talking about?"

"Shut your lying mouth!"

Ballinger's face blanched.

"Why, Hale!" he gasped. "Hale! Tell me what has happened!"

"I'm telling you this," said Jeff. "You don't get that land! You don't get it through your daughter marrying me, and if you've lied to me about withdrawing your claim I'm going to kill you!"

"Good heavens, man! I have never wanted that land enough to do what you seem to think I have done. I could have had it long ago if I had wanted to take it that way! I could have had it only last night. Jim Kellis was here, drunk, claiming he had the certificate your father filed years ago. Kellis intimated that he would sell it! I think he stole it from the land office! I was going to ride over to your place to-day to tell you about it! Now, Hale, if I wanted to be a thief and a liar, as you have intimated, I——"

He gasped, for Jeff had moved. Not toward Ballinger, however. In three leaps he had reached his horse and was in the saddle. The spurs sank into the animal's flanks so viciously that in desperation he stood on his hind legs frantically pawing the air. Then he came down, bucked furiously across the yard, then flattened out, and with stretching neck and flashing hoofs thundered into the wild growth of the big basin, sending the yellow dust skyward in great, ballooning clouds.

CHAPTER TWENTY

The distance from the Hour Glass to Kellis's cabin was about twenty miles and Jeff had not ridden very far when he drew his horse down. Ballinger's information had aroused in him a fierce determination to confront Kellis as quickly as possible, and for one wild instant his angry impatience had ruled him.

He knew better than to indulge his passions rashly. He had always fought against his reckless impulses, knowing that once they were unleashed they would master him, and he was aware that he had need of all his reason and his self-control.

He was now certain that Kellis had stolen the certificate and was trying to sell it. Whoever bought it from him would destroy it, of course, since its non-appearance at the land office before the first of the month would insure the title to the land in dispute being awarded to the first claimant. Ballinger had refused to buy it and Jeff knew that it would be offered to Dallman. If Dallman bought it and destroyed it the title to the land was certain to go to him. Dallman would buy it.

Jeff's horse was comparatively fresh, for his pace on the way to the Hour Glass had been little more than a walk, and while Jeff did not urge him now he permitted him to hold a brisk lope which covered the ground rapidly.

It was still early, and if Kellis had visited the Hour Glass the night before it was unlikely that he had ridden in to Randall afterwards. Kellis was lazy and shiftless, and it was probable that he was still in bed.

Kellis!

His contempt for the man had been so great that he had never for an instant suspected him of being connected with the land fraud. Dozens of times he had passed the man and had thought him unimportant. Kellis had no individuality. In a crowd he was simply a negligible unit; alone he was too insignificant to attract attention. And yet this man had become a danger and a menace. Moreover, he had once been regarded with something like affection by Ellen—by his wife!

Jeff viciously jabbed his spurs into the flanks of the horse and the animal bounded forward into a furious gallop. The pace accorded with Jeff's mood. Jeff writhed as a strange, new rage gripped him—a rage that tortured him because he could find no outlet for it. The rage of jealousy!

Kellis had written letters to Ellen. His wife! Ellen had written to Kellis. For four years they had exchanged romantic communications. And of course in those four years Ellen had entertained romantic visions. There must have been something between them—something of a serious nature to hold her interest that long. And that something would have to be love, for nothing else would last. Ellen had told him that she had once loved Kellis, but that since she had seen him again in the hotel in Randall, she loathed him. Well, perhaps that was the truth, but Ellen had lied so much that he didn't know whether to believe that statement or not. It was strange that if she loathed him she would have permitted him to visit her in the hotel.

The rage in him turned upon Ellen. He told himself that he hated her; that she could not be trusted, that she was an insincere, lying, impudent, and unscrupulous woman. Yet——

He had a mental picture of her now, standing straight and gazing at him with level eyes. He felt the charm of her. He had felt it from the beginning. It had gone through him, stirring his blood and filling him with enchanting visions. He had seen the calmness of perfect mental poise in her eyes; he had seen wistfulness; and at times he had observed reproach in their depths. Never, though he had searched for it, had he found deceit. She had lied, yet it had seemed to him that a woman of her type couldn't lie.

He saw her continually. Days when he had been away from the Diamond A he would ride along thinking of her; nights in his blanket he would dream of her. He had stayed away from the ranch house so that he might fight against the lure of her, but in spite of everything her charm pervaded him.

His thoughts ran, rioting, grim as the mood that possessed him.

Kellis was aiming at him, of course, was seeking revenge for the knockdown he had administered when Kellis had insulted Sadie Nokes. He couldn't kill Kellis, even though he yearned to kill him. But in some manner he must make him produce the certificate.

The horse ran steadily, tirelessly. The sun was not very high when from a distance Jeff discerned the roof of the Kellis cabin. A little later he rode out of the timber, dismounted near the cabin, and strode to the front door.

The door was open. The rear door also. The cabin faced east and the sunlight streamed straight through it, disclosing the pitiful interior.

There was only one room and only one window—cut in the north wall. It was uncurtained and the glass in it was cracked and broken. A bed stood in a corner. It was dilapidated and in disorder, dirty. Discarded wearing apparel was strewn around it and upon it. In another corner was a rusted cast-iron stove with some pots and pans partly filled with cooked food scattered upon its warped and discoloured lids; in the centre of the room was a small, rough table with some dishes upon its uncovered top. There were four broken down chairs, standing forlornly about.

That was all. The cabin had no human occupant.

Disappointed and impatient because it seemed that Kellis was not at home, Jeff strode to the rear door and looked out. In a small patch of grass under a tree near the rear of the cabin was Kellis's wife and child. The woman was just rising to her feet, having heard Jeff's step in the house.

She stood rigid when she saw Jeff, and twined her fingers together when she observed the cold glint in his eyes.

"Where's Kellis?" he asked.

"Jim away."

"Where?"

"What you want weeth him?"

"I've got some good news for him," he lied, grimly.

The woman grimaced and shook her head negatively.

"No, no!" she said. "You got no good news for heem! You Jeff Hale. You hurt Jim. Please, Mr. Hale!"

"Is Kellis around here?"

"Jim away."

"In Randall?"

"He no say.".

"How long has he been gone?"

"An hour—two hour—mebbe. What you want, Mr. Hale?"

"Where was Kellis last night?"

"Oh, he all right last night, Mr. Hale. He do nothing bad. You want heem because he do something bad? He do nothing bad last night. He over to see Mr. Ballinger. He come home early—ten o'clock, mebbe."

Ballinger hadn't lied—Kellis had been there. And Kellis had reached home about ten o'clock, so he hadn't seen Dallman last night. He was on his way to see Dallman now, however.

Jeff turned from the woman and ran around the house to his horse. He was in the saddle and riding away in an instant, while the woman followed him, running and calling unintelligibly to him.

Randall was only ten miles distant and if Kellis had left home two hours ago he was now in town, providing he had been headed in that direction. There was a chance that he hadn't gone directly to town and in that case Jeff might reach there ahead of him.

The horse was not spared now. Through the green aisles of the forest he flashed—a black bolt moving with sweeping undulations. Jeff knew the country thoroughly and he saved much time by heading the horse over dim cross trails and into little known levels where the footing was firm. As Jeff rode he scanned the country near him in search of Kellis. The high ridges that loomed momentarily in his vision received a glance, the gorges he passed were swiftly scrutinized, as were the little flats that were disclosed to him, the miniature valleys, the arroyos, and the natural coverts.

After Jeff reached the great upland which rimmed the mighty basin on the south he slowed the horse down and dismounted. To conserve the animal's strength he went on foot up the long slope, the horse following. For a brief instant Jeff paused, to search with swift glances the low country which spread around him in all directions. He could see no rider, so he mounted and rode westward, following the trail Ellen and he had ridden when they had gone to Randall to be married.

Later, emerging from the gorge down which he had ridden from the mesa, he saw the Randall trail stretching before him. The trail was empty, so Kellis was probably already in town.

There was still a chance that Kellis had not reached Dallman, and the black horse went down the long slope with sickening velocity. The headlong pace carried him far out over the floor of the valley, and he was within a mile of the town before he would permit Jeff to pull him down. He was loping sedately, however, when he reached the eastern end of Randall's one street.

Jeff rode along, searching for Jim Kellis's horse, which might have been at one of the various hitching racks.

Not finding it he rode to the livery stable, dismounted, and talked a brief time with Allen, the proprietor. When he left Allen he knew that Kellis had not entered town that morning. Allen had been sitting in front of his place since dawn and declared no one had ridden into town. A humorous remark trembled on Allen's tongue, but he withheld it. Instead of speaking he drew a long breath and held it, for what he saw in Jeff's eyes awed him.

Later, to a friend, Allen said:

"I don't know. But somehow I was glad I wasn't Kellis."

Kellis's wife had lied, of course. Kellis had probably been hiding somewhere in the vicinity of the cabin. And now, knowing that Jeff Hale was looking for him, Kellis would divine the reason.

Jeff was riding past the Elite when he glanced toward the restaurant and observed Sadie Nokes at the window, violently motioning to him. He nodded slightly to her, rode a little distance down the street, wheeled his horse, rode back, dismounted at the hitching rack in front of the Elite, and entered.

There was no one inside except Sadie, and the girl was visibly excited.

"You are in for it now, Jeff!" she said. "Mart Blandin sent a man to the Diamond A last night to warn you! Your wife told the man you were not at home!

"Dallman and Hazen and a bunch of farmers had a meeting last night in Hazen's office. Mart was there. Hazen has sworn in a lot of deputies, besides Mart and the other regular ones. They were all there. Hazen and Dall-man are wild because of the way you smashed them off their horses with Dallman's rifle! They intended to kill you that night! They had told Mart all about it, for they think Mart hates you. He's made them believe that! Now Hazen says it can't go on any longer. To-night they're going to organize a posse. They're going to capture you. Then they are going to shoot you and pretend they did it in self-defence. Don't you see why they are going to do that, Jeff? The day after to-morrow is the first and they are afraid you will do something desperate before then! Mart says it looks bad. The farmers are vindictive. Hazen says your wife's lying has saved you twice but that he'll see that she don't get a chance to lie for you again. Mart says if he was you he'd get out of town for a while, until this blows over. You can't fight them all, Jeff, and you can't do anything about the land. Dallman will get it. He's bragged to Mart that he's got things all fixed up at the land office. Get out of town, Jeff—and stay out!"

"Thanks. Rustle some grub, Sadie. I'll be back in five minutes."

He went out, swung into the saddle, rode to the livery stable, and told Allen to feed and water his horse. He stood for a few minutes in front of the livery stable, and saw Dallman walking on the other side of the street. He observed that Dallman saw him but pretended he did not, and he watched the man until he entered the doorway of a building far down the street.

Jeff returned to the Elite and sank into a chair at one of the tables. Sadie placed food before him and hovered near.

"You'll go away, won't you, Jeff?" she asked.

"No."

"Mart said you wouldn't. But you ought to. They'll kill you!"

Jeff did not answer. He finished eating, got up, and smiled gravely at the girl.

"You and Mart have been good friends," he said. "If you hadn't been keeping me informed about what has been going on in the last year or so, I reckon I'd have been dead a long time, now. Have you seen Kellis this morning?"

"Kellis hasn't been in town since—since I saw him in the hotel with your wife." Sadie reddened.

Jeff's gaze was meditative.

"You don't like my wife—do you?"

"I didn't—at first."

"Does that mean you like her now?"

"Yes. She is a good woman."

"In spite of the fact that she was in the hotel room with Jim Kellis?"

"She ain't the kind of woman that does that, Jeff. She couldn't help that. She wouldn't do anything to hurt you."

"Why?"

"Why! Why, you darned fool! She loves you!"

She looked keenly at him and laughed in amazement and derision.

"Don't you know that? I don't believe you do! Why, everybody knows that! It's in her eyes when she looks at you—when she talks about you! And you don't know it! My Gawd! Ain't men the fools!"

Jeff accepted the epithet in silence. There were several things about his association with Ellen that Sadie did not know. One was that she had married him through mercenary motives. Another was that she did not love him.

He had got no satisfaction from Ballinger. Ballinger was a good actor or a good liar—he didn't know which. But he was determined to get to the bottom of the mystery—the reason she had married him. And while he was waiting for the solution of that he'd settle things with Hazen and Dallman.

He left Sadie and walked down the street. He was aware that he was watched; that his presence in town was known to his enemies, for never had he observed so many men lounging about.

Sadie was right—his enemies were ready to act. Their interest in his movements was evident—so glaringly obvious that he wondered if they were not meditating instant action. His contempt for them was deep. They were farmers. Some of them wore guns, and perhaps a few might be able to use them. But he doubted it. The guns were in holsters that were strapped tightly to the waist above the hips. Some of the butts pointed forward, some backward.

They were not his kind of people. They were alien usurpers of the ranges, they did not belong in cattleland. They were plodders of the plough swarming slowly over the trails that had been blazed by the frontier riders. But as Gillman had said: "You can't stop them fellows from coming. A whole wagon train of them came in to-day. . . . we're through, Jeff."

Yes; they were through. Jeff knew that. He was contemptuous of the farmers, and yet he sympathized with them. They would have to endure much. But their coming marked the beginning of the end of the reign of cattle. Men like his father, himself, like Gillman and all the rest, would have to get out. They'd have to move farther west.

He did not blame the farmers for coming; he blamed Dallman for bringing them. Dallman was a pernicious influence in the country. He was bringing these people before the land was ready for them; he was stealing land and selling it to innocent victims of his greed. Every title would be clouded.

Jeff found himself entering the door of a little office. Above the door was a sign, reading: "Wade Dallman: Land, Titles, Surveys."

Jeff pushed the door open and entered the office. He stood before Dallman—for at his entrance Dallman got up and faced him. The colour drained from Dallman's cheeks, but he made a valiant effort to stiffen his muscles so that he might stand before his enemy with some semblance of steadiness.

"Dallman," said Jeff, "it all comes back to this."

He moved his right hand and the heavy Colt was out of its holster and balanced in his palm. "I'm through accepting your kind of law. Withdraw your claim to the Hale land and get out of town by the day after to-morrow!"

He stood looking at Dallman. Dallman did not move or speak. Jeff backed slowly out of the office. On the sidewalk he holstered his gun and walked down to the livery stable.

His horse was tired, so he borrowed another from Allen. He rode straight down the street, taking the trail he had ridden when entering town.

He was aware of the stares that followed him; he observed various groups of men in doorways, other groups clustered around various wagons. Faces were plastered against window panes. Sadie Nokes was right. His enemies meditated action.

CHAPTER TWENTY-ONE

From the floor of the valley the long upland trail over which Kellis would have to ride to reach Randall was always in sight, and as Jeff rode out of town he watched for a rider to appear there. It was unlikely, however, that Kellis would visit in town that day, for if he had been in concealment during Jeff's visit to his cabin he would suspect what the visit portended and would remain hidden until he was certain Jeff had left town.

Jeff had only one chance of getting possession of the certificate. That was to surprise Kellis, to come upon him before he had an opportunity to destroy the document, for it was valuable to Kellis only if he could sell it, and if he discovered that Jeff suspected him of having it he would destroy it out of pure malice.

Of course Dallman would buy the certificate to prevent it being restored to the land office. Jeff was certain it had not yet been offered to Dallman. Ballinger had been given first chance.

Jeff rode back to the Kellis cabin. He left the trail when still some distance away and rode carefully through the timber until he reached a point several hundred feet from the rear of the building. Concealed by a heavy growth of brush he watched the cabin.

Near a small outbuilding was a little corral built of cedar poles. There was no horse in the corral, and the absence of a horse would appear to indicate that Mrs. Kellis had told the truth when she had said that Kellis was away.

But Jeff did not believe that Kellis was away. He had no interests anywhere except in Randall. He had no friends and no neighbours who would receive him. If he had gone anywhere he would be in town, for that was where he would find Dallman.

For perhaps an hour Jeff continued to watch the cabin. Several times he saw the woman come to the door. Once she emerged and walked slowly around the cabin, evidently without purpose, and Jeff watched her narrowly to see if she would make any movement that could be construed as a signal. But she did not even glance into the surrounding timber. Once she paused and plucked casually and languidly at a wild vine that grew against the cabin wall; and for a time she stood at the southwesterly corner staring downward. There was something in her attitude that suggested weariness and discouragement. Jeff waited until she went into the house. Then he rode away, convinced that Kellis wasn't anywhere about.

He rode back to Randall and went directly to Bill Hazen's office, which was a small frame building set in the centre of a space between two other buildings. There was a hitching rail at the side of the office. The front door was open. Jeff entered and a tall, slender man of about Jeff's age greeted him with a smile.

The slender man was Mart Blandin, Sadie Nokes's lover and one of Hazen's deputies.

"Saw you in town a while ago," he said. He got up, walked to the rear door, opened it and spat, glanced out casually, left the door open, sauntered to the front door, spat again, turned, leaned against a jamb and whispered:

"Sadie tell you?"

Jeff nodded.

"They mean business, Jeff," warned Blandin. "They're goin' to organize at nine to-night. Hazen will be back, then."

"Where is Hazen now?"

"He rode over to Lazette yesterday. I don't know what for." He looked keenly at Jeff, adding slowly: "I hear Gillman an' the boys have quit. That leaves you playin' her a lone hand, eh?" He shook his head. "No use advisin' you lay low for a while, I suppose. Well, I reckoned you wouldn't. I got an idea it'll blow over—after the first of the month. I got it figgered out that they want to get you out of the way before the first, so's you won't be able to pull off any surprise party on them. Hazen an' Dallman hate you like poison since you bashed their heads in that night. There's nothin' you can do about the land, anyhow, Jeff. If you could manage to keep out of their way until after the first, I got an idea they——"

"Thanks, Mart," smiled Jeff. "You say Hazen will be back before nine?"

"About an hour after dusk, he told me."

"The others won't do anything until Hazen comes, eh?"

"No. Hazen's makin' it legal. He's runnin' it. Told the other boys to keep their hands off. So they won't start nothin' until he gets here."

"Has Jim Kellis been in town?"

"Ain't seen him."

"I've been hoping that if he does come to town he won't see Dallman," said Jeff. He smiled.

"I can fix that," promised Blandin. "There's an order to bring him in, anyway. Nothin' serious. Hazen wants to ask him some questions about that Hank Kroll hangin'. Hazen thinks he knows somethin'. If Kellis comes in I'll hold him. He won't see Dallman, alone."

"Leave word with Sadie if you get hold of Kellis," said Jeff. "I'll see her to-night."

"You hadn't ought to come to town to-night, Jeff," warned Blandin.

Jeff did not answer. He went out, mounted his horse, and rode out of town. He rode toward the Diamond A, following the trail that led straight down the valley, and he was aware that his departure was observed by many watchers.

His mood was now saturnine. He hadn't slept in twenty-four hours and he was physically and mentally weary. His friends had deserted him. He was convinced that Kellis had the certificate and would destroy it before permitting it to be found. Despite anything he could do the land would go to Dallman. His wife was a liar and a fraud.

The afternoon was almost gone when he dismounted at the corral gates and turned his horse into the inclosure. He carried saddle and bridle into the stable and placed them upon their pegs, then walked to the door and stood for a time staring grimly out into the valley.

He was considering his wife.

Half an hour later he was standing in the doorway of her room, looking at her with a steady, sombre gaze. He had appeared in the doorway while Ellen had been combing her hair in front of the mirror in the dresser, and she had turned when she had heard his step on the threshold.

He had never seen her looking more beautiful. Her hair was down, and she had caught the glistening mass in one hand and was holding it close to her breast so that one side of her face was screened by its filmy folds while the other was revealed with cameolike sharpness in the dim light that shone upon her. He had never seen her eyes so big or so lustrous. They were alight with wonder and embarrassment, but when she saw him standing there so rigidly, his gaze intent and sombre, she slowly straightened—defensively, he thought.

He moved slowly toward her, and when he was close enough he reached out and grasped her arms, the tightness of his grip betraying the passion he felt. She did not try to escape him, but stood erect, gazing straight into his eyes.

"What were you doing in the Navajo basin the night I found you in the cabin?" he asked.

"Why, I had been abducted, of course."

She had paled and her eyes were luminous.

"That's evasion," he said, contempt in his voice. "It's something I know. I want to know what you went into the basin for, why you were there at all?"

"I rode over to see Jim Kellis!" she returned, defiantly. "I told you once before that there was some romantic nonsense between us! I once thought I loved Jim Kellis well enough to marry him. I rode over there to do it—and met his wife!"

The statement accorded with Ballinger's version of the affair. He couldn't be jealous of Kellis. If she had told him about this when he had questioned her before he would have thought nothing of it. But after discovering that Kellis was married she had permitted him to enter her room at the hotel.

"You met his wife," said Jeff. "And you left. Which direction did you take?"

A certain gleam in his eyes warned her that he knew she did not ride toward the Hour Glass. And so she told the truth—with reservations.

"I—I felt so badly that I decided I wouldn't go home," she answered. She would never tell him the truth! He must never know of her wanton determination to marry the first good-looking man she met! She would admit anything but that!

"Which way did you go?"

"I rode toward Randall."

A cynical quirk appeared at the corner of his mouth.

"What did you expect to find at Randall?" he asked.

"Why I—" She hesitated, blushed, met his gaze again and continued: "Why, I don't know. I just wanted to go there."

"And then somebody abducted you," he added, mockery in his voice.

"Then *you* abducted me!" she declared.

Jeff shook his head.

"Too thin," he said. "You know better, too. Even if you made a mistake you'd know by now that I didn't do it. One of the Ballingers is lying."

"Oh," she said, "you have been talking with father!"

Well, her father didn't know what had been in her mind that night, and she wouldn't tell, no matter how Jeff pressed her! She didn't want him to know that she was the kind of woman who would marry the first man that came along. She wanted him to respect her! Her thoughts of that night had not been regretted, however. She had treasured them because they had brought Jeff to her.

"Yes. I told Ballinger about the monogrammed silk handkerchief I found in the cabin. I mentioned the rope I found in the slicker behind the saddle you used that night. Some of that rope was used to tie your hands. Your father told me Jim Peters followed you to Kellis's cabin that day. I think your father didn't tell all he knew. Did Peters tie you up?"

"It was not Peters—it was you!"

His grip on her arms tightened and she detected a faint paleness around his lips.

"That's getting monotonous," he said. "You're a liar, but you can't lie as cleverly as you think you can. I don't clearly understand what you and your father had in mind when this thing started—possibly you thought that if you married me your father would somehow be able to get his railroad through the valley. I don't know. I haven't the least idea how liars invent their lies. But here is the way you carried it out.

"You pretended to ride to the Kellis cabin. Perhaps you did. I don't know, and I don't care. Somehow, you and your father knew I would be in the Navajo basin that night, and Jim Peters leads you to the cabin, binds and gags you, and leaves you there. Then he rides back, looking for me and my men. He sees us hanging Hank Kroll and he lets himself be seen so that we'll chase him past the cabin, where he has left you. He placed your horse where we couldn't fail to see it, to make certain we would stop. He got away. After that it was easy. You overheard the boys talking about hanging Kroll, and you worked on that, thinking I would marry you to keep you from telling." The queer quirk twisted his lips again. "It wasn't that. I didn't care a damn about that." He laughed mirthlessly. "Sympathy, and perhaps a sense of decency, did it. And hell! I can tell you now that I think I loved you with the first look I got of you when you stood there in the moonlight that came into the window!"

"What!" she said, tremulously taunting him. "Did character have nothing to do with it?"

He laughed harshly and stepped back, releasing her arms.

"Character!" he said. "I think not. I always imagined it did. But I'm just like millions of other damned fools. I went crazy over a pretty face. Why, right now I'm glad I married you. In spite of the fact that I know you are a liar and that you lured me into marrying you, I love you! I love you in spite of the fact that Jim Kellis was found drunk in your room!"

"Oh!" she exclaimed, putting both hands to her face.

"Clever!" he mocked. He walked to the door and stood there for an instant looking back over his shoulder at her as she stood with her wonderful hair streaming down over her shoulders and her hands still covering her face.

"You'd better go back to the Hour Glass, to-night," he said. "You like to do your gadding alone, and to-night will be a good night for it. And get a train out of this country as soon as you can, for things won't be pretty around here from to-night on!"

He stood for another instant, looking at her. Then he was gone. Ellen could hear his booted heels striking the flagstones of the patio, could hear the musical jangling of his spurs.

That was all.

CHAPTER TWENTY-TWO

Ellen had some very definite ideas about her married life. She wasn't going to permit the marriage to be wrecked. The longer she knew Jeff the more determined she was to keep him. It made no difference to her what he said or how he treated her. She deserved all the harsh things he had said to her. She knew it and she wasn't going to hold it against him. She loved him. He loved her. He had told her so.

His black moods were another matter. He couldn't change his nature any more than she could change hers. And she didn't want him to change, for she loved him as he was, temper and all, just as he loved her in spite of the fact that he knew she was a liar.

But her face was pale and her lips set tightly together when at last she left her room, crossed the patio, and entered the living room. She was glad the elder Hales were not at home—they had ridden away early in the morning, telling Ellen they were going to Lazette. Possibly they would not return for several days.

Standing far back in the living room Ellen saw Jeff riding away. He had changed horses; he now rode a powerful, rangey bay. He was headed toward Randall.

Ellen had seen that Jeff was worried. She had observed the deep lines about his mouth, the new wrinkles that had appeared around his eyes, his unshaved face. Standing in her room he had seemed to be afflicted with a great weariness which was mental as well as physical. It was weariness such as would oppress a man who no longer cared what happened to him. It seemed to express contempt of everybody and everything, and yet it some-how conveyed the sinister promise of reckless violence.

She was certain he was riding into danger, but she had no power to prevent him. He did not trust her; he would not listen to her.

With her hands clasped over her breast she watched him out of sight. Turning then, she stood for a long time gazing at his picture which looked down at her from the shelf. She reached up, took the picture from its frame, and concealed it in the bosom of her dress.

It was almost dusk when she went out to the stable and placed saddle and bridle on her horse. She carried none of her belongings except Jeff's picture and a small revolver in a holster. She had no intention of obeying Jeff's orders. Her personal effects would remain at the Diamond A, for she intended to return. Jeff did not want her now, but some day he would be glad she had not obeyed him—she hoped.

After mounting she rode northeastward, up the great, sloping wall of the valley to the high level country. Before darkness finally encompassed her she had found the trail she sought and was determinedly riding it.

She was going to see Jim Kellis. She intended to appeal to the man's better nature. She was confident that Kellis knew where the missing certificate could be found, and she meant, somehow, to make him tell her how she might get possession of it. There must be a man named Lincoln somewhere in the vicinity or Kellis would not keep repeating his name.

At moonrise she was descending the big slope that led down into Navajo basin, and shortly afterward she passed the cabin where she had first met Jeff. How long ago it seemed! She had a yearning to stop at the cabin but she did not yield to it and presently the cabin was behind her and she was deep in the timber that had been the scene of her adventure with Dallman.

She had never been able to understand why Dallman had abducted her. Of course she remembered his words: "This is one time I even things with Matthew M. Ballinger," but she had thought then, as she thought now, that the threat was vague and indefinite. At any rate, what Dallman had in mind that night wasn't important because he hadn't succeeded in holding her. And she wasn't interested in Dallman, except that she hated him because of the names he had called her. Some day—if she managed to stay married to Jeff—she would make Dallman squirm because of those names! That is, if Jeff didn't kill him before she got a chance!

The forest was beautiful, but she was in no mood to appreciate it, though she was grateful for the mellow moonlight that disclosed the narrow trail winding sinuously between the trees. She had been riding not more than half an hour through the timber when she crossed the swale where she had fallen from her horse the night Dallman had abducted her. A few minutes later she was riding across a clearing to the door of the Kellis cabin.

There was a light inside—a kerosene lamp standing on a table near the centre of the room. Mrs. Kellis was sitting at the table, staring out through the open doorway. She had evidently heard Ellen's horse.

She got up as Ellen dismounted and was standing in the doorway when Ellen tied her horse to one of the slender porch columns and moved toward her. The moonlight was strong and she recognized Ellen, for she became suddenly rigid.

"Miz Ballinger?" she said. "What you want?"

"I am on my way to the Hour Glass," lied Ellen. "I started late and I am afraid I can't make it to-night. You see, I don't know the trail very well. I was thinking that perhaps I might stay here until morning."

"Huh." The woman's voice lacked cordiality; it even held a note of suspicion. She did not move.

"Why you start so late? You know heem far distance. Why you' husban' not come weeth you? Where you' husban'?"

"Mr. Hale had to go to Randall."

The woman shook her head with a violent, negative motion.

"You' husban' here to-day—two time. He look for Jeem. What he want weeth Jeem?"

"Mr. Hale was here to-day!" exclaimed Ellen. "Why, what did he want?"

"He look for Jeem. He come in. He look like he keel somebody! He ask for Jeem. I tell heem Jeem no here. He go away. He come back an' stay over in the timber, watchin' the cabin. He go away again. What he want weeth Jeem?"

"I am sure I cannot tell you," said Ellen. "But I am certain he didn't wish to kill your husband. And he isn't with me now—he is in Randall."

"You leave heem? He don' treat you right?"

"Oh, no!" smiled Ellen. "That isn't it. You think that because I am going to the Hour Glass——"

"What you ride this time of night for, if you don' leave him?"

Ellen resented the woman's impudent questioning, but she was determined to enter the cabin. She divined that Kellis wasn't at home. She didn't know whether she was disappointed or relieved. She was a little afraid of Kellis since his real character had been disclosed to her, and she doubted that she would gain anything by questioning him further. If she could convince Mrs. Kellis that her visit was entirely unpremeditated and incidental she might succeed in discovering something about the mysterious Lincoln. And if Mrs. Kellis permitted her to stay all night she would manage to search the cabin, for there was a slight chance that Kellis had the certificate in his possession.

"Oh, Mrs. Kellis, you mustn't say that," she said, smiling. "I wouldn't leave Jeff."

"You love heem?"

"Quite as deeply as you appear to love Mr. Kellis," said Ellen.

The woman's face flushed.

"What Jeff want weeth Jeem?" she asked.

"I can't answer that, of course," returned Ellen. "He certainly doesn't want to kill him, Mrs. Kellis. Jeff has never killed anybody, has he? I think, perhaps, he wanted to ask Mr. Kellis some questions about Mr. Dallman. You know, of course, that Mr. Dallman has been trying to take some of Jeff's land?"

"Yes. I hear that. Jeem talk sometime in hees sleep; sometime when he drunk. Jeem hurt nobody. You sure Jeff don' hurt Jeem? You not let Jeff hurt Jeem?"

"Certainly not! There is no reason why Jeff should hurt him."

And now because of a subtle change in Mrs. Kellis' voice Ellen knew that the woman's suspicions were almost allayed. So Ellen laughed and stepped back, reaching for the bridle rein.

"I think I shall ride on, after all," she said. "There is a good moon, and I think I shall be able to find the trail."

"No!" exclaimed the woman. "You no ride! You come in. You get lost—hurt, mebbe. Excuse me, please. I'm foolish, mebbe. I think everybody want to hurt Jeem. Please. You come in. You stay. To-morrow you go. Leave you' horse there. After while I put heem in stable. Come!"

She stepped back and smiled at her visitor.

Ellen entered.

She had no intention of staying in the cabin all night, and one glance at the interior almost dissuaded her from taking the chair Mrs. Kellis offered her. But she must appear to appreciate the woman's hospitality, and so she sank into the chair and smiled.

Mrs. Kellis was now eager. She darted here and there, making ineffectual attempts to tidy up the room, insisting that her guest remove her hat and be comfortable. She, herself, could not wear a hat. Too heavy. The mantilla was best. Cool, in the sun. A hat was hot. Why did American women wear hats?

She chatted volubly. Her voice, now that her suspicions were gone, became flatteringly soft and solicitous. Mr. Ballinger was a great man. Reech (rich). Never, anywhere, was there a ranch like the Hour Glass! The Hales were wonderful people, too. How long had Ellen known Jeff Hale?

Ellen answered many questions, and failed to answer many others because apparently Mrs. Kellis did not expect them to be answered and went on asking others without waiting.

She made excuses for the appearance of the cabin, for Jim's lack of ambition, for their poverty. Jim was a good man. People didn't understand Jim. Babies! They were a bother. But they came. One couldn't help that. They were wonderful, though. Her baby looked just like Jim. Jim loved the baby.

For perhaps an hour Ellen sat, nodding and smiling. But there were times when she hardly heard Mrs. Kellis. Once she interrupted Mrs. Kellis. Did Mrs. Kellis know where Mr. Kellis was?

The woman gave her a sharp glance and shook her head.

She didn't know. Jim had left the cabin about daybreak without telling her where he was going. He seldom told her anything about his movements. For a time following the answering of the question Mrs. Kellis was silent. Then, as Ellen asked no more questions she resumed her chatter.

Meanwhile Ellen was inspecting the room with her glances.

There was a battered dresser in a corner with several drawers in it. If Kellis had the certificate would he conceal it in the dresser? Hardly. Yet she would search there when the opportunity came. There was a shelf on the wall above the dresser, and upon the shelf was a small metal box, together with a pipe, a leather tobacco pouch, and a comb. The box would be peered into.

There wasn't much else. The stove, the bed, the table and the chairs. A faded steel engraving on the wall near the bed. The picture was tacked to the wall. It was unframed, discoloured with age, its edges were torn and frayed.

But the long, homely face portrayed on the faded paper was distinct enough. It may have been the way the light shone on the portrait, or it may have been that Ellen's dawning comprehension intensified her vision, for the sad and patient eyes that gazed so calmly at her appeared to flicker with faint, ironic inquiry. It was as if they were saying: "Well, here I am! You didn't expect to find me here, eh?"

How simple it seemed, now that the mystery was solved!

Ellen's heart was suddenly pounding hard. She assured herself that she wasn't excited, that there was nothing to get excited over. If she had not misinterpreted Kellis's drunken declarations; if she had calmly reasoned the thing out, she must have known what Kellis had meant when he had told her that Lincoln would not talk.

It had been like solving a puzzle. Mystery, bafflement, and then amazingly rapid understanding. She was now aware that she had studied the picture for many minutes before she had realized that the face in the picture was that of the martyred President, Lincoln.

She wasn't excited. She had been for just an instant. Now she was calm, cold, determined. She deliberately turned her back to the picture so that if Mrs. Kellis were watching she might not suspect her interest, and quietly asked if she hadn't better go out and water her horse. It had been hot and the animal had been long without a drink.

No; the woman said, she should not bother with the horse. Besides, she didn't know where the water could be found. Right away she, herself, would go out and water the horse. Then she would put him in the stable and feed him. She went out, smiling.

Only an instant Ellen waited. Only until she heard Mrs. Kellis speak to the horse. Then she was out of her chair and at the picture of Lincoln. She had no time to be careful, so she tore the picture from the tacks and slipped a hand into the aperture. Instantly her searching, eager fingers gripped a paper. She drew it out, opened it, quickly examined it and thrust it into the bosom of her dress, where Jeff's picture reposed.

She had it! There was no doubt that the paper was the missing certificate. She had seen Adam Hale's name on it, the land-office stamp, the engraved border, the flowing signature of the land agent, and the date.

She drew a deep breath of triumph and made an involuntary bow of gratitude toward the picture. As she bent her head she heard the swish of some object hurtling past her, and she straightened, startled, to see a long knife sticking in the wall, its haft quivering.

She knew the knife had been thrown with murderous intent, as she knew that the voice of the knife-thrower belonged to Kellis. His shrieking curse and the thudding of the knife in the wall above her head appeared to come simultaneously.

She glanced backward as she darted toward the rear door. Kellis was leaping toward her from the front door. She had never seen such demoniac rage in any man's face, and for an instant as she fled her muscles faltered on the verge of paralysis. Then terror strengthened her, and she was over the doorsill, running toward the timber that fringed the clearing.

As she reached the edge of the timber fright drew her gaze backward, and she saw Kellis falling headlong through the rear doorway. He had evidently stumbled over the sill.

Ellen ran on without any idea of direction. For the timber was strange to her and there was no trail for her to follow.

She had not gone a hundred feet when she heard Kellis crashing after her. He was cursing. He was muttering, too, unintelligibly, whining and mewing like a desperately harried animal. The sounds he made terrified her.

She ran on, seeking the aisles that appeared to offer good footing. She soon discovered that there were traps and pitfalls everywhere. She got into many of them. A dozen times in half a mile she fell. Thorns clutched at her garments and scratched her face and hands. She could hear Kellis coming after her. He crashed heavily through brush that she dared not try to enter. He leaped over deadfalls which she had to go around, and his superior strength and sure-footedness gave him an advantage that was certain to win him victory in the end.

However, twice it seemed she was to escape him, for twice heavy clouds covered the face of the moon, and in the darkness she changed her course and veered sharply from the course she had been following. Once she thought she had lost him, for she could no longer see him or hear him. However, she did not linger and presently, at a little distance she saw him clamber out of a dry arroyo. The moonlight shone clearly upon him and she saw that his face was hideously contorted. He stopped, drew a gun from a holster and levelled it at her. She stopped and stood, incredulously watching him. The powder belched at her and she heard the bullet whine as it passed her.

She turned and ran, moving in zigzag fashion among the trees. She heard the crashing of the gun again and again, heard the bullets thudding around her.

Strangely, although Kellis was a man and was naturally stronger than she, he did not appear to gain upon her. She was aware that his cursing had grown louder and that there was a high, screeching note in his voice. Its timbre had changed. There had been a ring of command in it. Rage, too, but a sane rage—the rage of baffled human hate.

But there was nothing human in the cries that now filled the timber. There was a wail in them, a shrill, quavering, senseless and querulous crying which sounded so strangely in Ellen's ears that curiosity prompted her to pause and turn.

About a hundred yards from her she saw Kellis. He was limping. He had evidently hurt his right leg badly, for he was holding the knee as he moved toward her, and dropping almost to the ground at each step. But he was coming. And when he saw that she had stopped he yelled hoarsely at her and came toward her faster than ever. She screamed at sight of his face and ran on.

She ran until in sheer weariness she was forced to drop to the bole of a fallen tree to rest. Somewhere back in the seemingly endless stretch of timber through which she had passed was Kellis. She did not see him. But listening, she heard him—heard the crashing of twigs and branches that marked his progress.

She had no idea where she was; she had lost all sense of direction. One section of the forest was exactly like any other section. The moon was now directly overhead. When she finally saw Kellis coming toward her, still limping, she got up and went on again.

She would have circled around Kellis in an effort to get back to the cabin and take possession of her horse, if she had known which direction to take. For all she knew she might now be going toward the cabin. She had no hope of finding a trail in the timber. This was the Navajo basin, and she remembered that Jeff had told her there was no trail through it.

But at this minute she wasn't very greatly concerned over the possibility of her escape from the basin. What she must do was to keep away from Kellis. She was tired, and her progress was slow, and yet she was still strong enough to keep Kellis at a distance. And it seemed that Kellis had used all the cartridges for his gun. He did no more shooting. In fact, she was almost convinced that he no longer had the gun.

She went on, slowly but steadily, watching Kellis, keeping him at a distance. She had been going for more than an hour when she observed that on each side of her the timber was growing thinner. She paused, quickly apprehensive, and looked back. She had been travelling over a mesa—a great, timbered tableland. Thinking only of Kellis and being unable to see far enough ahead to discern the character of the country, she had walked out upon a narrowing wedge of land which ended in a ragged, rocky butte that sloped sharply downward toward the lower country.

She was in a trap!

She ran swiftly to her right, hoping to slip by Kellis before he became aware of her predicament.

Kellis also hobbled in that direction, so she turned and ran the other way until she saw that Kellis was still active enough to intercept her. Moreover, it seemed to her that the contemplation of her imminent capture had endowed the man with remarkable agility, for he now hopped toward her with amazing strides, his injured leg dragging limply, like some sort of a superfluous appendage. As he came closer to her she saw his face clearly, and she knew that he had lost his reason.

His face had no expression whatever. His eyes held only a blank stare and his open mouth was drooling saliva. If he had not been coming directly toward her she must have thought he did not see her. He said nothing, but there issued from his loose lips a flow of sound, a steady, monotonous whining. It was unlike any sound that she had ever heard before. Appalled, but still courageous, she turned her back to him and ran to the edge of the cliff. Pausing there for an instant and glancing back, she observed that he was still hopping toward her. Swiftly turning, she faced him and clambered over the edge of the cliff, sliding downward until she was suspended by her hands. She had seen a ledge below her, and had thought she would be able to reach it by dangling her legs. But the ledge was farther down than she had estimated; her toes did not touch it.

She released her grip and dropped. The distance was not great, for the shock was slight and she had no difficulty in maintaining an upright position, though for an awful instant she swayed outward.

She did not hesitate to see if Kellis had reached the edge of the cliff, but got down on her hands and knees and began to crawl along the ledge, which ran along the face of the wall under a great, jagged, bulging rim-rock.

The ledge grew narrower. She reached a spot where it merged into the wall and vanished. The moonlight was still good and she looked around her. She could hear Kellis again. The strange, mewing sound he made seemed to come from the point on the edge of the cliff that she had vacated. Kellis was probably looking for her. Perhaps he would think that she had missed the ledge and had gone tumbling down the sharp slope to the valley below. She resolved to stay where she was until she was certain Kellis was coming after her.

Straight down for perhaps a dozen feet was a sloping section of wall out of which projected jagged points of rock. From her position the rocks looked slippery, but from various fissures grew gnarled, rootlike branches of nondescript brush which appeared to be strong enough to support her weight. Beyond this section it seemed the descent would be easier. She would have to go down, anyway, whether Kellis followed her or not, for she realized that she would not be able to retrace her steps.

For some time she rested on the ledge, hoping that Kellis would not attempt the descent. But presently she heard a slithering sound and she knew he was sliding over the edge. She was moving downward when she heard Kellis drop to the ledge. Almost, she felt, he had gone over. For she heard him scrambling around, and cursing.

She descended backward, her face to the wall, and when she was about half way down the stretch she saw Kellis crawling along the ledge above her. He made no sound when he observed her, but he halted for an instant and seemed to watch her.

She went down until she reached a huge slab of rock which seemed to have broken from its position somewhere above and dropped to its present resting place. It had lodged against a huge rock outcropping and appeared to be balanced there precariously. She carefully slid around it, observing as she moved that Kellis had reached the point of the ledge above where she had been forced off.

She was near enough to Kellis to get a good view of his face. She thought some of the blankness of his expression had been replaced by slyness. His mouth had closed a little, and there seemed to be a queer, malignant quirk to his lips. But there was no gleam of sanity in his eyes. They were wild and staring.

However, some portion of his brain was functioning, for he was casting rapid glances here and there as though searching for a place to descend. She thought she saw fright in his eyes when once he stared downward, and she was certain he shrank backward as if the prospect of descending dismayed him.

When she saw him pick up a rock from the ledge beside him she comprehended the meaning of the action. Swiftly she threw herself flat and slid down the slope, recklessly trusting to chance. She saw the rock leave his hands, watched it strike the wall near her and go bounding down the slope to the bottom of the valley. Long after it struck the bottom she heard other rocks slithering and sliding after it. A light, feathery dust arose and hovered over the slope.

She got behind a rock that was not quite large enough to shield her, and crouched there. Another rock, hurled by Kellis, struck close to her and bounded over her. Then another, and another.

She heard Kellis shrieking, and looked up to see him crazily running back and forth on the ledge—hopping grotesquely, rather, dragging his limp leg.

"Damn you!" he yelled. "I'll kill you! I'll smash you to smithereens!"

CHAPTER TWENTY-THREE

After leaving Ellen at the Diamond A Jeff rode toward Randall. He rode slowly and darkness overtook him while he was still about five miles from town. Then, instead of continuing on the Randall trail he left it and cut across the valley bottom into the country west of town. There, apparently being familiar with the section, he found a trail and rode it northwestward until he reached a point where the trail ran through a dry arroyo.

Dismounting, he led the horse behind a dense growth of wild brush, trailed the reins over his head and left him.

Jeff walked to the western end of the arroyo, which cut into a section of upland country which was brilliant in the moonlight, dropped upon a boulder behind a dense clump of tall mesquite, and sat there, sombrely regarding the trail.

Apparently Jeff had judged the time accurately, for he had not been sitting on the boulder very long when he saw a rider come into view on the west trail. The rider was in view for all the distance down the slope. He was coming at a moderate speed, his horse in a steady, rocking lope.

Blandin hadn't lied.

When the rider reached the head of the arroyo he slowed down because of the shadows and the uncertainty of the trail, and when he reached the clump of mesquite behind which Jeff was sitting on the rock, the horse was moving at a walk.

And then Jeff's voice, cold and sharp, floated through the mesquite:

"Reach for the sky, you mangy pup!"

So swiftly that the action seemed to be accomplished with a single movement, the rider brought his horse to a halt and raised his hands high in the air. He had turned his head and the shining moonlight revealed him as Bill Hazen.

He had recognized Jeff's voice, but he said nothing as Jeff emerged from beyond the mesquite and confronted him.

Jeff's gun was rigid at his hip, but not more rigid than his muscles as he stood there in the moonlight watching his enemy. Hazen had never seen Jeff in his present mood. He was apprehensive at the sight, for he gulped twice and seemed to settle heavily in the saddle.

At Jeff's command he gripped his gun carefully and delicately with forefinger and thumb and dropped it into the sand of the trail. He appeared to realize that he must obey quickly and without objection.

" 'Light!" ordered Jeff.

Hazen swung out of the saddle and dropped to the ground without lowering his hands. Silently he faced the sombre figure of his enemy.

"Turn!" ordered Jeff.

Jeff searched Hazen's clothing. He found no other weapons. With Hazen standing motionless Jeff drew a rifle from a saddle sheath on the sheriff's horse, tossed it into the mesquite clump, and then inspected the slicker that was strapped to the cantle.

He stepped aside.

"Get up and ride straight down the arroyo!" he commanded.

Hazen obeyed, still keeping his hands above his head except when he was required to use them for an instant in order to mount. Then, followed by Jeff, he rode down the arroyo to where Jeff had left his horse. There, at Jeff's command, Hazen halted, and waited until Jeff was in the saddle.

By this time Hazen seemed to have partially regained his courage, possibly realizing that since he had not been shot at once he was to escape that fate altogether.

"Seems you're makin' a lot of fuss about somethin'!" he jeered.

"More than you're worth," answered Jeff. "You know I'm not in the habit of shooting men who can't shoot back. But I've no objection to cracking your head with the butt of my gun. Make no mistake, Hazen. I'm yearning to kill you. Whether you live to get where I'm taking you depends on yourself. Get going—north!"

"Hell!" exclaimed Hazen, "That'll be Navajo basin!"

"Exactly. Just let your horse lope smooth and easy."

Hazen was reluctant, but he had no choice, and he sent his horse across some level country northward, toward a long slope that could be seen in the distance. Beyond that slope was a wilderness that few men had ever penetrated. It loomed, dark and forbidding, a mysterious country.

For an hour Hazen rode steadily, with Jeff not more than twenty or thirty feet behind him. The two riders crossed the level, descended the slope and were riding straight into the solemn darkness of the forest when Hazen suddenly halted his horse, swung around and faced his captor. Hazen's face was now pallid with fright.

"You can kill me right here, damn you!" he shouted.

"I'm glad to hear you admit that you need killing," said Jeff. "I've known it for more than a year. I'll be glad to accommodate you. If you are not riding in ten seconds you'll be plenty dead right after that!"

He sat motionless, his gun drawn, watching Hazen.

Before the ten seconds had passed Hazen was riding again. Some of the resistance had gone out of him; the belligerence of spirit which had provoked him to halt and face his captor had been quelled by the steady and saturnine eye which had met his.

He was in ignorance of Jeff's intentions. Jeff had told him nothing. Jeff had not revealed his knowledge of Hazen's plans to organize the posse of farmers for the purpose of lending a legal atmosphere to his own execution; he had not intimated that he knew anything about Hazen's plans. He would give Hazen no information whatever.

When they entered the timber Hazen again hesitated. But presently he went on again without speaking.

To Hazen's amazement they ultimately found a trail. Where they came upon it Hazen could not have told, or could he ever find it again. It seemed they had been zigzagging and circling in the timber for two or three hours when the trail appeared, but by that time the sheriff had lost all sense of direction. If Jeff had left him at that moment he could not have found his way out of the timber. He was lost and his manner betrayed his helplessness.

The trail was a faint one, running in irregular fashion from one aisle of the forest to another, circling around low, wooded hills, doubling back and forth to skirt deadfalls and sometimes descending to miniature flats or rising to dizzy heights at the rims of great, ragged buttes.

Hazen found nothing more to say. He seemed resigned, dispirited, and he rode forward, slouching in the saddle in a manner that was singularly in contrast to his usual arrogant attitude.

About midnight the trail led them down into a little flat close to the bank of a small stream of water. At a little distance from the water's edge was a small cabin built of logs.

The cabin was dark, and Jeff signed to Hazen to halt.

Jeff called, and after an interval a voice answered:

"That you, Hale?"

Jeff replied, and he and Hazen rode forward.

Two men emerged from the cabin doorway. They were men who occasionally visited Randall. Hazen had seen them several times, and knew them as Dell Hart and Jess Givens. He had been told that they were outlaws. Once, when they had lingered in town too long, he had ordered them to leave.

He listened, now, to the conversation carried on between the three men. They did not lower their voices; it appeared they were very frank in discussing him.

"So you want us to take him with us an' lose him?" said Hart. "Well, he's worthless, anyway. Nobody will miss him."

Hazen watched the two outlaws as they talked. Their faces were villainous, and Hazen knew that if they took him with them, anywhere, he would not return.

He learned from the conversation that Hart and Givens were about to leave the country anyway. Pickings were not good. They were going north, straight through Navajo basin, through one hundred and fifty miles of forest wilderness.

"What's the use of botherin' with him," said Givens. "Why not——" Significantly he tapped his gun holster.

"He's not worth even that," said Jeff. "But he's an officer."

"Of what?" asked Hart. "Of the law? Well, I don't know. I've heard of the sort of law he runs, an' it don't amount to anything. For himself. His law. Him an' Dallman. Shootin' him wouldn't be injurin' the law."

"He's no good," said Jeff. "But I haven't been able to bring myself to do it. I had thought of it. Twice. But it would have been like killing a sheep."

"He's yellow, of course," said Givens. "Everybody knows it. But why should that save him? He's just one of them accidents you hear about. Somehow, he got the most votes. That makes him represent the law. But such law! He's been sheriff for more than a year an' he's never arrested anybody. Brag an' bluster an' pose."

"Well, we can't let him go," said Hart. "He'd go right back to town an' start to strut. Mebbe he'd have nerve enough to bring a posse here. He'd be sure to do that if he could be certain we'd gone."

"If you boys would let me go I'd ride straight to Lazette an' resign," interjected Hazen. He was pallid again; he gulped his words out.

Nobody seemed to hear his voice; nobody looked at him. He felt he had not spoken distinctly enough, and so he repeated his words. As before, they were ignored.

"The best way to do is to end it right now," said Givens. "What do we gain by taking him with us? I sure wouldn't lose no sleep, watchin' him nights while we was ridin'."

"We'd be nervous," added Hart. "If we'd be in camp an' he'd take it into his head to turn over in his sleep, I'd throw my gun on him, thinkin' he'd be meanin' to cut our throats."

"We couldn't always be keepin' him ahead of us," said Givens. "If he'd fall back we'd have to plug him. We ought to do it right now. It would save trouble."

"Well," said Jeff, "you boys do as you think best. I'm turning him over to you. Do what you please with him. I'm ridin' back to town. But maybe you'd like to know what he was intending to do to-night." Jeff told them what Blandin had said, and when he concluded there was a short silence.

Hart and Givens looked at Hazen.

Jeff had not mentioned Blandin's name, and Hazen seemed amazed to discover that Jeff knew of his plans.

"See!" said Hart. "He didn't mean to give you any chance. Why should you give him any? If you don't want to kill him, why I——"

Hart's gun seemed to glide into his right hand.

"I'd be willin' to give you boys my resignation right now," said Hazen. "You could send it on to Lazette. I'd light out of the country an' never come back!" He wiped his moist forehead with a handkerchief. His hands trembled; his knees were sagging.

"After we kill him we could toss him into that narrow canyon," said Givens. "Nobody would ever find him. That's a better way than havin' him resign. He might change his mind."

"Don't kill me, boys!" begged Hazen. "I ain't done nothin' so awful bad. Nobody's been hurt. I'd write a confession, sayin' me an' Dallman was workin' together to get the Hale land. I wouldn't dast come back."

"We could try that," said Jeff. "You boys take him into your shack and set him to writing."

They led Hazen into the cabin—Givens and Hart. Jeff waited outside. Just before daylight Hazen and the other men emerged.

There was no word spoken. Hart and Givens stood near the door of the cabin. Jeff had vanished, though his horse was grazing near the edge of the clearing.

"I'd ride north," suggested Givens, as Hazen mounted. "That way you'll be certain to miss town. I'd keep on missin' it."

CHAPTER TWENTY-FOUR

Hart and Givens found Jeff lying in a grass plot sound asleep. He had been in the saddle for nearly forty-eight hours, had ridden three different horses—two of them to exhaustion—and now nature had overcome him. Givens covered him with a blanket.

"Hazen was lucky," said Givens, looking down at Jeff. "There was a time when he wouldn't have got off like that." He shook his head. "He's changed. He's got a temper like a sidewinder with family troubles, but lately he's kept a hold on it."

"School," said Hart, "and marriage. Both learn a man somethin'."

"Sure," agreed Givens. "Hazen an' Dallman wouldn't be here no more if she hadn't married him when she did. He was seein' red about that time. Seems like he's about ready to break out, now, though. Killin' a sheriff is one thing. Killin' a polecat like Dallman is another. If I was Dallman I'd be pullin' my freight!"

The afternoon sun awakened Jeff. He had turned and the glare was in his eyes. He sat up, gazed about him and saw Hart and Givens seated near him, watching him.

Hart grinned at him.

"You was bushed, I reckon. It's three, mebbe."

"Hazen gone?"

"He's ridin north. He'll be missin' town plenty."

When Jeff got to his feet Hart handed him two pieces of paper. One bore Hazen's resignation; the other was his confession of his illegal association with Wade Dallman.

Jeff placed both in a pocket. He gazed into the north.

"I'm thanking you boys," he said. "Killing him wouldn't be a proper deed for a married man. She ain't used to it." He smiled. "She's law-abiding."

Givens soberly watched him.

"I know how it is," he said. "I was married once. A man considers. There's Dallman. Say the word an' we'll take this off your hands."

"It's past that," said Jeff. "I've spoken to him."

Jeff mounted his horse and rode into the forest, following the faint trail used by himself and Hazen. The sun was still high when he reached the arroyo where he had waited for the sheriff, and in another half hour he was riding down Randall's one street.

To-day did not end the period of grace he had given Dallman, and he could not strike until that time arrived. But he was hoping that he might find Kellis in town, and he knew that his own presence might provoke Dallman to commit an indiscreet action that would hasten the crisis.

He dismounted in front of the livery stable and led his horse inside. He merely nodded to Allen and went outside again, walking slowly down the street. He saw Blandin and another deputy standing in front of the sheriff's office and although his gaze rested momentarily upon them he gave no sign that he recognized them. He was looking for Dallman, and he knew Dallman would be looking for him.

It seemed to him that he was an alien in his own land. This town had been here when he had come. Only a few shanties at first, he had watched it grow until now. Every building in it was familiar to him. Yet to-day it was strange. A new atmosphere hovered over it—a hostile atmosphere. The street seemed different, the buildings were not the same, the people were strangers. He knew, however, that nothing had changed. The change was in himself. What had happened was that the town had finally revealed itself as an enemy, and he was considering it as he would consider a human enemy who had once been a friend. He was scanning it cynically, as he would scan a false friend's face, finding defects where he had once observed charm, detecting insincerity where he had once seen loyalty.

He knew that he had few friends here. Most of the men who watched him as he moved slowly down the street were farmers who were waiting for the signal from Hazen—a signal that would never come. They were studying him, appraising him. No doubt some of them were already visualizing him dangling at the end of a rope. They knew him by reputation, and not one of them would risk attacking him. Yet they would act quickly enough if organized.

He was contemptuous of them and did not even glance at those he passed.

It seemed to him that the town was unnaturally calm, that all normal activity had ceased. Some wagons were on the street, but these were motionless. They were standing before various hitching rails. They were driverless; the horses were drowsing. The silence seemed sepulchral and served to strengthen the illusion of strangeness that had already afflicted him.

His enemies were watching him. He knew that. They were watching him and were wondering what had become of Hazen. They were like a flock of sheep deserted by the bellwether. They were waiting, leaderless, for instructions. They would do nothing until their leader appeared.

He wasn't interested in the farmers. He was searching for Kellis and Dallman, one or the other, or both. He did not see either in any of the doorways he passed, and so at last he began to enter the various saloons and gambling houses.

He spoke to no one, but stalked through the doorways, grimly scanned the faces that were turned toward him, and stalked out again. It was remarkable how doorways were cleared for his entrance, and amazing how quickly they were filled again after he passed. Twice he tried the door of Dallman's office, and therefore the watchers knew it was Dallman he sought.

But Dallman was not visible. No one had seen him.

CHAPTER TWENTY-FIVE

However, Dallman was in town. Early on the preceding evening he had made arrangements for the meeting of the farmers' posse, and in the darkness near the stable where Ellen had once overheard Hazen and Dallman planning, the posse had waited for Hazen to appear. They had waited until midnight and had then dispersed, leaving Dallman nervous and apprehensive.

For Dallman knew that Jeff Hale's word to him had been final. He must leave town or meet his enemy in a fair fight.

Dallman had no desire to fight and he had hoped by taking the offensive with the posse to avoid the prospective meeting with his enemy. But Hazen had not appeared.

Dallman did not sleep. He still hoped that Hazen would come. He sat all day in his office, with the door locked, scanning the west trail from behind the heavy curtain of a window. Hazen did not appear.

But Dallman had seen Jeff Hale coming over the west trail, and he instantly divined the truth—that Jeff had met Hazen. To be sure he did not know and could not suspect what had happened to Hazen, but the fact that Jeff was riding the trail that the sheriff should be riding convinced him that Hazen would not appear.

Dallman yielded to a sudden panic of fear. He knew, now, that he should have heeded Jeff's warning. There was rage in his fear, and as he let himself out of the rear door of his office he was wondering if he dared conceal himself and shoot Jeff before his hour of grace ended.

He might try that.

He ran through the refuse in the rear of several buildings until he reached a door that was familiar to him. The door was not locked and he pushed it open, stood for an instant on the threshold and glanced about him to see if he was observed by anyone outside, then stepped inside and swiftly closed the door. He stood against the door, panting a little. He was aware of a strange nausea which he knew had not been provoked by his short run from his office. The feeling had come upon him a few times before—always when facing danger. Fear!

He did not attempt to delude himself. He was afraid of Jeff Hale. He had always been afraid of Jeff, even while he had been trying to steal the Hale lands. However, he had thought that Jeff would not dare resort to violence, for the law was in Randall and Jeff must conform to it the same as all the citizens of the town. Besides, Hazen was with him, and he had relied upon Hazen to protect him. But Hazen wasn't here now. Hazen's absence made a difference.

Dallman felt that Hazen had deserted him. Somehow Hazen had learned that Jeff Hale was coming to town. If Hazen hadn't met Jeff on the trail he had found out about it some other way. He knew Hazen feared Jeff. Hazen hadn't admitted it but his fear had been disclosed in various other ways.

Dallman discovered that he was trembling. He still stood at the door. In front of him was another door, opening upon another room. Dallman was in the kitchen. The next room was a bedroom. A third door led from the bedroom into the front room of the building, which was used as a store room. The third door was not in line with the other two, but was a little to the right, so that Dallman could only see one of the jambs. By leaning a little to the left, however, Dallman could look into the front room, where he could see various articles on shelves. The store held a miscellaneous stock—groceries, notions, drygoods. Not much of anything but a little of everything needed by the average small purchaser.

Dallman could hear someone walking about in the store. He waited until he was certain only one person was in the store, and then he called, softly:

"Dell."

There was a stir, a step on the floor, and a woman appeared in the third doorway. She craned her head, peered into the kitchen, and saw Dallman.

"Wade!" she said.

She moved toward Dallman and came far enough into the kitchen so that light from one of the rear windows shone upon her. She was young, but there was about her a singular atmosphere of untidiness which was not entirely a matter of personal appearance. It was in a certain sly, veiled gleam of the eyes that one got his impression, and in the full, sensuous lower lip and flare of the nostrils. Vast experience with men had given her a hard sophistication which was unmistakable. Randall knew her as a widow—Della Lane.

"What are you doing here at this hour?" she wanted to know. "Damn it! Don't you know better than that?"

"I'm in trouble, Dell," answered Dallman. "I've got to hide! Jeff Hale is in town, looking for me!"

Della's lips curved scornfully.

"You and Hazen are bunglers!" she charged. "Why didn't you organize your farmers last night?"

"Something's happened to Hazen," Dallman told her. "Hale came in the west trail. I've got an idea that he met Hazen and downed him. I'll be next. He warned me to get out of town!"

"What are you going to do?" asked the woman.

"I don't know. I've got to think it out. He's a fast man with a gun. I don't think I'd have much chance with him."

"Seems like the best thing would be to get out of here, then," suggested Della. "The safest, anyway."

"I've got to think it over. I'll stay out here a while. You go on back to the store."

For an instant the woman stood, silently looking at Dallman. Her face was expressionless. At last it seemed to soften with sympathy.

"All right, Wade," she said. "You stay here and think it over."

She left Dallman. Dallman heard her walking about the little store.

An hour passed. Della appeared at the kitchen door to see Dallman sitting in a chair, his head bent forward, resting in his hands.

"There's hell in his eyes, Wade!" she whispered. "He has passed the store twice. Once he looked in—just a glance. He means to kill you! It seems everybody knows it. Everything has stopped. Everybody's watching him. He's going from one saloon to another, and he isn't drinking, for he comes right out. People are standing around, watching him. Blandin and another deputy are right across the street. They've been watching him, too. He is not paying attention to anybody. He don't look at anybody. He acts like a caged animal. But he's cold, Wade. I never saw him look like that before!"

Dallman did not answer. He knew, though, that various men knew he was in town and that sooner or later Hale would find him. Hale would stay in town until they met.

Dallman got up and walked back and forth in the kitchen. He would have to do something, but he was certain he would not go out in the street and face Jeff Hale with a gun in hand. He thought of that, and saw himself sinking into the dust. He saw people coming toward him, saw them looking down at him, curiously examining the place where he had been shot. The mental picture horrified him. He tried to quit thinking about it, knowing the effect it was having upon him, but he kept seeing it.

At the end of another hour Della again appeared in the doorway. She seemed to be far away and her voice had a note of terrible calm.

"He's been at the door of your office twice," she said.

Della vanished.

Dallman ceased walking. He now stood in the doorway between the kitchen and the bedroom. He was pale, but there was a new light in his eyes—a strange mixture of malice, cunning, and hatred.

Hale was looking for him. By this time everybody in town knew Hale was looking for him. They knew Hale was hunting him, that Hale intended to kill him. Well, he had a right to protect himself, hadn't he? There was a fool custom to the effect that a warning to leave town must be answered by obeying or by meeting the enemy face to face. But Hale's warning had not been a public warning. Nobody besides himself had heard it!

That made a difference, didn't it? A great difference! Dallman drew out his six-shooter, inspected it and moved toward the third doorway with the weapon dangling from his right hand. At the doorway he paused and curiously stuck his head around the jamb. He saw Della sitting on a bench near the front window. Her back was toward him. She was sewing something, and he knew she was covertly watching the street for the reappearance of Jeff Hale.

The sun had gone down. Twilight had come. In the room where Dallman stood, out in the street, everywhere, was the solemn hush which in the high altitudes presages the imminence of night.

Dallman whispered, and it seemed to him that his voice must have been heard in the street.

"Della!" he said.

Della turned. Slowly she rose and walked toward him.

When she entered the bedroom and saw him standing there with the gun in her hand her face paled and she stood rigid.

"Get out of here!" he said, a ring of cold command in his voice. "Go somewhere! I'm taking my end!"

Della stared at him for an instant. Then she caught up a shawl from the bed and went out the rear doorway, closing the door after her.

The store was not more than a dozen feet from front to rear. The small front window sash, swung upward upon hinges, was open. Flattening himself against the partition that separated the store from the bedroom, Dallman waited.

Only part of his head and the muzzle of his six-shooter were visible from the street. The gun was rigid, for it was held tightly against the doorjamb, and its muzzle was pointed toward the street.

"Looking for me, eh?" sneered Dallman. "Well, come on, damn you!"

CHAPTER TWENTY-SIX

Apparently Dallman was not in town, or at least if he was in town Jeff was not able to find him. Aware that he was being watched and his every movement noted, he could not go into the Elite for fear of drawing suspicion upon Sadie.

Several times he passed the Elite. He saw Sadie inside, sitting at a table. Once he met her gaze fairly, but there was no sign that she had anything to communicate to him. Her eyes expressed nothing but apprehension.

He kept walking slowly back and forth from one end of town to the other. He had entered all the saloons and gambling houses, and had not seen Dallman.

The sun was low. He stood for a moment in front of the livery stable, which was almost directly across the street from the hotel where Ellen had stayed overnight, and where she had met Kellis, and rage blazed in him as he looked at the building.

"Lies!" he said aloud.

He had told her the truth. He loved her. He loved her more than he had ever loved anything. He had loved her from the beginning. He had fought against it, but it had conquered him. An aching regret seized him. He kept seeing her as she had appeared when he had surprised her by suddenly entering the door of her room at the ranch house—when he had told her that the end had come. He couldn't get that picture out of his mind. He had seen it during every waking moment since. He was seeing her now as she had gazed at him through the glistening strands of her wonderful hair; as she had appeared, her face framed in it, watching him reproachfully.

That silent reproach was one thing he couldn't understand. It was a contradiction. She had lied to him, and cheated, and yet she was able mutely to rebuke him, to make him feel that he had injured her by refusing to believe in her.

Well, he had told her to go, and by this time she was out of his life. He would never see her again. He had made it plain enough to her, and all the time he had been talking he had been aware that he wanted her to stay. Yes: he would have her stay. He would take her, knowing her to be a liar and a cheat.

He saw Mart Blandin again. Blandin was alone, sitting on a bench in front of the sheriff's office. There was no one within a hundred feet of him.

Jeff moved toward Blandin. He had been in town for several hours and had spoken no word to anyone. Perhaps if he talked with Blandin for a few minutes he could relieve the terrible tension that had gripped him, could calm the cold, deadly rage that seethed in him.

He stood before Blandin, looking down at the man. He remembered the pieces of paper in his pocket—Hazen's confession and his resignation. He passed them over to Blandin.

"Your boss has left the country," he said.

He stood facing the street while Blandin scanned the papers. Blandin did not look up; he seemed to speak to the sand in front of him which was darkening as the colours of the afterglow faded from the sky.

"So he's gone," said Blandin. "This makes me sheriff—if I want it." Blandin's voice leaped. "Why, damn it, Jeff, I can run Dallman in on the strength of this!"

"You're not touching Dallman!" said Jeff. "I'm going to kill him."

"Why, yes," said Blandin, gently, "I reckon that's right. You've got a right to kill him. He'd ought to be killed for what he done to your wife."

Jeff turned.

"Dallman didn't do anything to my wife, Mart. I'm going to kill him for what he's been trying to do with our land."

"Didn't, eh?" said Blandin. He now looked up and met Jeff's gaze. "Didn't do anything to your wife! Lord! Don't you know it was Dallman that abducted her?"

Jeff's muscles leaped, became rigid.

"Talk!" he ordered, sharply.

"Why, shucks!" said Blandin, "I thought you knew. I overheard Dallman an' Hazen talkin'. Hazen an' Dallman was runnin' that gang of rustlers. They was both down in Navajo basin the night you hung Hank Kroll. The man that was with Kroll that night was Hazen, himself! I've knowed it but I didn't dare say anything.

"Dallman was down there, too, but he'd gone off alone to meet some of the other rustlers. He run into Ellen Ballinger—found her stretched out, senseless, after she'd fell from her horse. Dallman was scared Ballinger was goin' to file on your land, and would mebbe get it away from him, so he figures that if he'd take Ellen an' hide her for a while he'd be able to make a deal with Ballinger. You spoiled that. I've been wantin' to tell you, but I figured I'd better not as long as Hazen was runnin' things. An' sometimes I couldn't understand how you wouldn't know it. I figured Ellen would know who had abducted her."

Jeff turned from Blandin. He did not want Blandin to see the fierce joy that shone in his eyes.

Ellen was innocent. The abduction had not been planned by the Ballingers. The calm light that he had seen so often in her eyes had not been deceit or duplicity but consciousness of her own truthfulness. Many times had her expression baffled him. He had thought her a marvellous actress and liar, and he had permitted her to see the contempt in his eyes. And all the time he had been treating her unjustly she had made no complaint. She had endured suspicion and insult, always insisting that it had been he and not another that had abducted her. He would reach her before she left the country. Failing in that, he would follow her east and tell her what a fool he had been.

But before he set out to find her he would finish with Dallman. If he lost her the fault would be Dallman's. Dallman was to blame for all his troubles.

He stepped away from Blandin, and the latter whispered to him:

"He's in town, Jeff. I saw him this afternoon, in his office. He'll know that you are lookin' for him. By this time some of his friends have told him. He'll be hidin' somewhere, waitin' to shoot you in the back. Every time you've passed a buildin' or a doorway, I've jumped, expectin' him to shoot. Watch yourself!"

Jeff walked down the street, eastward. He was across the street from Della's store, and was facing the front of the building. Dusk had fallen, but through the window of the store he caught a glimpse of a face and a glint of dying light shining for an instant upon metal.

He leaped sideways and a bullet whined past him. The muffled crash of a heavy pistol was followed by the musical tinkle of falling glass. Before a second shot could follow, Jeff was across the street, crouching against the front wall of the building adjoining that from which the bullet had come. He had located Dallman.

There was no space between the buildings for quite a distance down the street, but he found one presently and plunged into it. He expected to reach Dallman from the rear of the building from which the shot had been fired. He felt that Dallman would be there, waiting, watching, expecting an attack from the front.

Dusk was deepening into darkness, and he had some trouble locating the building. When he found it he drew his gun and entered. The interior was dark, but he soon discovered that Dallman had fled. Della, too, had gone.

He stood in the rear doorway peering out. From a point somewhere in the dusk behind the buildings he heard the rapid beating of hoofs. The sound developed suddenly from a heavy silence, and so he knew that a man had mounted and was riding away.

Dallman, of course.

Jeff turned, leaped through the rooms and the store and reached the street. He saw a horse and rider flitting over the east trail, heading up the slope that led out of the valley.

Jeff turned, intending to run to the livery stable to get his horse. He saw a horse and rider bearing down upon him from the west, and he leaped aside to keep from being run down. The animal came to a sliding halt in a heavy dust cloud, and the rider slid down.

The rider was Blandin.

"Just what I thought would happen," he said. "He tried to pot-shot you! I seen him light out of the back door. He missed, an' he knows you'll follow him. He'll run like a scared rabbit. But this horse will ketch him. Run his head off, if you want to!"

Jeff leaped into the saddle. Presently the watchers in the doorways saw two dust clouds drifting over the upland trail. The clouds were visible for a little while, then they vanished.

CHAPTER TWENTY-SEVEN

Ellen was not frightened by Kellis's threats. She was curiously calm and alert for she realized that her life depended upon her ability to keep distance between herself and him. His marksmanship was bad, and his supply of rocks could not last long. He would smash her if he could, of course, for he had already demonstrated his eagerness to do so, and so his threats did not disturb her.

She knew that she dared not risk moving from her present position as long as Kellis continued to throw at her, for the slightest injury would slow her movements and perhaps permit Kellis to catch her. She was confident that as long as she retained her agility and her senses she could keep away from him.

The brilliant moonlight disclosed every feature of the great declivity. While Kellis continued to throw rocks at her she found opportunity to look about her and to estimate her chances of reaching another position in case he should decide to descend to her. Close to her was an expanse of glassy rock perhaps a dozen feet wide. She could not escape over that. But above was a narrow ledge which projected out over the rock and ran downward to a huge mass of broken granite that appeared to be strewn over a little level.

As she faced the wall the section of broken granite was on her left. On her right was a perpendicular drop into a shadowy cleft. She could not move in that direction, nor could she go any farther straight down from where she crouched. A backward glance told her that at a little distance the wall dropped straight to the valley below.

Once, glancing down into the valley, she was afflicted with a sudden nausea; she held tightly to the rock and closed her eyes. But she knew that she must conquer that weakness or she would never escape. So, deliberately, while Kellis crouched on the upper ledge and glared at her, she scanned the country below her.

And instantly the dizziness passed. For it seemed not so far, after all. Nor did it appear that a fall into the green depths would be so terrible. For the moonlight, working its magic upon the wild growth of the valley, transformed it into a gently undulating sea of soft, green velvet.

For an instant she had forgotten Kellis. She was reminded of him when she heard him screaming curses at her. Apparently a new frenzy had gripped him, for she saw him slipping over the ledge, his good leg searching, the injured one dangling.

Instantly she clambered over the edge of the rock in front of her and started for the narrow ledge above the expanse of glassy rock.

By balancing perilously she gained the narrow ledge. It was not wide enough to permit her even to crawl over it on her hands and knees, so she lay flat on her stomach and wriggled over it. When she reached the huge rocks on the little level she sank beside one of them, gasping.

She saw Kellis in the position she had occupied. He was not behind the rock, however, but was stretched out upon it face down, holding tightly to its edges with both hands. His face was pallid, his eyes were malignant.

But Kellis was frightened. He was clinging to the rock as a certain variety of ivy clings to the face of a brick wall, and Ellen, breathlessly watching him, was convinced that the shock of the fall to the rock had momentarily restored his reason. She felt that as long as his sanity stayed with him he would not move. He was a coward, and if he had been in his right senses he would not have followed her.

Anyway, she was no longer afraid of him. He had lost the revolver, and he could not throw rocks at her from his present position. She doubted if he would have the courage to attempt to follow her over the ledge.

She sat watching him, regaining her breath. Kellis still clung to the top of the rock. He continued to glare at her.

For perhaps an hour Ellen sat there, resting, and then she began to seek a way to descend. The night was going. The moon was far over in the west and would presently vanish altogether.

She crept over the rocky level to the edge farthest away from Kellis. At the edge of the level was another outcropping of rock which ran like a ridge at an angle down the huge slope to another ledge. The distance was perhaps a hundred feet, and Ellen was certain she could descend without difficulty.

As she halted at the edge of the level she turned and saw Kellis watching her. Her first step downward left only her head visible to him, and he must have divined that she was escaping him for he shouted profanely.

She paid no attention to him. For a little while as she descended he was invisible to her, and then when about half way down she saw him again. His head was twisted in her direction.

When she reached the lower ledge she rested again. She was growing confident of her ability to make the complete descent, and she no longer feared Kellis. She could see him still clinging to the flat rock. At the distance from which she looked at him he looked as if he had been stuck there.

She felt in the bosom of her dress. The certificate was still there, and the photograph of Jeff which she had taken from the shelf in the Diamond A ranch house. She must get the certificate to the land office.

At the side of the ledge upon which she sat—toward Kellis this time—was another section of jagged rock that jutted out from the main wall. Just below the rocky section was a deep channel, a miniature gully, formed undoubtedly by the erosive action of the elements. It seemed to her that from the end of the gulley to the floor of the valley was not a great distance and that the hazards decreased as the valley grew nearer.

Confidently and boldly she stepped off the ledge among the rocks. She descended carefully, however, and slowly, giving her entire attention to her task. She had reached the bottom of the rocky section and had turned to look at Kellis before venturing into the gully. She saw Kellis wildly scrambling upward to the ledge above the rock upon which he had been lying. His voice reached her. He was screaming violent curses.

He was hopping upward like a great one-legged animal, his injured leg seeming to flap wildly with each muscular movement. He got to the upper edge of the rock, leaped upward and gripped the edge of the narrow ledge along which Ellen had squirmed.

He grasped the edge of the ledge and tried to pull himself upward. It seemed his hands must have slipped at the first effort and that he had not strength enough to succeed in a second attempt, though he tried. There was a time when Ellen saw him gripping the edge of the ledge with one hand, and she knew that the edge sloped sharply, for she had had to cling tightly even while resting her entire body upon it.

Kellis might have returned to the safety of the flat rock. But he made no attempt to do so. Instead, he tried to cross by gripping the ledge first with one hand and then the other, swinging his body sideways each time he attempted a fresh grip on the ledge.

His hands kept slipping off the edge of the ledge. His progress grew slower. He reached the middle and hung there for a time with both hands. Ellen observed him glancing to his right and left and knew he was beginning to realize that he was doomed.

He hung there, motionless.

Ellen saw him turn his head and glance backward to the glassy rock beneath him. She called wildly to him and started to clamber up toward him. But she was hundreds of feet distant, and before she had gone a dozen feet his hands slipped off the edge of the ledge.

He dropped slowly, heavily, landing on his knees. Desperately he clawed at the glassy surface of the big rock, and it seemed that for an instant he was lying there, motionless. Then, slowly, he began to slide downward. He was still sliding slowly when he went over the edge of the rock, and with both arms outstretched he seemed merely to float downward into the shadowy space beyond the edge of the rock.

Cringing from the sight and yet held in the grip of a terrible fascination, Ellen watched him. So great was the distance he had to fall to reach the green, velvety sea at the bottom of the valley that he seemed a long time falling. He turned over and over, slowly, gracefully, like an aërial acrobat who is confident of the position of the net in which he is to land; and he sank so gently into the soft green of the valley that Ellen felt for a moment that he could not be injured.

She wanted to climb down instantly, to help him. But the sight had unnerved her and she sank to her knees, trembling. She knew better than to think he had not been hurt by the fall, for she had heard a faint crash at the end, as of branches breaking with his weight.

By the time she reached the floor of the valley the moon had gone down behind the high peaks. A heavy darkness engulfed her. She climbed to the top of a huge rock and crouched there until daylight. Then she got down from the rock and went in search of Kellis.

He had sought to kill her, but she could not leave the vicinity without determining how badly he had been injured. She spent two hours searching for him, and when she finally found him she shuddered and ran from the spot. He was lying flat on his back, his eyes open and staring.

Ellen started across the valley through the dense, wild growth of the virgin forest. There were no paths or trails to guide her. But she had watched where the moon had gone down and she knew that the Hour Glass should be in nearly the opposite direction.

When the sun came up she walked straight toward it, but she was so tired that her progress was slow, and she had to stop frequently to rest.

The trees did not grow as close together as she had supposed when she had viewed them from the higher country. It was apparent that no axes or fires had ever destroyed them. Great, gnarled cottonwoods stretched their mighty branches upward, magnificent old giants that demanded space in which to thrive, their huge roots extending far in all directions and sucking the sustenance of the soil to the exclusion of all other growth. They were the monarchs, and even the brush that encroached upon them was etiolated and stunted. The newcomers and the upstarts of the forest remained at a distance.

The sun was almost directly overhead when Ellen pushed her way out of a tangle of undergrowth and came upon a small stream of water. She was suffering from thirst and eagerly approached the stream, knelt at a convenient shallow, and drank, using her cupped hands.

The water was clear and cool, and she felt refreshed when she got up to resume her search for the Hour Glass.

She crossed the stream and went on a little distance through the trees. And then suddenly found herself crossing a faint trail that seemed to run north and south through the forest.

Exclaiming with delight, she paused and considered. She had been travelling eastward, she knew, but the Hour Glass was northeastward from the Diamond A and from the Kellis cabin, so that if she followed this trail she might find an eastward trail that intersected it. Then she would come out of the forest somewhere near the Hour Glass. If no east trail intersected she could keep on following this trail until it took her out of the basin.

But she had grown so tired that her feet seemed to have become leaden weights. She walked grimly on, though, until under a mighty cottonwood she came upon a fallen giant of the forest which in toppling to its final resting place had crashed through the branches of the cottonwood. The deadfall was in a deep shade. Ellen stopped and found the silence soothing.

She decided she would rest for a few moments, and she climbed upon the fallen trunk and leaned her head wearily against a convenient branch. She must have fallen asleep, for though she had heard no sound she suddenly became aware that a horse and rider were near her. They were not more than a dozen feet distant, and they must have been there for some minutes. For the horse was contentedly grazing upon a clump of bunch grass, while the rider was sitting crossways in the saddle, watching her.

The rider was Bill Hazen.

CHAPTER TWENTY-EIGHT

Ellen sat erect, and Hazen grinned at her. He was obviously enjoying her astonishment.

Ellen's first sensation was one of relief. For Hazen was sheriff of the county. He represented authority and stability and, to her, safety. In a little while now she would be upon the right trail. Perhaps Hazen would even take her to the Hour Glass, permitting her to ride behind him.

She entertained such thoughts until, expressing her delight at his appearance, she smiled at him. Hazen's answering smile was not that of a public official intent upon performing a service for a woman in distress. It was a smile which expressed cunning and passion.

Ellen was frightened. She glanced about and observed that she and Hazen were alone. And now she remembered that Hazen was Jeff's enemy. In her delight over seeing him she had almost forgotten.

Hazen slid out of the saddle and walked close to her. He stood, watching her, his gaze roving over her from head to foot, noting her torn and dusty garments.

"Where's your horse?" he asked.

"I left him at Jim Kellis's cabin," she answered, truthfully.

"What did you leave him there for? Decided you like walkin' better?"

She knew she did not dare tell him the truth, so she lied.

"I was at the Kellis cabin to see Mrs. Kellis," she said. "Father wanted her to do some work at the Hour Glass. I took a walk through the forest while waiting for her, and got lost. I fell and when I got up I had lost my sense of direction. Then I found this trail and thought it might lead to the Hour Glass. It does, doesn't it?"

"Not to-day. This trail leads north."

"Will you please put me on the right trail? You don't need to bother much. I can walk. I am in a hurry. Will you show me the trail?"

He smiled at her, shaking his head slowly from side to side.

"You're too pretty to ride alone, Mrs. Hale. I'm goin' to invite you to ride with me."

"Thank you. Then you are going to the Hour Glass!"

"You're gettin' things all wrong," he said. "I'm not goin' to the Hour Glass. I'm goin' to keep right on, goin' through the Navajo basin. It'll take four or five days of ridin'. Travelling double it will take longer. It's a lonesome ride an' company will be acceptable."

"Father will reward you," she said, deliberately ignoring the significance of his words.

"He won't reward me," he grinned. He took a step toward her, holding out his arms. "Come on," he said, "I'll help you mount."

She got up and ran swiftly along the trunk of the tree. He followed, running beside her on the ground, leaping over the dead branches in his path, crashing through the smaller ones. He was grinning confidently, knowing that in the end he would catch her.

When she had gone as far as she could she leaped off the tree, fought her way furiously through some impeding dead branches and ran southward over the trail she had found. She did not look around, but she heard Hazen coming after her. He was laughing.

She was too tired to run fast or far. Desperation had supplied her with strength for a few minutes, but before she had gone far she felt her muscles begin to lag. She ran on, though, until she could go no farther. Then she ran behind a tree, hoping to hide from Hazen. But Hazen saw her and leaped toward her. One of his clutching hands gripped her shoulder. She jerked away, and the cloth ripped. Terrorized, she screamed.

Then she heard a flurry of hoof beats—and a voice:

"Why, it's Hazen! An' Jeff's wife!"

She turned and saw two riders. They had evidently reached the spot over the south trail, for their horses were facing the north. They were not a dozen feet distant. One was grinning felinely at Hazen over the barrel of a heavy revolver; the second rider was staring at Ellen.

"Playin' tag with the lady, Hazen?" said the rider who was holding the gun. "Gettin' rough, too. Tryin' to tear her waist off. Thought you'd be half way out of the basin by this time."

Hazen did not answer. He stood, staring downward, his eyes sullen.

"Lift his gun, Jess!" snapped the first rider.

The man called Jess slipped out of the saddle and deftly drew Hazen's gun from its holster. He ran an experienced hand over Hazen's clothing in search of other weapons. Finding none, he grinned at his companion.

"He's clean, Dell," he said. "This is the gun I gave him."

"Turn around!" Dell ordered. Hazen obeyed and Dell looked at Ellen.

"Ma'am," he said respectfully, "we're friends of Jeff Hale. Last night Jeff visited our shack, bringin' this jasper with him. Mebbe you know him—he's Bill Hazen. He was sheriff, but he ain't any more. We understood he was headin' north as fast as he could travel. But it seems he didn't. We are headin' north, too, figurin' to leave the country. But we wasn't hurryin' none, an' we find Hazen ain't far ahead of us. In fact, we find him entertainin' Jeff Hale's wife. We know that whatever's been done has been done by Hazen, but we'd like to know what it is."

Ellen told him, including her experience with Kellis. At the end the riders exchanged glances, then both looked at Hazen, who seemed to cringe.

"That's it, eh?" said Dell. "This guy is playin' Romeo an' Little Red Ridin' Hood. Thinks he's a wolf with women, eh?" He smiled broadly at Ellen.

"Right now you're wantin' to go some place, eh?" he added.

"To Jim Kellis's cabin," said Ellen. "My horse is there, you see."

"Sure," said Dell. "That's easy. Jess," he added, "you just ketch Hazen's horse, will you?"

Jess jumped his horse forward. They saw him ride beside Hazen's animal, seize the dragging rein and come toward them. When Jess came up Dell dismounted and motioned for Ellen to come to him.

"You'll ride my horse, ma'am," he said. "I'll take Hazen's. The trail is plain. You ride this trail for about two miles. Then you hit another, crossin' it. You turn to your right an' keep goin'. After a while you strike the big trail runnin' from the Hour Glass to Randall. It runs right past Kellis's place."

Dell helped Ellen mount. After she was in the saddle she looked straight at Dell.

"What are you going to do with Mr. Hazen?" she asked.

"Why, Hazen is goin' to continue his trip, ma'am."

"With you?"

"We're figurin' on goin' part way with him, ma'am. So we'll be sure he's goin' where he's goin'."

"Oh," she said, "I was wondering. You see, it is not pleasant to be in this forest without a horse."

"It ain't, ma'am, for a fact."

"And—and—I think Hazen didn't mean anything, after all. He was merely foolish."

"Yes," said Dell, "foolish."

"Sure," added Jess. "Foolish."

Both men laughed. But there was no mirth in their laughter and Ellen glanced at them, puzzled. They stood, waiting for her to be off. And yet they seemed in no hurry, did not seem to be eager to see her go.

"Well," she said, "I thank you."

"Shucks," answered Dell.

"You'll remember about the trail," said Jess. "Turn to the right."

"Tell Jeff there'll be no mistake about it this time," said Dell. He flashed a strange smile at her. "He'll know what that means," he added.

His eyes were enigmatic. His gaze dropped; he seemed to become suddenly interested in a hummock at his feet. Jess had turned his back to her. His arms were folded. He too was staring downward.

"Well, good-bye," said Ellen, "and I thank you again."

She sent Dell's horse along the trail. She was strangely perturbed, and when she had ridden perhaps half a mile she turned in the saddle and looked back. The men were standing where she had left them. But now they were facing her, watching her.

She rode on, realizing that she must have slept long on the tree trunk, for the sun had gone down over the rim of the basin, and the wonderful pageant of the afterglow was visible. The strong, soft colours tinted the treetops and sent long bright shafts of varicoloured light through the aisles of the forest. Dominating the sky was an effulgent flood of orange and gold.

Slowly as she rode the colours faded to slate and purple and tones of gray. Then suddenly the light dimmed and the forest darkened. A solemn hush descended. Faintly to her in the dead and heavy silence came the sound of a shot. It reverberated in slowly diminishing waves until it ceased altogether and the heavy silence reigned again.

Ellen shuddered, and rode on. She reached the cross trail, turned to her right and went on into the deepening darkness. When an hour or so later she came to the broad trail running from the Hour Glass she recognized it. And now, no longer in doubt as to her whereabouts, she rode swiftly.

Tired as she was, she intended to ride to Lazette, to deposit the certificate in the land office. There must be no delay about that. But first she would stop at the Kellis cabin for food, for she was famished.

She rode fast along the wide trail, for she was familiar with it, and when at last she saw a light shining through the trees ahead she rode more slowly, knowing that she would find Mrs. Kellis at home. She would have to tell Mrs. Kellis what had happened to her husband. She dreaded to witness the woman's grief, but she must tell.

However, when she reached the front door of the cabin after dismounting from the horse and tying the animal to a tree at the edge of the clearing, she saw no one inside. An oil lamp burned on the table in the centre of the room, and as Ellen stepped inside her gaze went to a piece of paper on the table near the lamp. An empty cup had been placed on the paper to keep it from being blown away by the breeze that swept through the house. Curiously, Ellen bent forward and read:

I am tired to live like thees. I see you throw knife at Ellen Balinger. You will keel her. Whisky make you crazy. For long time I theenk I dont love you. Now I know. Some day you go crazy an keel me an babby. I go way.

There was no name signed to the note, but Ellen knew the writer had been Mrs. Kellis. The woman's poor romance had been shattered.

Ellen stood for a long time leaning on the edge of the table looking down at the note. When she finally stood erect again she had decided to ride on to Lazette. She could not endure staying alone in the cabin; she preferred to be out under the stars to sitting here, brooding over what had happened. For she kept seeing Kellis lying at the base of the great slope; she kept hearing the faint report of the pistol in the forest.

She got a drink of water from a pail that stood on a shelf near the stove, and paused for an instant in front of a mirror on the wall. Then she walked to the front door and gazed out.

The moon had come up while she had been in the cabin. She must have been inside longer than she had thought, for the moon was high. It was bright, too, as bright as it had been last night while she had been running through the forest.

Standing in the doorway she heard a horse coming—running fast. An instant later there was a smother of dust at the edge of the clearing. She saw a rider throw himself off his horse and come running toward her. He leaped upon the porch and the light from the lamp inside shone full upon him.

Ellen stepped back into the room, slowly retreating until the table was between her and the rider. For the rider was Wade Dallman. He was trembling and there was a wild glare in his eyes. But he was amazed to find her in the cabin, for he stood in the doorway and shouted:

"You? You? Damn you, what are you doing here?"

CHAPTER TWENTY-NINE

Like Kellis, Dallman seemed to have lost his reason. His face was pallid, his eyes were blazing with a light that she had never seen in the eyes of a sane man. His muscles were tensed. He stood in the doorway with his legs spread far apart, his arms hanging at his sides, his hands clenched, the fingers working and straining as though he was striving to drive the nails into the flesh of the palms. His shoulders were hunched forward, his chin was thrust out, his mouth was open in a terrible pout.

However, Ellen knew Dallman was not insane. He was merely in the grip of a mighty emotion. Fear!

That was it. Dallman was afraid of something. What that something was Ellen had no means of discovering, and yet she could read fear in his eyes. There was rage in them, also, and cunning, but fear was the dominant emotion.

He did not wait for Ellen to answer his question, but asked another:

"Where's Kellis?"

"Kellis isn't here."

Dallman leaped into the room. He ran from corner to corner, searching, throwing things aside, tumbling furniture out of his way. He was searching for something. He went to the bed and ripped off the quilts. Raging, he pulled off the mattress and kicked it violently aside. He peered under the bed, into and behind the old dresser that stood against a wall. He ran, breathing heavily, to the stove and looked behind it. His gaze swept the walls, the floor. From a point near the stove he glared at Ellen.

"Where's Kellis's rifle?"

"I didn't know Kellis had a rifle."

Dallman's face blotched. He seemed to swell with rage.

"Damn that slut!" he shouted. "She's taken it!" He stared at Ellen with the furtive, shifting gaze of a desperately harried animal. She could tell that he was involving her in some meditated action. In the heavy silence that had come with the cessation of his activity, Ellen could hear only his shrill breathing. Suddenly even that sound ceased. Dallman was holding his breath. His head was cocked to one side, to his right, and he appeared to be listening for an expected sound. As Dallman's head was inclined to his right, Ellen divined that he expected sound to come from that direction, which was from the direction Dallman himself had come.

Ellen also listened, and it seemed to her that she could hear a faint drumming, as of a horse running. She looked at Dallman and saw that his face had grown pallid again.

He leaped at her, gripped her arms, held her and shook her savagely.

"Listen, you!" he said, his face close to hers. "You're goin' to die damn quick if you don't do what I tell you! Understand? I'll blow hell out of you!

"Jeff Hale is comin'. He's after me—chased me from town! He's close. If I could have found a rifle I would shoot him when he comes over that ridge out there. But I'm no match for him with a six-shooter. My horse is out there in the clearing. He's hid an' Jeff won't see him. I'm slipping out the rear door. You stand in the front door so Jeff can see you, an' bring him into the shack that way. Keep him inside until I get away. If he asks if you've seen me, tell him you haven't. I'm goin' to hang outside by a window and if you don't come through I'll blow you apart if it's the last thing I do!" He shook her again, so hard that she reeled dizzily. "You hear me?" he asked.

"Yes."

"You'll do as I tell you?"

She nodded.

And now, unmistakably, came to them the rapid drumming of hoofs on the trail.

Dallman leaned over the table and blew out the light. He seized Ellen's arms from behind and shoved her to the front door—out a little distance upon the porch, where the light from the moon shone directly upon her. She heard Dallman's step in the room behind her—she waited expectantly to hear him step down from the rear doorway. She would have heard him if he had done so, for on the ground just outside the rear door was a wide wooden platform with loose boards covering its top, and these would creak and clatter with his weight.

She heard no such sound, and so she knew that Dallman was still in the room behind her. His voice came again.

"I'm stayin' here for a minute or two," he said. "If you don't come through I'll bore you right through the back!"

"All right," said Ellen, calmly.

She knew now that Dallman intended to kill Jeff. She had known it from the instant he had told her that Jeff was coming. For if he wished merely to escape he would have had time to disappear into Navajo basin. He could have kept right on going and by this time he would have had a mile or so of dense forest between himself and Jeff. His search for the rifle had betrayed his intentions. Ellen knew that he had ridden here purposely. He had expected to find Kellis, had expected to use the man's rifle. He had told her how easy it would be to shoot Jeff as he came over the ridge near the edge of the clearing.

Dallman did not intend to leave the cabin. He was now standing inside, probably near the rear doorway, in the darkness. The shack faced south so that the cleared space in both front and rear received the full light of the moon. Concealed in the semi-darkness of the cabin Dallman could shoot down anyone who entered the front or rear door. That of course, was just what Dallman intended to do.

Ellen heard the hoofbeats grow clearer. She had ridden the trail several times, and knew that Jeff was now coming across a sand level just beyond the base of the ridge that Dallman had referred to. Presently he would burst into view on the crest of the ridge. As she waited it seemed to her that her brain had ceased functioning, and that her body was paralyzed. She could not think and her muscles refused to do anything except to hold her body rigid. She wanted to shout to Jeff, to tell him of the danger that threatened him, to tell him to go back, to stay away. She knew that if she did that Dallman would kill her, but she would have been willing to die to save Jeff.

And then there was a leaping silhouette on the crest of the ridge, a smother of dust on the near slope, and Jeff appeared at the edge of the clearing.

Jeff seemed to see her instantly, for he stopped and stared at her. The moonlight was so clear that she could see the expression of amazement on his face; could observe how he stood rigid, looking at her. She knew that she was equally visible to him.

Jeff had descended the slope of the ridge a little to the west of the doorway, so that if Dallman were watching from a position near the rear door he could not have seen Jeff when he stopped to stare at Ellen. And although Ellen was standing just outside the door, she was a little west of its centre, so that her right arm and shoulder could not be seen from inside the cabin—by Dallman, especially, standing near the rear door.

Ellen's lips now formed words, but she was powerless to utter them. And Jeff, his amazement changing to eagerness and delight, was walking toward her.

"Ellen!" he said.

"Oh, Jeff!" Ellen found herself saying, and wondered if the voice was her own.

And then, as if the sound had broken the paralysis which had gripped her, she quickly pressed the index finger of her right hand to her lips and as quickly removed it and motioned to Jeff to go around the west side of the cabin to the rear door.

Jeff paused again. Then apparently quickly interpreting the motion he gazed keenly at her for an instant, and obeyed her.

Ellen stood rigid, motionless. She did not know for certain if Jeff had understood her, but she was aware that he was always mentally alert, and he must know of course that her signals to him had been significant of the unusual. Also, he was pursuing Dallman, and she felt that it would be his conviction that Dallman was in the cabin, or in the rear of it. She hadn't been able to warn him in words, but she had cautioned him in pantomime, and now she must trust to his wisdom.

But there was a way in which she could create an illusion in Dallman's mind; a trick by which she could keep his attention centred upon the front doorway while Jeff cautiously approached the rear door. She waited an instant and then she spoke, lowly, as if Jeff were standing near her.

"Why, Jeff!" she said. "How did you happen to come here to-night?" And then, quickly, pretending that she was not giving Jeff an opportunity to answer her, she added:

"You didn't expect to see me here, did you? Now don't pretend that you did! No; don't come in that way! The side, Jeff! The side, dear! There's a beam there! Don't you see it? You're so tall you'd be sure to bump your head on it. Now be careful not to fall over that bench! Now stand there for a minute until I look at you. I haven't seen you for a week, you know, and I want to——"

She paused, unable to say more. The strange paralysis was creeping upon her again, bringing incoherence, atrophy. It seemed to her that even her breathing stopped. There was a long interval of silence so deep that it seemed to her that she was standing alone in a place where all sound had ceased. An age. An interminable period. A monstrous and horrible hush.

Then came a hoarse and profane exclamation, a sudden scuffling as of a man in heavy boots swiftly turning. Then two thunderous reports and the sound of a heavy body falling.

She could not look; she dared not. She hadn't the strength or the courage. She covered her eyes with her hands and stood there, waiting.

CHAPTER THIRTY

Jeff had been amazed to see Ellen standing in the moonlight just outside the door of the cabin. He could not explain her presence in the vicinity, but her warning signal he interpreted correctly. He knew Dallman was in the cabin, for he had not been far behind the man in the race from town; he had seen Dallman heading toward this spot and he had observed Dallman's horse standing in the timber near the edge of the clearing. He suspected that Dallman was inside the cabin waiting for him, expecting him to rush through the front doorway and be killed.

A new rage surged through him at sight of Ellen's torn garments and dishevelled hair. It was down on her shoulders, a glistening, filmy, negligent cascade. Her white face shone through it, and he saw that her lips were forming words that she could not utter. She was covered with dust, and he felt that Dallman had attacked her.

He moved cautiously toward the rear of the cabin. There was no window on that side and he knew Dallman could not see him. Also, he heard Ellen talking, speaking his name, and he was aware that she was pretending, trying to create in Dallman's mind the impression that he, Jeff, was moving toward her.

Her voice became fainter as he reached and turned the rear corner of the cabin. When he got to the rear door and peered stealthily inside he could hear her voice more clearly. And then he saw Dallman.

The land shark, unable to control his impatience, had stepped to the centre of the room; he stood there, bent forward, waiting and listening. He had been deceived by Ellen's trick, for his gun was out, held rigidly at his side as he waited for his enemy to step into the doorway. The moonlight, entering the east window of the cabin, shone full upon him. In his impatience he had emerged from the sheltering shadows. And now it seemed he was beginning to distrust Ellen. He could see her, even as Jeff could see her, standing just outside the door in the moonlight. But she was no longer talking. She was standing there, rigid as a statue, and her hands were covering her eyes. Suspicious, Dallman stepped forward, far enough to peer out of the front doorway. Seeming to realize that he had been tricked, he cursed, turned. Jeff shot him—once.

Dallman's gun went off, the bullet ploughing into the cabin floor in front of him. Dallman went down slowly, his knees striking the floor first.

His hands went out in front of him, and for a few minutes he rested there on his hands and knees, his head drooping. Then he fell, face downward, his arms doubling under him, his legs slowly straightening.

Jeff walked to the man and stood for a time looking down at him. Dallman was still.

Jeff left Dallman and stepped softly to the door, where he stood for an instant looking at Ellen, who still stood waiting, afraid to uncover her eyes and turn.

"I'm thanking you," said Jeff.

Ellen turned swiftly.

"Oh!" she exclaimed, and swayed toward him. Then she was in his arms, and he was holding her tightly.

"I didn't want to kill him," he said, regretfully. "I've been fighting against it. I went into town, looking for him. I would have killed him if I had found him there. He tried to shoot me when I wasn't expecting it. That stirred me. But chasing him here I got over it. I would have been satisfied if he had got out of the country. Then when I saw what he had done to you, I had to go through with it. I waited until he turned. He had his chance. He had his gun in his hand. I think he meant to kill both——"

She didn't tell him the truth, then—how it had been Kellis who had been responsible for her torn clothing and her bedraggled appearance—she just held tightly to him, knowing that something had happened to change his opinion of her, and that she had him—had him at last.

CHAPTER THIRTY-ONE

They rode—first—to the Diamond A.

Jeff's father and mother had not returned, and they had the house to themselves. However, they lingered there only long enough to permit Ellen to change her clothing, and then they set out for Lazette, to file the certificate that Ellen had found.

They met the elder Hales in Lazette and Jeff gave Adam the certificate to file.

"You was right all along, daughter," Adam told Ellen. "I knew it."

Ellen blushed.

"Mebbe some other folks didn't," added Adam. "But I reckon they do now." He looked at Jeff and patted him on a shoulder. "Shucks, boy," he said, "you knew it too, but you was harder to convince."

When they left the Hales and Lazette their faces were serious.

Riding to the Diamond A Ellen had related to Jeff the story of her experience with Kellis, and Jeff had sent a man to Randall to tell Mart Blandin where Kellis's body might be found. "He'll find Dallman in the Kellis cabin," Jeff added, speaking to the messenger. "Tell Mart I'll come in if he wants to see me about the killing of Dallman."

Jeff knew, however, that Blandin would not ask him to come in. For Blandin, as well as a number of other people in Randall, knew that the killing had been justifiable.

And now, riding eastward from Lazette, Ellen and Jeff finally came to a trail that was familiar to both. The trail led to the Hale cabin in the Navajo basin, where the two had met for the first time. Ellen looked at Jeff when he turned into it, but said nothing.

They were still serious, and so they rode on, saying little, until late in the afternoon they halted their horses in front of the cabin, and dismounted.

"We'll grub here," said Jeff. "I'll do the cooking, and you will compliment me as you did during that breakfast. We'll stay here until morning, and then we'll ride to the Hour Glass. There's a lot of things I've got to say to your dad."

The meal was finished after a while, and darkness had come when they went out upon the veranda and sat upon its edge, close together. The night song of the forest insects had begun, but their voices made the only sound that disturbed the solemnity of the night.

"How did you discover that Dallman abducted me?" asked Ellen.

"Mart Blandin told me. Dallman had boasted about it to Hazen. I was a fool to doubt you," he added. "But what I will never be able to understand is how you could mistake Dallman's voice for mine."

"I didn't," she said, dropping her gaze from his.

"Didn't? But you said—you were positive that——"

"I lied, Jeff. I knew it was not you. But Jeff, when I saw you standing before me in the moonlight—when you came in to cut the ropes that bound my hands—I—I wanted you. And I lied to get you. And I would lie ten thousand times to keep you!"

She snuggled into the arms that suddenly encircled her.

"And Jeff," she said, "I never loved Jim Kellis. I believe I only recognized his weakness and was sorry for him. I am still sorry."

"I know it," said Jeff. "I get older and wiser."

"And less and less a wild man. Oh, Jeff, we are going to be so happy!"

"Sure."

"But Sadie Nokes——"

"Shucks. Sadie Nokes is Mart Blandin's girl. They are going to be married next month. Mart used to send word to me through her."

"But the way she looked at me!"

"She was suspicious—thought you were after the land."

They were silent after that, listening to the voice of the great, virgin wilderness that encompassed them. They were facing happiness and the future was bright and alluring. And yet in the voice of the wilderness Ellen found a note of sadness, for she kept seeing Jess and Dell and Hazen as they had stood in the fastness of the basin, watching her as she rode away upon one of the outlaws' horses.

"Tell Jeff there'll be no mistake this time," one of the outlaws had said to her.

She wondered about the words as she wondered about the faint report of the pistol, which had reached her ears as she had been riding away. It seemed she could hear it now—the sound gradually diminishing until it died away altogether. But life, she knew, is like that. Sadness in happiness. One always lurking near the other. . . .

THE END

www.ingramcontent.com/pod-product-compliance
Lightning Source LLC
Chambersburg PA
CBHW050747250626
47155CB00005B/1958